THE
TASTERS
GUILD

Also by Susannah Appelbaum:

The Hollow Bettle
The Poisons of Caux, Book I

Library of Congress Cataloging-in-Publication Data
Appelbaum, Susannah.
The Tasters Guild / Susannah Appelbaum; illustrated by Jennifer Taylor. — 1st ed.
p. cm.—
(Poisons of Caux ; bk. 2)
Summary: Eleven-year-old Ivy Manx sets out with her friends for the dangerous city of Rocamadour, where poison and the evil Tasters Guild rule, in the hopes of finding a door to the sisterland of Pimcaux and fulfilling a great and ancient prophecy.
ISBN 978-0-375-85174-2 (trade) — ISBN 978-0-375-95174-9 (lib. bdg.) —
ISBN 978-0-375-89619-4 (e-book)
[1. Poisons—Fiction. 2. Voyages and travels—Fiction. 3. Kings, queens, rulers, etc.—Fiction.
4. Fantasy.] I. Taylor, Jennifer (Jennifer Ann), ill. II. Title.
PZ7.A6445Tas 2010
[Fic]—dc22
2009028710

THE POISONS OF CAUX

BOOK TWO

THE TASTERS GUILD

SUSANNAH APPELBAUM

illustrated by Jennifer Taylor

Alfred A. Knopf   New York

For Harper and Henry,
the Winds blow just for you

Contents 🌿

Previously, in Book I, *The Hollow Bettle* xi

Part 1: Templar

Chapter 1 The Calligrapher 3
Chapter 2 Ink 10
Chapter 3 Peps 15
Chapter 4 Thwarted 20
Chapter 5 The Child of the Prophecy 26
Chapter 6 Alewives 36
Chapter 7 The News 38
Chapter 8 The Tapestries 41
Chapter 9 Delivery 48
Chapter 10 The Secret Language of Flowers 52
Chapter 11 The Deadly Dose 55
Chapter 12 Dumbcane's Shop 57
Chapter 13 C Is for "Crow" 60
Chapter 14 Scourge Bracken 63
Chapter 15 The Elevator 67
Chapter 16 Departure 70
Chapter 17 Six 77

CHAPTER 18 The Cure.................................. 80

CHAPTER 19 The Charm 86

CHAPTER 20 Troubled Waters........................ 89

CHAPTER 21 Foul Mood 92

CHAPTER 22 A Cautionary Note..................... 95

CHAPTER 23 Fog...................................... 100

CHAPTER 24 The Snodgrass Toad 103

CHAPTER 25 No Vacancy............................. 106

CHAPTER 26 Rhustaphustian 111

CHAPTER 27 Tribunal................................. 118

CHAPTER 28 The Gallery............................. 121

CHAPTER 29 The Cafeteria........................... 125

CHAPTER 30 Farewell 128

CHAPTER 31 Springforms............................ 132

CHAPTER 32 The True Nature of Plants 140

CHAPTER 33 The Uninvited Visitor 142

CHAPTER 34 Peps's Story 148

Part II: Rocamadour

CHAPTER 35 Red..................................... 152

CHAPTER 36 Gripe 157

CHAPTER 37 The Wall 160

CHAPTER 38 Mind Garden........................... 166

CHAPTER 39 The Sewer 170

CHAPTER 40 Down....................................176

CHAPTER 41 Bitter Swill.............................180

CHAPTER 42 The King's Flower.......................182

CHAPTER 43 Malapert................................184

CHAPTER 44 The Riddle 188

CHAPTER 45 The Reply...............................190

CHAPTER 46 Tea and Sympathy.......................193

CHAPTER 47 Professor Breaux's Moonlit Garden........197

CHAPTER 48 The Ladder..............................201

CHAPTER 49 The Plan................................208

CHAPTER 50 Something That Grows....................212

CHAPTER 51 Truax 216

CHAPTER 52 Kingmaker 218

CHAPTER 53 The Catacombs..........................222

CHAPTER 54 Hallowed Ground 228

CHAPTER 55 Capture.................................231

CHAPTER 56 Gloamwort 235

CHAPTER 57 The Final Exam 238

CHAPTER 58 The Dose................................246

CHAPTER 59 Shadow.................................250

CHAPTER 60 Arrivals 255

CHAPTER 61 Caged Reverie 258

CHAPTER 62 The Petition 261

CHAPTER 63 The Chapter Room.......................264

CHAPTER 64 Breaux's Bouquet........................271

CHAPTER 65 Flight..................................274

CHAPTER 66 Truax 277

CHAPTER 67 The Crypt. 282

CHAPTER 68 Hallowed Ground 285

CHAPTER 69 The Pimcaux Doorway 289

Part III: Pimcaux

CHAPTER 70 Not Pimcaux. 294

CHAPTER 71 Wilhelmina 299

CHAPTER 72 A Change of Attire. 305

CHAPTER 73 The Ribbon Tree 310

CHAPTER 74 Four Sisters 314

CHAPTER 75 Six. 316

CHAPTER 76 Klair and Lofft 319

CHAPTER 77 Thin Air. 323

CHAPTER 78 Clothilde. 327

CHAPTER 79 The Grange. 331

CHAPTER 80 Mr. Foxglove. 335

CHAPTER 81 The Masquerade 341

CHAPTER 82 Reunion 344

CHAPTER 83 The King. 347

CHAPTER 84 The Thorn 355

CHAPTER 85 The Ring. 360

CHAPTER 86 Caucus. 363

APPENDIX 367

THE HOLLOW BETTLE

The Deadly Nightshades were cruel and villainous rulers, and in that they took great pride. They enjoyed misery, so naturally they perpetuated mistrust and deceit among their subjects. Replacing Caux's long traditions of scholarship and healing, King and Queen Nightshade preferred instead to use herbs to poison rather than cure. To dine in their uneasy realm of Caux was to take your very life in your hands—indeed, you were unlikely to survive your next meal without a Guild-accredited taster by your side.

Poison Ivy did not need a taster at all—she was a poisoner of some skill and therefore quite well suited to detecting it. Yet, somehow, she got not one taster—but two. The first, Sorrel Flux, tried to kill her. Flux was idle and, Ivy would soon learn, a servant of the evil forces bent on her destruction. The second, Rowan Truax, was escaping the powerful Tasters' Guild, and its evil Director, Vidal Verjouce.

But with Rowan's help, Ivy would eventually make it to Templar—and hopefully to Pimcaux—to fulfill a secret and ancient Prophecy.

There was once a time when poison was not the way of the land. It was a time long ago—of earlier, magical kings. Caux's wisest sages still whispered of this great Prophecy, which told of the coming of a child who would cure their King—their one, true King—the Good King Verdigris, who lay ailing in a self-imposed exile in the sisterland of Pimcaux.

The Noble Child of the Prophecy, as it turned out, was Poison Ivy, whose penchant for making exquisite and deadly poisons—with her vast knowledge of herbs—also lent itself to healing. On the run in the ancient land, Ivy and the taster Rowan were pursued by a gruesome Outrider—a tongueless servant of the Tasters' Guild. Ivy left behind her uncle's tavern and her beloved crow, Shoo, taking only her red bettle— a hollow jewel with the power to ward off poison.

The pair traveled deep within the ancient forests in search of her missing uncle Cecil, an apotheopath, or healer. With the help of *The Field Guide to the Poisons of Caux*, her friend Axle's masterwork, they reached the walled city of Templar, where the Deadly Nightshades were taking refuge from the Windy Season.

There, Ivy discovered the Doorway to Pimcaux in the Nightshades' castle—but too late. The Winds slammed it shut, leaving the corrupt Sorrel Flux and her mother, Clothilde, on the other side, and Ivy to fend off the murderous impulses of the Guild's Director on her own.

But her hollow bettle hatched—it was in fact something of a butterfly—and, indeed, all the bettles in the land followed suit. Vidal Verjouce retreated to the Tasters' Guild to plan his revenge while all of Caux celebrated the end of the evil Nightshade regime.

Yet there still remained the great and ancient Prophecy.

Ivy and Rowan must together enter the foreboding city of Rocamadour—and the Tasters' Guild itself—a city that no outsider has ever successfully penetrated. There, the two must find the only other Doorway to Pimcaux.

Part 1

Templar

Plants—all plants—have secrets. To unlock them is power, as the apotheopaths knew.

—The Field Guide to the Poisons of Caux
Axlerod D. Roux

Chapter One

The Calligrapher

Hemsen Dumbcane's withered skin was pasty from a lifetime of library work. He was a sour man whose eyes had long gone rheumy and uncooperative, and he routinely wore a powerful magnifying lens clipped to his thick spectacles. He preferred his small, unobtrusive shop empty, and for most of his long career, he had only one client. But what a client he served! Hemsen Dumbcane was a master calligrapher to the secretive Tasters' Guild—producing the majority of its inscrutable documents—trusted with its most top-secret work and given access to its very private Library.

Although it was newly unfashionable, the royal seal of King Nightshade still hung over the dusty front door of Hemsen Dumbcane's shop, on the busy Knox bridge, right beneath the large, pointed quill indicating his trade. He figured the unpopular royal seal kept his store quiet, which was how he needed it to be in order to practice not only his calligraphy but also his more secretive, and highly lucrative, secondary trade. For

Hemsen Dumbcane was a crook of enormous proportions—stealing and forging ancient, highly valuable, and oftentimes enchanted documents from Caux's libraries and private collections and then selling them on the black market.

Hemsen Dumbcane had been slowly relieving the land of its ancient maps and pictorials, testaments and charts of odd, indecipherable symbols for his entire career—one spanning many long years. That was a lot of missing paper, although for each he would toil to replace the original with a clever fake, copying it perfectly and returning the counterfeit undetected. Since many of the ancient tableaus were considered to be irreplaceable magical texts, Hemsen Dumbcane was distinctly responsible for the dilution of the ancient wisdom of earlier—and more respectable—kings than his most recent benefactor, King Nightshade.

At present, in his quiet shop, a drop of perspiration hung threateningly at the tip of his nose. Pausing, the calligrapher wiped his face with his damp kerchief, catching the offending droplet in the nick of time—lest it sully his work on the desk beneath his gaze. Before him, his final forgery.

A masterwork.

He had stolen it from its hiding place in the very chambers of the Guild's fearsome Director, a scroll of such beauty and value that he could not bear to be without it. At great personal hazard, he now toiled to produce a counterfeit before his transgression was discovered.

He heard nothing of the little bell that now rang from the

front of the shop, a signal of the unusual presence of a customer. He continued his work, though burdened by a great nervousness that had settled upon him in the middle of the night. For the past week Dumbcane had found himself distracted mightily from his sleep, from his shop duties, from everything. And today brought no relief. He tried to clear his mind and complete his final task, concentrating upon the dark weave of images amid the strange text. His shaking hand attempted to duplicate the sheen of the golden serpent before him.

There was quite a lot of traffic on the Knox bridge this morning, owing probably to some festivity, a festivity that Dumbcane—if he chose to acknowledge it at all—would find entirely uninteresting. The town had turned out for some mindless event, and compounding the traffic was an annoying amount of construction on the bridge. He had little to do with the life of the city—having long ago aligned himself with the thieves and scoundrels that made up his network of contacts, and the darker sides of Caux from which he profited.

The little bell rang again sourly—indicating that the door had shut once more. Presumably, someone now awaited him. This time Dumbcane was alerted, and he sat bolt upright, upending a small pot of black ink, a few pages before him scattering to the floor. Quickly he wiped the ink blot with his elbow—a lazy swarm of dark fruit flies escaped his arm just in time, only to come together again and settle hungrily on the stain.

Peering about the dark room cautiously, he craned his neck

toward the door, his earlier nighttime anxieties returning. One large eye—magnified by his calligraphy lens—regarded the shaded room fearfully.

"What?" he hissed. "Who's there?"

"Hemsen Dumbcane?" came a nasally response.

"Who wants to know?" Dumbcane leaned out a little further into the gloomy room. With a start he relieved himself of his ever-present magnifying lens—flipping it upright quickly—but not before he was afforded the shock of one of the biggest noses ever to grace a face, a nose that indeed marked its wearer's lineage.

A nose as long as a sausage could only belong to a Taxus.

Dumbcane at once regained his composure. A half smile even made an appearance across his sallow face. Although he had had dealings with the Taxus family over the years, these two before him were new. But he knew the type.

"What, gentlemen, can I do for you today?" Dumbcane asked.

"We are looking for a certain document," the elder and larger of the two Taxuses responded. This was Quarles Taxus, a man who really never achieved much in his life by respectable means. In fact, over the family's long and feuding history, there had been but one Taxus upon whom any amount of success had been visited. That was Turner Taxus, and he was now dead. Turner Taxus had risen through the ranks of the Nightshade army to a respectable position, only to consume for his last meal some poisoned soup.

Quarles and his cousin, the more diminutive Qwill, had in their kinsman's early demise found their particular calling. And that was to deliver vengeance upon the irksome taster who was the cause of Turner Taxus's poisoning. (The contract and subsequent rules between taster and charge are arcane and intricate, but call for the taster's surrender should he be responsible for the untimely end of his employer.) The Estate of Turner Taxus approached this task with uncharacteristic dedication—the tenacity of a dog with a bone. There was, of course, a sizable reward offered for the capture of the renegade taster, and this reward was, in Quarles's eyes, nearly theirs.

"We have it on good authority that you have in your possession a document belonging to us." Quarles indicated the ordered stacks of Dumbcane's archives, pointing, seemingly, with his long and crooked nose.

The small, dark hairs on the back of the calligrapher's thin neck rose up in alarm, and he was overcome with a fit of coughing.

"I hardly think that's possible," he told the pair as soon as the distressing rattle in his lungs stopped. "You see, I've never met the two of you, er, gentlemen, nor had the pleasure of any business dealings with you, so, you see, it would be simply impossible that I might have something of yours." He looked over the wire rims of his glasses to see if the two Taxuses were convinced. "So, if you'd excuse me, I'm in a bit of a hurry—"

"Dumbcane." Quarles somehow doubled his girth while

lowering his voice several octaves—a talent gleaned from years of tavern brawls. "How would you know you don't have it when you don't even know what it is? And don't you worry. It's not one of those old maps here of *questionable ownership*—"

Dumbcane blanched, his hand at his mouth in horror.

"And nor do we care to discuss that subject further—do we, Qwill? Unless . . . unless we are forced to. If you cannot produce our Epistle, we will report your doings to the proper authorities—and seeing as you currently lack royal patronage, you would surely be held accountable for all your crimes." Quarles looked around the dim room, satisfied. "Besides, I'm not leaving without it, and since it seems that you have travel plans yourself . . ." There was indeed an overstuffed satchel at Dumbcane's feet, from which a mass of scrolls and parchments protruded beside a tidy purse stuffed to the seams with minims and scruples. "You'd better get busy looking wherever it is that you keep these, er, things."

"Epistle?! Epistle?!" Dumbcane's voice broke, and with it he relinquished all attempts at remaining calm. "What Epistle? What sort of Epistle do you want? There are *thousands* of Epistles. You have to be more specific before I can even begin to help."

"We want the Epistle of the taster Rowan Truax. It belongs to us under the rules of the Tasters' Guild—since he was responsible for the death of our dear, dear cousin Turner."

In Dumbcane, there was suddenly the distinct impression

that no familial love existed between the departed and these two, but having to produce for them such a minor document made him nearly shake with relief.

"Oh, yes, why didn't you say so? Quite a common Epistle, yes, indeed. A taster receives his Epistle in a special ceremony at the time his training is complete, along with his robes. A signature required, I do believe. The taster and the Director. I should—yes, I think I do—have it right back here in my files. Truax you say? With a T? If you'd be patient—I shan't be long."

Indeed, Dumbcane's filing system rewarded him greatly with the proper form—everything was meticulously alphabetized with a highly ornate font. Abandoning any of his usual orderliness, he calculated that he would just have time to finish his endeavor if these two irksome visitors would only leave.

So it was that, with shaking hands, he quickly found the Truax file. But in his haste and elation, as he placed the handsome document upon his worktable and kicked closed his drawers, he failed to notice that upon retrieving it, he had inadvertently grabbed a second, more tattered page. These both he then delivered to the two distant relatives of Turner Taxus, who left immediately thereafter—but not before the larger of the two took notice of the calligrapher's error.

Quarles eyed the odd page—for it was much older and printed upon the finest parchment, and showed distinct signs of having survived a fire.

Evidence of a fire upon such an ancient document might not be notable to a Taxus, or similarly to one who mistook his history lessons for naptime. But in Caux, there was at one time a notable fire—a truly evil fire—at the foot of a steep tower in the ancient town of Rocamadour. The fire was sparked by the wicked King Nightshade and overseen by the Director of the Tasters' Guild, the notorious Vidal Verjouce, and the fuel that fed it was the many majestic tomes and charts of a dying King. This fire, it was thought, was the end of all but a very few magical texts—books capable of delivering the reader much more than a history lesson.

Dumbcane cursed this fire—for very few ancient works survived it.

In the splendid Library at Rocamadour, before most of Caux's masterworks were reduced to ash, Dumbcane purported to be performing the work of a scholar. He examined tome after splendid tome, and when something pleased him, he would simply take it. This he did by secretly unwinding a thin silk thread from under his tongue, which he would then lay across the page of interest, nestled near the binding. Closing the book, he would occupy himself for a matter of minutes, and when he returned, the page would tear completely free. He would then hurry back to his small shop to begin to duplicate his pilfered goods, and return the forgeries to the place of the originals.

At first the magical texts resisted him.

He seemed perfectly incapable of reproducing the sparkle of life that made the texts at once so desirable and valuable. The originals seemed to practically jump out from the page, while his own tries were flat and lifeless.

That is, until the recipe.

In these ancient apotheopathic texts, Hemsen Dumbcane sometimes found handwritten notes in the margins, obscure symbols from an ancient pen. Early in his unlawful career, he never considered these commentaries to be of much value—in fact, just the opposite: he looked upon them as the work of a vandal, sullying the sacred texts. A rude distraction.

But then he came across one such notation, in the same discreet scrawl as the rest, which described for the scribe the recipe for what would be the secret of his success: the ancient formulation of the special inks that composed the magical works, the very works he so admired. Once the formula was mastered, Dumbcane was free to practice his illicit talents without any fear of discovery, so convincing was the result. Nothing could defy his genius at forgery. He simply learned to ignore the caustic stench and the strange, small flies that seemed perpetually attracted to these new, potent inks.

He began to expand his repertoire.

With this ink, he was now capable of great genius. The ink seemed to enchant the page, infusing life across its papery surface. With ease—almost too much—Dumbcane produced one magnificent forgery after the next, beginning simply with the alphabet and from there moving on to spectacular feats of duplication, all the while driven not by creativity but by wicked ambition.

Ink crusted his cuticles and saturated his pores.

Now, as Dumbcane readied himself to depart the bridge, he stood and surveyed his beloved shop for the last time. As he did, his eyes settled on his earliest accomplishment, the ornate alphabet he had produced as his very first experiment with the new inks. The letters were tacked to the peeling wall, intricate lines with many showy flourishes. Each was wreathed in a border, and the calligrapher had taken pains to draw various objects that commenced with that letter—in this way, the letter *A* contained an acorn.

Over time, dust had been allowed to settle on them all, and the years had been unkind to many—indeed, most. He had to squint at the faded parchments. With a stained hand, he wiped away a veil of dust. A favorite, his early attempt at a capital *P*, he had painted with a brush made of a single hair from the belly of a silver mink. He could barely make it out. It seemed in fact to be fading before his eyes—the glorious rolling hills of the land of Pimcaux were withering, the landscape darkening as if before a storm. He rubbed his tired eyes as he often did, but the anguish he was feeling merely doubled.

In fact, the alarm that had torn him from his restless sleep that night returned in full force, and the old scribe found his knees beginning to buckle. He leaned against the wall. Over the past several weeks, he had noticed things, small things—but peculiar, inexplicable occurrences that when totaled together in the dark of night on his lumpy mattress haunted him in a way to which he was quite unaccustomed. His shifty eyes alighted on his drafting table in the corner, in particular, on a haphazard collection of his homemade inks.

For weeks, Dumbcane had been noticing his stolen apotheopathic manuscripts behaving strangely. The once bright, aligned script of some was now dim and smudged, and the neatly ruled lines at times descended into complete chaos. The text of others, incredibly, seemed to have vanished entirely—as if made from invisible ink. His life's work—his collection of stolen parchment, scrolls, and charts of untold value—was vanishing before his eyes!

This curious turn led Dumbcane to the conclusion that

either someone was trying to ruin him or some ancient and powerful magic was afoot—or both.

As he cowered before his beloved alphabet upon the wall, the letter *V* glinted in the shadows at the tail end of the abecedarium. Vultures circled a shadowy tower. It was always a dark one, drawn in a moonscape and featuring a ring of stars commonly seen in Caux in the winter sky. But as Dumbcane now observed, it seemed at once to draw him in and lash out—and the small scribe felt a potent flash of true terror. Unfathomable, he told himself, that he should be made so fearful by something of his own hand! Something of ink and paper. A trick of the light perhaps. Or of the dark.

Vidal Verjouce, he thought with a start.

He must depart—at once.

And with that, the proprietor of the dim little calligraphy shop on the Knox bridge turned his back on his workshop, unwittingly leaving his last masterpiece unfinished, and departed hurriedly—not bothering with the lock.

Chapter Three

Peps

The bustling Knox was a bridge of much renown, older, perhaps, than even the walled city of Templar that it served. The Knox was wide and stout and as strong as its years, and was home to some of Caux's oldest and most distinguished proprietors. Where a railing might normally be found, it boasted an eclectic array of precarious storefronts, some even of multiple floors, saddling the bridge itself on either side. These shops roosted above the wallowing waters of the river Marcel indifferent to everything but commerce, while beneath them a long line of trestlemen inhabited the lower level of the bridge.

That is, until recently.

Peps D. Roux, who considered himself to be a dashing example of Caux's rare and ancient race of trestlemen, would point out that it was he and he alone who had braved the tyranny of the Nightshade regime, while all other trestlemen had quietly departed and passed the most recent—and embarrassing—chapter in Caux's history out of sight.

This fact seemed important to Peps, as he was being forced to relinquish what had become quite a deluxe apartment for one diminutive man—or man of any size, for that matter. (Trestlemen were of course quite small in height, if not in girth.) Peps indeed had remained loyal to his trestle heritage during the reign of the Deadly Nightshades and, in refusing to leave, had inherited the entire underside of the Knox—a palace by anyone's standards. In knocking down the walls, he had created, together with his companion the cobbler Gudgeon, an expanse of luxury to rival none.

And now he was being forced to give it back—or most of it—since many of the exiles (or *cowards*, as Peps preferred to call them) were returning from their hiding.

So Peps, characteristically, had come up with a unique solution for himself. As he cast about a morose eye from his mullioned windows, draped on either end with the most luxurious of silk velvet, he saw below him the many houseboats that were moored upon the banks of the Marcel—and from there his discerning eye alighted upon the finest of the fleet, the most tasteful and sedate vessel ever to loll in the slight waves, the boat whose name was stenciled on its blunt stern in fine gold leaf: *Trindletrip.*

And Peps decided at once that the boat of his friend, the chef Trindle, would make a fine home for him for the near future, since it met both of the flamboyant trestleman's conditions: first, that it was an enviable place to lay one's head, and second, that it would accommodate nicely the parties he was accustomed to throwing for himself. Buoyed by his own clever decision, he neglected to consider the very real fact that only ill fortune awaits any trestleman who chooses to live upon—rather than over—the water.

And so this day found Peps with a handful of local riffraff he had hired to help him move and an armful of plush pillows he was unwilling to hand over. Peps was shouting orders to the indifferent youths upon the Knox, just as a paler-than-usual Hemsen Dumbcane emerged from his shop and started off away from the city.

"What's he up to?" Peps stopped his instructions, seeing Dumbcane's retreating figure and haunted expression.

Residing beside Dumbcane for all these years had produced nothing in the form of neighborly courtesy. The two were just as much strangers as they had been on the first day the calligrapher set up shop, and this distrust of each other produced—at least in Peps—an addictive curiosity. Hadn't Hemsen Dumbcane learned calligraphy by copying his father's will and liberally writing himself into it? Peps's eyes narrowed at the fact that the normally reserved calligrapher had not even bothered to lock his front door.

The trestleman thoughtfully fingered a satin tassel on one of his overstuffed cushions and took a moment to reflect. Something like this should be reported to Cecil Manx, at the palace. The Steward had warned that these times, while they were awaiting the reappearance of the Good King Verdigris, were treacherous. There was real reason to distrust Dumbcane, Peps concluded, since he was the last merchant on the Knox—or, for that matter, anywhere—to still display the royal seal of the evil King Night-shade, and the collection of dubious visitors to his small shop at nightfall was worrisome.

But, Peps reflected as he scrutinized his loutish movers, he wasn't really sure that anything was amiss, was he? Might this wait until a better time, like over aperitifs and finger food at Trindlesnifter's later? Surely that would be more civilized. He pictured himself with Cecil Manx, the Steward of Caux and famed apotheopath, at a lovely table at Templar's finest restaurant.

His gaze returned to the retreating calligrapher.

Odd. A haze of small, annoying flies was retreating with him. They swarmed about in a daze, pressing on with the diminishing figure of the scribe. And then he noticed something that made his blood run cold. At first the trestleman mistook it for the lazy cloud of insects. But no. It was as if Dumbcane brought along with him a residue of darkness from his shop, a sort of peculiar shadow emanating from his coattails, tingeing the very air a deep gray.

Dumbcane pulled his hood up and threw his heavy satchel over his bony shoulder. In his wake, the newly planted window boxes and flowerpots of the Knox—all part of the bridge's face-lift—shriveled and withered, and soon were nothing but an inky black ash.

Peps turned to run, still with his armload of fancy cushions, his leisurely day of overseeing his move to the *Trindletrip* forgotten.

Chapter Four

Thwarted

Peps sprinted, watching the receding Dumbcane and his particular dark blight upon the bridge's potted plants from over his shoulder. Running forward while looking backward never accomplishes much, and indeed, he soon met with the rear end of a large, burly worker—sending his cushions scattershot about him. Yet the man barely noticed the intrusion and continued to peer eagerly ahead into the deepening gathering.

"Move along!" Peps shouted up at him, but no answer came.

An enormous crowd clogged the Knox. Peps darted around with great agitation, trying to find a place to squeeze himself through trousered legs, but when he was greeted, it was roughly and he was admonished to wait his turn.

"Wait my turn?" Peps huffed. "I am on an errand for the Steward!"

"Errand or not, I been waiting all morning on this lame leg— an' no one's busting in to see 'er before me!"

Appalled, Peps took a measured look about him.

There was simply no passage.

Above him, he noticed, was the new and terribly exciting sign announcing the ancient city of Templar's return to its proper place as capital of the land. Earlier in the day, it had been hoisted high into the air with the help of a thick length of rope and an over-worked donkey. Both rope and donkey were an integral part of an elevator system on the bridge, lowering an iron cage to and from the water below. It was meant for passengers—a small few at a time—but more often than not, it was overloaded with supplies and wares arriving from various water routes.

Peps regarded the plaque for a moment. Gold leaf proclaimed in glorious script:

Templar, Capital of Caux

It was a celebration of a sign, one signaling the banishment of the evil King and Queen Nightshade. Poison was no longer the way of the land, and the citizens of Caux had reason to be proud—not only of their long heritage in the healing arts but also of recent triumphs over the darker side, the Deadly Nightshades, who had ruled with such greed and spite.

But this was one celebration that for Peps would have to wait. He noticed that the crowd thinned a bit to the sides, and there

Peps spied a rickety wooden ladder leaning against a nearby storefront. He glanced again behind him at the blighted flowerpots—but Dumbcane was no longer visible. With a heavy heart, Peps began heaving himself upon the rungs.

He was uneasy with heights. There were many of his kind who lived below wondrous trestles that spanned dizzying gorges and glorious cliffsides, but not Peps. Ballads had been written about such men, and in better times were sung at trestlemen gatherings, functions that had ceased entirely under the Nightshade regime. No such ballad existed about Peps D. Roux, and any composer would be hard-pressed to find much adventure in Peps's personal history. (The song would be brief and celebrate such things as his taste in formal wear and his prized golden tooth.)

Peps crept forward uneasily atop the thatched roof. It was quite a view—the ramparts of the Templar palace, the carefully executed stones of the walled city, gleaming cobbles of the many twisting streets below. But Peps refused to be distracted from his errand, instead preferring to inch forward on all fours as the memory of the departing Dumbcane bolstered his courage. Coming finally to the source of the congestion, the trestleman peered over the edge nervously.

A cart, of sorts, met his eye.

This was not unusual in the daily life upon the bridge in and of itself. But this small, canvas-topped cart was drawing an enormous amount of attention. A line—if it could indeed be called that, possessing neither order nor visible rules—snaked its way across the Knox, twisting and turning and finally boiling over onto a small square where Crossbones and Thrashweed streets collided at the city gates.

He looked about the crowd gathered below him, a wisp of steam penetrating the chill air. The colorful horde was gathered in every available space, the expectant faces muffled by a patchwork of cloaks and hoods. The people had come in droves, despite the unseasonable cold, and had amassed upon the cobblestones—swaying from lampposts, even dangling off of the small balconies that perched along the plaza.

Amid the pushing and shoving, small snippets of conversation floated up to Peps. ". . . Made his warts shrivel right up—every last one of 'em dropped off during that thunderstorm last week! And, where they landed, toadstools grew! I tell you, though—he's now developed a taste for yeasted bread, and makes himself loaf after loaf from sunup till sundown! We're *buried* in loaves, so many he bakes—why, I haven't seen the cat in weeks!"

"My cousin Herrick came to see her, troubled by indigestion, and a day later his appetite returned—and with it a strange new ability to call the birds down from the trees and have them entertain him with sweet music all the day long! Only, he was quite soon burdened by their unbearable weight, a whole forest's worth of birds upon his shoulders day and night—and now it is his great wish that she make them go, and perhaps attend to his ailing back."

The tremendous crowd beneath Peps continued in such medical discourse, complaining of their various ailments that they hoped to have addressed, exchanging one story for the next.

The trestleman began to wonder at how he was to get himself down. He regarded the sky, in which black clouds clotted out much of the daylight. High above the clusters of sloping rooftops, a single soaring bird—a vulture. It circled lazily, lower and lower.

There was a figure at the front of the crowd, the object of everyone's attention. It was a familiar one to the trestleman, and he squinted in disbelief. A wormholed plank of wood stretched between a pair of barrels, and behind it was seated his young friend Ivy Manx. She wore, besides her leather workshop apron, a look of earnest determination and a slight frown upon her brow. Her golden hair was tied back with a piece of string, and above her—Peps could just make it out—dangled a small plaque that was even more thrilling to the citizens of Caux than the new Templar sign. The notice was written in the carefree script of a young girl.

What Ails You?
Consult the Child of the
Prophecy
Miracle Healer on Duty
~Donations Appreciated~

Chapter Five
The Child of the Prophecy

The Prophecy to which Ivy's plaque referred was a great and ancient one, passed down from generation to generation by a few wise scholars, and until recently had been all but forgotten. Even the parchment upon which it was written was lost—presumed burned in the terrible fire at the Library of Rocamadour. But the Prophecy was known—in full or part— by a select few and predicted that a child of noble birth would heal Caux's ailing King. This child, as it turned out, was Poison Ivy, a young girl with a penchant for making exquisite and deadly poisons—a talent that, with her vast knowledge of herbs, also lent itself to healing. The King was none other than the Good King Verdigris, Ivy's great-grandfather.

The Child of the Prophecy was currently being greatly disobedient.

It wasn't that she was practicing an illegal brand of medicine, exactly. True, apotheopathy had once been forbidden under the Deadly Nightshades, punishable by death in the kingdom of Caux. And no one could claim she was a licensed apotheopath—this was a reward for only a select few, after years of arduous study such as her uncle had endured. (Study, it should be said, was not one of Ivy's strong suits.) But she was, after all, an indisputable expert on herbs and plants, the potencies of which could be used to cure as well as harm.

And now Ivy was practicing her own secret brand of medicine, working on intuition alone, and, indeed, to the great satisfaction of the citizens of Templar.

By her side was her good friend Rowan Truax. The errant taster was on the run from the dreaded Tasters' Guild, where he had learned his trade, only to practice it disastrously—killing twenty of King Nightshade's men and the man he was specifically charged with protecting. The Tasters' Guild meted out horrendous punishments to tasters who defied their Oath, and Rowan knew the day would come when his past would catch up to him. But thoughts of Guild retribution—and of its fearsome Director, Vidal Verjouce—were forgotten for today, in favor of remedy and vitality.

Rowan held a thick clipboard and saw to the needs of the lengthy line. He prepared each patient, prepping them with a series of questions. He peered in between toes and under bandages. He inspected tonsils, carbuncles, and boils. And then he moved the citizens along swiftly to Ivy for their cures.

Upon a little alcohol stove, Ivy was preparing a tincture. She crumbled various dried herbs and, with the tip of a pocketknife she produced from her apron, scraped the spots from a small toadstool and flicked them in, too. The brew exhaled a weak puff of smoke, and Ivy added more of the mushroom, frowning. With a sudden *snap*, the potion produced a sulfurous cloud, and when it finally cleared, Ivy was regarding her patient thoughtfully.

"Tonight before bed, drink this. One thimbleful only."

The patient nodded earnestly and watched as Ivy drained the mixture through a thin funnel and into a small glass vial, one quivering drop at a time. Thinking for a moment, she pried open a small pillbox she pulled from an equally small pocket and, with a set of tweezers, added what appeared to be a grain of dust. The potion turned a steely blue, and then a brilliant sapphire.

"Pollen of witch hazel," she confided, satisfied.

Producing a cork from her apron pocket, she sealed the ampoule.

"Repeat nightly for one week, and—" She stopped. Something had caught the girl's eye, and her outstretched arm froze midreach. She gripped the potion.

"And?" The confused patient leaned in, trying to retrieve his tonic.

The odd gathering on the Knox was growing. Some un-invited guests were arriving—from the sky. The dark speck Peps had noticed in the clouds had now descended, and it was bringing friends. Landing about them were great dark birds—enormous vultures. Their ugly heads were naked of feathers and blood-red.

Ivy blinked.

She forced herself to turn her attention back to her patient even as the grim creatures continued to arrive from above.

"Repeat nightly for one week, and—your carbuncles will be gone," Ivy continued, writing the directions on the label in illegible script. "Guaranteed!" She smiled. "Or your money back."

Rowan cleared his throat.

He had great faith in Ivy's knowledge of botanicals—he had seen her potions do miraculous things and had sampled them himself. But her blithe guarantee made him nervous.

Earlier, he had taken her aside.

"Ivy, must you make promises like that? We won't even be *here* in a week!"

Indeed, they were meant to depart quite soon for Rocamadour—a destination that left a cold feeling of dread in the taster's stomach. The ailing King of Caux, the Good King Verdigris, was somewhere in Pimcaux. And if they were to help him, they needed to infiltrate the Tasters' Guild—no easy task—and find the only remaining Doorway to Pimcaux. Only then could Ivy fulfill the Prophecy.

"Rowan," she had teased, "have you no faith in my abilities?"

Rowan must have looked unsure, because a new, sulky pout appeared on Ivy's face.

"Besides, the guarantee makes the medicine work better." She sniffed. "Everyone knows that."

He doubted her uncle made such rash promises but thought it an unwise time to remind her of such. In fact, the thought of the famed apotheopath and Steward of Caux was not a comforting one to Rowan currently. Ivy's uncle was kindhearted and forgiving, but Rowan knew she was being greatly defiant by performing these renegade cures— Cecil expected his niece to follow in his own apotheopathic footsteps, which required patience and study. For the twelfth time that afternoon, Rowan regretted agreeing to assist Ivy.

These were his thoughts as he finally noticed the shadowy visitors—and the ever-darkening sky.

Vultures were landing everywhere now, it seemed; the sky was dark with them. Ungraceful when grounded, a few raised their wings in displeasure, shaking out an unpleasant amount of dust and releasing their particular smell—that of decay— throughout the plaza, and it became impossible for the townsfolk not to notice.

"Where are they coming from?" Ivy shaded her eyes as she squinted at the sky.

Rowan shook his head. Vultures. They were streaming in from the east. Could it be? He dropped his ordered clipboard, the pages tumbling about the cobblestones. Mad panic settled in, and the townsfolk scattered hastily.

"There's only one place I know of," he shouted, his voice strained.

"Rocamadour?" Ivy called. She had seen them there, from the safety of a train, hovering in the air around the piercing black tower. "What are they doing here?"

Rowan felt his stomach sink to the very cobbles of the bridge.

"I think I know that, too," he said miserably.

With surprising quickness, the bridge, and the plaza before them, were emptied—and vultures were perched upon Ivy's makeshift workplace, tearing it apart. Glass vials, powdered herbs, and alcohol tinctures were scattered, their inadvertent combinations creating a sour smell. Corks and stoppers were lost, skittering beneath the barrels and bouncing along the cobbles. Ivy and Rowan huddled together in the midst of the chaos.

There was a great cacophony; the vultures appeared to be greeting each other. Feathers flew and dust stung Ivy's cheeks. Soon Ivy and Rowan became aware of a single cloaked figure amid the unsettled birds. It was hard to tell where he began and the birds ended, since the clouds had stolen most of the morning's light. As he swung his heavy cloak about him, Ivy thought for a moment that he, too, possessed wings.

The vultures hissed, drawing themselves up menacingly. The dark figure allowed his gaze to settle upon the cowering pair. He held aloft a twisted cane, and for a brief, horrible

instant, Rowan thought his worst fear was before him: here stood the Guild's appalling Director. He would be made to account for his misdeeds—here, in Templar. Rowan's mind reeled at the vision of Verjouce's sightless eyes—awful scarred pits, the result of his own hand.

But it was not Vidal Verjouce.

There was no wicked barbed cane but rather a weathered staff of twisted wood. Ivy's uncle stepped forward, letting his gray hood fall from his head.

"A token"—Cecil Manx gestured at the uninvited guests—"from the Tasters' Guild."

He regarded the birds thoughtfully, and then his eyes fell upon Ivy's sign. She felt the color rise in her cheeks. Cecil took in the small plaque and regarded the two children wearily. And then he did something utterly and completely surprising.

He smiled.

"Mrs. Pulch thought I'd find you here."

Mrs. Pulch. Ivy scowled at the mention of her tutor—the silly woman seemed inclined to withhold nothing—any confidence, any secret, was soon unlocked and displayed for all of Templar to see, and it was Ivy's great misfortune to have told her where she'd be.

But Cecil's smile was short-lived.

Up on the rooftop behind her, Peps was in quite a precarious position.

Peps had been holding on to the small flower box upon a nearby dormer, watching Ivy in action, his mouth agape. At first, he could not fathom why all of Templar was so eager for a conference with the girl—but it was not long before he put two and two together and, finding his mouth open, closed it disapprovingly.

The trestleman was not disapproving for the reasons you might think. Peps had been known as an opportunist—in fact, simply for personal gain he had for years impersonated his famous brother, Axlerod D. Roux, the reclusive author of Caux's most famous book, *The Field Guide to the Poisons of Caux.* No, Peps was suddenly feeling inconvenienced by all these people—his big move was stalled, delaying a grand welcoming party, and he had a new and uncomfortable question as to how it was that he was going to get down from the roof and deliver his message to Cecil.

He tried, unsuccessfully, to get Rowan's attention—the taster was the closer of the two, and at one point the young man walked within earshot, but he failed to hear Peps's cries. Looking over his shoulder, the trestleman shivered at the Marcel below. The river was swollen and murky—how had this change passed him by? It was a dark, inky black. He frowned at the odd clumps floating in it, and a foamy scum congealed at the river's edge, gnawing the shore. But before the trestleman could puzzle over any of this, the sky fell in.

Large, dark shapes careened down from above in small spirals, coasting on a damp wind.

Peps shrieked at the arrival of the Rocamadour vultures—they landed roughly, skidding along the rooftops, tearing at the thatch with flashing talons, and hopping as they attempted to fold their enormous wings. He saw, to his great horror, several ratty birds take to his steamer trunk and china hutch. His precious rolled carpets were being trampled and befouled, and several sharp beaks were ripping into his piles of velvet cushions, disemboweling the stuffing.

He could no longer witness the destruction. Sheltering his eyes, he felt a dark veil blot out the view. Peering from between shaking fingers, he saw the veil take form, a form with craggy black feathers—massive ones—and dark, terrifyingly blank eyes.

A vulture—safely double the size of the diminutive trestleman—was rearing on him, neck scruff ruffled into deep trenches, bald head bobbing, wings beating a horrible dance. A stale wind licked the trestleman's nose as the bird neared, and he found himself involuntarily reaching for his handkerchief. With trembling hands, he dropped the fine red silk, and he watched helplessly as it was carried away by the breeze. As he reached desperately in a vain attempt to catch it, his foot slipped, and he lost his balance.

It was then that Cecil Manx saw Peps take one step, and then another, and finally, off-balance and arms windmilling frantically, tumble head over heels into the dreary waters of the river Marcel below.

Chapter Six

Alewives

As Peps found himself following the billowing red handkerchief over the side of the roof, he thought, not for the first time, of Wilhelmina.

Wilhelmina! his mind called out as the wind rushed by his ears.

Wilhelmina! he thought as the murky Marcel grew closer.

But Wilhelmina was gone, he knew, as indeed all the alewives were, and there was no hope of her interceding in his doom.

There had been a time in Caux's recent and dismal history when the Good King Verdigris was ill, despondent, and weak. His beloved daughter, Princess Violet, had been poisoned in Caux's sisterland of Pimcaux, where she had lived in a castle by the sea.

The King's grief grew so that it was all-encompassing—as grief can do—and soon he left his duties to his trusted advisor. A dark shadow fell over the once-proud King; his posture stooped, his face grew old. This advisor soon saw the King as vulnerable and, possessing no feeling of pity, began to ruthlessly whisper poison in his ear. This was none other than Vidal Verjouce, who was amassing all the kingly powers he could and dispensing them as if his own. Despite impressive efforts (and a showy investigation), Vidal Verjouce could find no culprit in the princess's demise. Meanwhile, he quietly groomed his pupil, Arsenious Nightshade, to succeed the Good King. And on one awful day this was accomplished—leaving Caux with a new ruler, whose legacy, along with Vidal Verjouce's, was grim and deadly.

In the time before the Good King Verdigris departed for Pimcaux to be closer to the memory of his daughter, a great many misdeeds were done at the behest of Vidal Verjouce. One such miserable event was the banishment from Caux of all the alewives.

If not an alewife, who, then, would see to Peps's safety as he bore down upon troubled waters?

The answer, Peps soon realized, was no one.

He hit the water hard and flat upon his profound stomach.

Yet, as he sank, he thought he heard in the watery distance the silvery thin chime of an alewife's bell.

Chapter Seven

The News

Cecil pulled his cloak in tighter, raising his hood. His eyes strayed to the far edges of the quay. All was quite silent, except the sloshing of the river against the tethered houseboats, an occasional squawk from the unwelcome vultures. Rowan held his breath, looking about desperately.

"Can he swim?" he asked Ivy's uncle.

"Somewhat," Cecil replied, scanning the water's slick surface. A dead fish bobbed gruesomely before them, caught in a web of knotted rope. Cecil moved away quickly along the bank, with Rowan urgently trying to keep up.

"Somewhat?" Rowan repeated, more worried than ever.

"Trestlemen have an uneasy truce with the water. Under ideal circumstances, that is. But the Marcel has changed. It runs dark."

Rowan's panic grew, and his mind cast about for a reason Peps might have found himself so high up on the rooftops— and with a growing sense of responsibility, he realized sickeningly that it must involve him and Ivy. The apotheopath was contemplating a small dinghy when Rowan was distracted by movement.

"Look!"

Something was indeed advancing on them—making slow and erratic progress from beneath the bridge. The silhouette wobbled unsteadily and stopped at one point to crouch beside a stone bench—resting, apparently, and gathering strength.

Cecil and Rowan were quickly by the trestleman's side, the Steward removing his own cloak and laying the small man down upon it. Rowan's initial relief was shattered as he eyed the proud trestleman.

Peps was a sad sight indeed. His clothes—his fantastic cloak with pearl embroidery—were in tatters, and his face and palms possessed unseemly and painful abrasions. He was completely beside himself and for the first minute could not find the strength to voice anything more than a high-pitched squeak.

After composing himself as best he could, the trestleman looked down at his cloak, and the shock of his presentation sent him yet again into a mute panic.

"My—my cape!" Peps finally managed, fingering the once-splendid detailing along the collar. As his hand passed over the lovingly assembled pearl beading, the gems disintegrated upon touch into dust. The trestleman recoiled.

His eyes were burning from the fetid water, and he reached for a small pocket, searching for his handkerchief, but stopped, remembering it was lost. He sagged, dissolving suddenly into tears.

"Peps, what were you doing on the roof?" Cecil asked.

Peps sobbed. "I was trying to find you to tell you the news."

"The news?" Cecil's brow lifted.

"Dumbcane. Hemsen Dumbcane."

"The calligrapher?" Cecil demanded, wary.

"You asked me to keep an eye out for any suspicious behavior, you know, and just this very morning Dumbcane packed himself up and left the Knox. It struck me immediately as highly irregular, and I had no doubt you'd wish to know. He had a sack of scrolls with him, and he seemed in a hurry."

"Hemsen Dumbcane," Cecil repeated sharply. "Did you see where he went?"

Peps shook his head. "I came straight here to report to you."

"By way of the river," Cecil replied kindly.

"One other thing . . ." Peps paused, trying to formulate his thought.

"Yes?"

"There was something odd." Peps's whisper was fading, and he could barely be heard. Cecil and Rowan leaned in. "As he went along the Knox, it seemed—I don't know how this could be, but it seemed as if everything he passed withered and died."

Chapter Eight

The Tapestries

owan was being punished. He had been remanded to the palace for his part in the morning's curing capers. He was to have no further contact with Ivy, who was similarly assigned to the Apothecary to complete her studies with Mrs. Pulch.

Being punished at a palace had its benefits, Rowan was realizing. There were many places to entertain oneself, many treasures to admire. He was sure he had gotten the better of the deal.

He stood now quite still before a panel of an enormous tapestry.

The seven tapestries—all marvels of creation and relics from the magical reign of King Verdigris—depicted a series of garden scenes, and the particular one that interested Rowan was the final in the sequence. Amid the lush forest and abundant plant life, a young lady in a cloud-white dress stood so lifelike that she might have very well stepped out of the scenery if Rowan had but extended her his hand.

Yet Rowan was not interested in her. He stared at the woven wool, at a black gloss that perched upon the lady's delicate shoulder, so dark that the light from the flickering lamp he held was gobbled up in its small, starched form.

Rowan was staring at the image of Shoo. Ivy's old crow had been so full of life when he knew him, and had rescued them on more than one occasion. Now he was captive to these tapestries, taken hostage when Cecil had spoken the ancient words that made the gardens within the weave come briefly to life.

He tapped on the darkness, the scratchy wool warm with his breath, and his lamp revealing—could it be?—a flicker of life in the bird's inklike eye. For the briefest of moments, the taster was certain he saw the room behind him—and his own likeness—reflected in the crow's eye. But then it was gone, only fiber and weave remaining.

"You'll catch the thing on fire if you get any closer," came an old voice from behind the former taster.

Axlerod D. Roux's small steps were soft, and he hadn't meant to startle Rowan, who jumped back in alarm. The famous author of Caux's most treasured reference book, *The Field Guide to the Poisons of Caux*, and informal sage and historian, stood beside the boy.

"Courage!" Axle grinned at his young friend, but his smile faded at the sight of Shoo, captive in the intricate weave. "One last look?" the trestleman asked.

Rowan nodded. "He's off—the whole thing's off to Underwood today."

By decree, Cecil Manx was having the entire seven magisterial panels reinstalled in the underground palace of the former King, where they had been confiscated by Queen Nightshade. (She had indeed been quite fond of them—particularly the ever-so-lifelike image of her namesake, the belladonna plant.) Finally, the panels would be back where they belonged.

"He looks happy. Not bad for an old crow," the trestleman said.

Rowan stepped back further, nearly tripping over the sprawling body of Poppy, the bettle boar, who had earlier made herself quite comfortable in his shadow. Her ears now perked at the stone doorway just beyond Rowan's golden circle of light.

"I was admiring the garden beside him," Rowan confessed.

"Ancient hands wove these, ones with great and magical knowledge."

"In the *Guide*, you write of Flower Code," the taster recalled, referring to his favorite book, Axle's own *Field Guide*.

Axle nodded, a twinkle in his eye. He had always thought this young man well read.

Rowan, encouraged, continued. "So—here." The taster pointed. "There's maiden heart and shrew's berry growing beside Shoo and this lady. According to the Code, that means *imprisoned soul* and *unfinished business.* Is it simply a coincidence?"

Axle was silent for a moment, admiring the weaving.

"There's also an acorn there, beside the maiden," the trestleman commented.

"Acorn—that's *eternal life,* isn't it?"

Axle paused. "Or *imminent death,*" the learned man added thoughtfully. "It depends on how it is presented."

"Which is it, then?"

"The Secret Language of Flowers is everywhere. One need only recognize it for what it is."

Rowan waited.

"Then—and this is the hard part—one must be able to comprehend it. Take all the bits and pieces and put them together into a language. Plants have much to say, much to teach. Except for the really basic meanings, it is a talent beyond most."

Indeed, in this, Rowan realized, the difficulty lay. If the natural world outside the door was a vast and intricate language, what might it be saying?

"The Secret Language of Flowers is a lost language, a dead one—one of ancient kings. *Whosoever speaks to the trees speaks to the King,*" Axle quoted. "Nature has retreated now and does not want to be interpreted."

"Really?"

"When you use plants to poison and harm, you are not

using plants as nature intended. So nature retreats, becomes separate and distant. Angry. But"—Axle's voice became suddenly more confident—"there is hope! There are signs that the plant kingdom awakens. When Cecil uttered the ancient words before the Nightshades and the tapestries temporarily came to life, there was an unintended effect. Things are simply more potent, more *alive* now. It's as if the tapestries never fully retreated."

"A lot of good it did Shoo in the end," Rowan said bitterly.

The pair turned again to the weavings.

"Who's to say this is his end?" Axle mused. "He's surprised us before," he reminded Rowan.

Indeed, the taster remembered Axle feeding the crow Ivy's potent elixir, watching Shoo's remarkable return to life. Rowan, too, had been saved by this potion, but his memories of that were steeped in humiliation—he had suffered the indignity of being poisoned. He was truly a taster of little talent.

"Who is it that Shoo perches upon?" Rowan changed the subject. He squinted at the image of the lady, a bemused look upon her face, but one that held something else in it, too—a cloying complexity. She was amazingly beautiful.

Axle was silent, frowning. He was a man of great learning, and when confronted with an unknown—not very often—his brows knit.

"It's one of the great mysteries of these tapestries," Axle said finally.

"And this panel." Rowan gestured to a nearby nighttime scene. He could just make out the dim imagery of a tidy, disciplined garden. It was so obscured that it seemed to be made of threads cast from the blackest ash, the thickest tar, the deepest moonless night. The woolen clouds swirled about the sky in an unfriendly manner, and the entire copse was surrounded by a very ornate, very imposing wrought-iron fence. "It seems that a storm is brewing," the taster decided.

"Quite so," agreed the trestleman.

As the taster peered into the dimness, he rose up on tiptoe in an effort to get closer, although feeling a great revulsion for the piece. Behind him Poppy bristled. Rowan could not help but feel that something was there, *someone* was there, just out of sight. Peering closer, he was struck by a slight scent of mildew. Off to one side was an abandoned folly—a small, circular building with a peaked roof, at one time meant for doves.

He was interrupted by the clatter of hurried heels hitting the stone hall behind him. The bettle boar snorted, alarmed, but it was merely a page who appeared, greatly out of breath, his chest heaving dangerously against his waistcoat.

"Ah—Masters Truax and D. Roux—I'm so pleased to have found you!"

Rowan frowned at the sight of the usually crisp servant.

"How is Peps faring?" Axle asked, hoping for further news.

"He mutters only that the waters are, well, *unfriendly*." He paused, appearing to weigh his words carefully. "He talks of a Wilhelmina, sir."

"Wilhelmina?!" Axle asked sharply.

The servant nodded nervously.

"Who is Wilhelmina?" Rowan asked.

Axle was silent, a furrow upon his brow.

"I have not heard that name in many years," the trestleman finally said.

"Here, I've brought your greatcoats," the servant urged.

Rowan turned to the page. "Did you see to that . . . *delivery?*"

"Of course, Master Rowan. It has been done." The servant held open Axle's small cloak.

"Oh, I am quite capable of doing up my own jacket," Axle muttered.

"Of course, sir. But do hurry. The Steward awaits you both upon the Knox."

Chapter Nine

Delivery

Above the Apothecary, in her current work-shop, Ivy's thick books on herbs and plant lore sat unopened, despite her uncle's admonition that she approach her studies with more seriousness. He had dismissed her from the bridge with a withering look—saying she had done enough healing for one day and Peps would be attended to quite well without her. Ivy sat, chewing on a pencil, staring out the window at the hulking visiting birds.

As it often did these days, the image of Pimcaux, her small but tantalizing peek through the Doorway, returned to her. Her mother had entered, imploring her to come. Clothilde looked, in that last image Ivy had of her, stricken and sickly against the yellow fields beyond.

Sorrel Flux had gone instead.

The thought of Sorrel Flux—her malingering former taster and servant to the Tasters' Guild—in Pimcaux was almost too much for the girl to bear. The small, pasty man spread enormous blight in his wake. He had been about to tell her—before the wild Winds of Caux slammed closed the heavy door—just who her father was. From the sniveling look of pleasure upon Flux's yellowed face, Ivy knew she was not going to like the news.

"Young lady," came a shrill voice from the front of the room. "Page 137, if you please."

A series of alembic copper vessels boiled away merrily in the workshop, spewing their concentrated essences, and a vast array of misted bell jars held living specimens—Ivy's attempt at a garden. In the corner, a smoke bush, with its lazy pom-poms of wispy florets, puffed away, now and then sending up small crescendos of perfumed haze. Her uncle's favorite snap-dragons strained testily toward the window, pushing and shoving, competing for the pale autumn light.

Mrs. Pulch was a tedious woman, Ivy had immediately decided, and there was something about her tutor that made Ivy resist all attempts to study her texts. She sighed and, dragging out the book in question, propped the massive thing up on her table. But her distraction was complete. She thought then of Peps and desperately hoped her friend was all right. She remembered the look upon Rowan's face at the arrival of the frightful vultures—and that brought her to the very thought she had hoped she might avoid for a while. The small worry that kept her fidgeting through her long lessons was this:

The Prophecy remained unfulfilled.

She had yet to get to Pimcaux and cure King Verdigris.

And the only known Doorway to the magical sisterland was hidden deep within the Tasters' Guild, at Rocamadour, where they were headed soon.

Mrs. Pulch was clearing her throat and adjusting her reading glasses, eager to begin memorization drills on elemental tables, when a clattering jangle announced someone at the workshop door.

Ivy jumped to attention, but her tutor's position beside the entrance made it impossible for Ivy to get there first.

"Hello?" Mrs. Pulch called through the door, hand on the knob.

"Delivery," came the answer.

"Delivery?" Mrs. Pulch frowned. The Steward had informed her that there were to be no interruptions in the girl's lessons, under any circumstances.

"Delivery from the palace," the disembodied voice tried again.

These must have been the magic words, for in Mrs. Pulch's mind, great things come from palaces.

The door popped open, and a boy held out an enormous brown-paper-wrapped cone—a bouquet.

"For Poison Ivy." Mrs. Pulch scowled at the card, reading, then waving, and dismissing the boy without even a minim.

"For me?" Ivy grabbed at the thing, but Mrs. Pulch moved swiftly—she possessed the advantage of years of tutoring, enabling her to anticipate any number of strategic maneuvers in her young pupils.

With a prim brow raised, Mrs. Pulch explained that she would be confiscating the delivery until lunchtime.

So it was that Ivy Manx sat down to learn her elemental distillation temperature tables, which, as they sound, are hard enough to memorize without the added distraction of a partly delivered flower arrangement a mere few feet away.

Chapter Ten

The Secret
Language of Flowers

Finally, it was time for lunch. Mrs. Pulch normally took hers right where she sat for most of the day, in the straight-back chair at the front of the workshop, removing a frugal sandwich from her embroidery bag. But today was Friday, to Ivy's great elation, and on Fridays Mrs. Pulch had another engagement.

So Ivy sat with her nose buried deep in *The Field Guide to the Poisons of Caux,* her friend Axle's wildly popular reference book. It was a borrowed copy—Rowan had kindly loaned her his own, slightly jumbled version for their stay in Templar.

Before her, the bouquet.

But not any bouquet.

To be sure, it was quite an odd-looking collection of leaves and twigs, filled with strange and wild clippings, some potent and fragrant herbs, even a fungus or two. The arrangement itself was peculiar: uneven, asymmetrical, and even possessing several upside-down flowers. Not entirely a nosegay. The bouquet was from her friend Rowan Truax, and it was a code.

Page 746 of Axlerod D. Roux's famed *Field Guide* begins a long treatise (entitled "The Secret Language of Flowers") of various and ancient meanings assigned to the vast floral population of Caux's gardens and woods. While the origin of the coded meanings remained unclear, Flower Language was said to come from a time when plants behaved according to their true natures, and their names illustrated these natures variously. In this way, one might be kept up all night by the barking of the dogwood tree, or the rays of the sunflowers might light up the eastern sky.

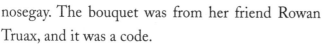

This magical time was long gone, but what remained of it was embodied in Flower Code. Axle maintained that with the help of his book, it was entirely possible to carry on a witty conversation *in complete silence* while enjoying one of Caux's many gardens or woods.

The Secret Language of Flowers was just as fusty and particular as the man responsible for recording it in writing. Not only did each flower, herb, or bough have a precise meaning, but its position in the final bouquet, and its presentation—whether, for instance, it was stripped of leaves or bark, or placed upside down—expressed an even deeper meaning, and in this way one's preciseness was limited only by one's creativity. So it was that a sprig of witch hazel could be deciphered as either *protection* or *jeopardy,* while foxglove might mean *honesty* or *insincerity.*

Rowan's bouquet managed to be quite detailed. He gave a specific update on Peps's condition (lady's slipper for *resting comfortably,* sapbreech for *enjoyment of hot beverage*) and mentioned an amusing encounter between the bettle boar Poppy and an enormous stray cat (cat's-claw and pig's ear). But most curious to the young girl was the bouquet's mention of a meeting. A meeting at a storefront upon the Knox.

Chapter Eleven

The Deadly Dose

I t was Mrs. Pulch's habit to meet her colleague on Smudgepot Lane, at the end of which, coincidentally, her favorite tavern could be found. Together, Mrs. Pulch and her friend and companion Mrs. Spittlethread would dine in the somewhat dignified interior of The Deadly Dose. There, Ivy's tutor was happy to detail the Child of the Prophecy's great and miraculous healings to Mrs. Spittlethread, whose unfortunate profile and nervous fidgeting were more than a little suggestive of a parrot.

Mrs. Pulch was quite proud of her commission with the Noble Child, and occasionally she was inclined to brag. Like many in Caux, Mrs. Pulch was an enthusiastic storyteller in her own right and at times would not hesitate to insert a few of her own flourishes. From The Deadly Dose, these tall tales spread through the population of the tavern; from Smudgepot Lane, they quickly made their way down Savory Street (where the well-to-do took their tea), darting across the city, and eventually even breaching Templar's stone walls and on to all of Caux. And since the people of Caux were nothing if not creative, with each telling, Ivy's incredible feats of healing grew more and more dexterous.

And soon expectations of Ivy's abilities rose until all of Caux was discussing the ancient Prophecy, and the very future of the land rested upon the young girl's head.

Today Mrs. Pulch had a larger audience than usual. The Deadly Dose was more crowded than ever, for many of the displaced patients of the Child of the Prophecy had found their way from the Knox to safety (and a hot lunch) behind the tavern's doors.

So it was that when Ivy made her way quickly past The Deadly Dose, Mrs. Pulch saw none of it. In her hand was a cup of hot buttered rum, and from her mouth came a new and exciting triumph of the Noble Child, who, for the second time in the day, was sneaking away from her studies to the Knox.

Chapter Twelve

Dumbcane's Shop

owan's bouquet had been specific about the location of the shop, but Ivy—being an expert poisoner but only a mediocre lock picker—sighed with relief when she came upon the open door. She felt the wall for a switch, and in the corner beside a desk, a tired bulb blinked to life. The filament was old and ineffectual, and the light seemed unwilling to leave its small corner, so Ivy was forced to wait while her eyes adjusted to the dimness. She did so before the wall of Dumbcane's illustrated alphabet, and she thought at first she was experiencing a trick of the stingy light when her eyes fell upon the showy letters.

In the dusky shadows of the small shop, the letters shifted and moved within their ornate boundaries, shimmering eerily as if caught by a breeze.

She leaned in to examine what was Dumbcane's letter *B*.

Seated on the top cascading hump of the capital letter was a delicately drawn bettle, flaunting its wings. But what technique—what ink! It shivered and shuddered, seeming to flap its crystalline wings within the dim shop. Ivy was at once reminded of her own red bettle—the flash of light coming from its hollow core. Said to have the power to protect the bearer from poison, these gemstones were once valued above all riches in Caux—but Ivy had loved hers because it reminded her of the tavern she had called home. With the fall of the Nightshades, her own bettle had hatched, bringing with it a cascade of colors, as all the other bettles in the land had hatched along with it. And then, with one parting visit, it was gone.

She looked again at Dumbcane's depiction of a bettle. He had taken liberties. Although very much a bettle, it lacked the glorious beauty and grace most would readily associate with such a thing; it was in fact rather ugly, and Dumbcane had chosen to draw it with a nasty-looking human head upon its shoulders—a head currently delivering a miniature scowl to Ivy.

"Eww." Ivy recoiled and nearly tripped over something at her feet. "What—?"

An extraordinary animal greeted her eyes. It was a cat, in fact—but it took Ivy a full moment to come to this conclusion. It was quite large, for one, and, incredibly, amazingly dirty. Matted and lumpy, its gray fur was splashed with dark paint— no, *ink*, Ivy now saw. And it was simply crawling with fleas. But although the insects jumped about the poor animal's ears and scruff, it hardly seemed bothered by them.

And the smell.

Ivy found herself stepping back, involuntarily, pushing up against the yellowed papers of Dumbcane's display.

"Hi, kitty," Ivy tried.

The cat was unresponsive and wore a look upon its large moonface that was indecipherable. Ivy flattened herself further against the wall. In the stalemate that followed, a disturbed page drifted lazily from the wall to the ground between them—but not before Ivy caught a good look at it. What she saw upon the page was preposterous, and she stepped forward. The cat growled menacingly.

"Oh!" Ivy exclaimed, eyeing the creature narrowly. "So it's going to be like that, is it?"

The rickety door of the calligrapher's shop burst open then and a stream of light poured in, slashing across the parchment at her feet.

"Ivy?" came a familiar voice. "What on earth are you doing here?"

"Uncle Cecil! Axle! Rowan!" Ivy smiled, reserving a wink for Rowan. "You must come look at this! There's a picture near this cat that looks *exactly* like me!"

Chapter Thirteen

C Is for "Crow"

hat cat?" The Steward of Caux stepped forward in the small shop, and years of accumulated dust fell upon his shoulders. Ivy blinked. Indeed, the curious cat was gone.

"Yes, what cat?" Rowan asked tentatively. He was highly allergic and sniffed the air nervously. He regretted leaving Poppy at the palace—she possessed the appropriate animosity for just these sorts of wretched creatures.

"That's strange." Ivy grabbed the parchment from the floor. "Never mind. See, here! The girl in this drawing. Doesn't she look exactly like me? And there—on the fence. The crow! It's Shoo! I'd know him anywhere." In fact, a crow was perched upon an ancient and dilapidated iron fence.

The group peered in at the page. The paper was yellowed and fragile, the drawing made long ago. It was Dumbcane's attempt at the letter *C*. In it, a small girl with golden hair stood beside a locked gate with a large crow by her side.

"Hmmph," Axle grunted. "It *does* possess a particular resemblance." The trestleman turned to the Steward. "Cecil?"

Cecil looked closely at the parchment and then, with a new urgency, around the shadowy shop. "Apparently this Hemsen Dumbcane possessed a vivid imagination."

His eyes came to rest upon a sad collection of flowerpots in the store window. They contained nothing but cobwebs and ash.

"*C* is for 'Crow,'" Rowan realized, talking to Ivy. "And there are cinquefoils pictured, too." The taster was referring to the flower that made up the Good King's crest. "Of course! *C* is for 'Child'—the Noble Child!" He examined the page closer and could make out some sort of vast garden nearby, but the paper was profoundly faded.

"Strange, though. This appears to have been drawn a long, long time ago." Rowan shrugged.

Ivy rolled the page up and, finding an empty pocket in her apron, stuck it in.

The adults were busy now rifling through the cast-off documents and odd pens, brushes, and blotters that made up a regular part of Dumbcane's trade. Axle looked distractedly down at his feet where the calligrapher had carelessly abandoned a stack of scrolls. One lay open, only partially completed.

"He seems to have been quite a talented forger."

"And quite prolific." Cecil unfurled a nearby parchment recklessly, holding it out toward the small light. A dark look passed between the Steward and the trestleman, and they hastily made their way over to Dumbcane's chaotic drafting table.

"There's only one place I know of where so many ancient, magical texts might still exist," Cecil said carefully.

"Rocamadour," came Axle's bitter response.

Ivy and Rowan, from their vantage point, could see the out-of-favor Nightshade seal that still hung from the calligrapher's storefront. It creaked in the slight breeze.

"Where do you suppose he went?" Rowan whispered.

"If there's a brain in his head, away from the Tasters' Guild," Ivy replied.

"It hardly matters. Once Vidal Verjouce discovers he employed a thief, he'll stop at nothing to find him."

Ivy looked around at the untidy mess of papers, a few now bearing muddy footprints. She saw that Hemsen Dumbcane had an archive of inestimable value and power. What would the Guild's Director do when he discovered his wealth of magical scrolls were forgeries?

Chapter Fourteen
Scourge Bracken

Something caught the apotheopath's eye, a small corner of a nearly transparent parchment peeking through the chaos on the tabletop. He pushed aside several stacks of orphaned leather book jackets and various discarded scrolls.

It was Dumbcane's final opus—a parchment only partially completed, the original of which was now in the hands of the Taxus Estate. Upon it, surrounded by tiny, impenetrable script, appeared to be the image of a half-finished door. A golden snake lay coiled at its center—a knocker of sorts.

Axle peered at the piece with interest. At the edges of the document where the scribe had left off working, the interrupted lines seemed to fret and wiggle with a real desire to be completed, pittering about like songbird tracks, nearly alive.

"They possess a quality of Verdigris magic, although they most certainly are fakes," Axle muttered. "A complete impossibility. Consider for a moment just what sort of supplies he must be using to create works of such convincing reality."

"He would need the tools the ancient King employed," Cecil was concluding. "The quills, the parchments—those are relatively easy. The ink, now that's another story."

"It was said that in the ink the enchantment lay, that without it the pages would not appear as they do," Axle added. "But the recipe was lost."

"Apparently not." Cecil scowled, angrily rolling up the forged page.

Rowan, meanwhile, was drawn to the back of the room, where a thin slice of filtered sunlight was allowed through the thick, faded curtains. At first it seemed that this area was merely for storage—Hemsen Dumbcane had left in such a hurry that his penchant for tidiness was disregarded entirely. The floor was strewn with yellowed, curling papers and ribboned rolls of large, ancient-looking charts. In the corner lay an open and disemboweled filing cabinet.

Curious, Ivy had joined Axle by the calligrapher's worktable, and the two stood on tiptoe and looked about the clutter. Reaching across the desk, she grabbed one of the discarded tins, dirty with age and crusted over with a dark and flaky patina. Ivy twisted the lid. She tried again, harder. Then, with all her effort—the thing was cemented shut—the lid released, and at once the room filled with an overbearingly sharp smell, causing the gathering to cough and quickly cover their faces.

"Aaag! Be careful!" Cecil cried.

With watering eyes, Axle helped Ivy to slam the cover

back upon the tin, but in doing so, a small spill ensued, and the noxious ink puddled in a trembling pool on the desktop. A cloud of flies appeared, as if from nowhere.

This was quite a quandary.

"Scourge bracken!" Axle choked on his words. "Dumbcane has been making ink from the scourge weed!" He took several steps back from the offending pool. Indeed, Axle's worst fears were realized. In his efforts to duplicate the ancient works and successfully replace the originals with his forgeries, Dumbcane had been using ink made from scourge bracken, the most potent and dangerous plant known—one of great volatility and impetuousness. Axle profoundly feared it. One need be a powerful and mighty King indeed in order to handle its dark and unpredictable character.

"Scourge bracken? Where did he find it?" The weed, Ivy knew, was long thought to be extinct. She felt suddenly light-headed.

The threesome watched the dark blot hesitantly. There it sat, refusing to bleed from its borders, a plump little puddle with an altogether unusual sheen—a shimmer like quicksilver, and behavior to match. A small air bubble remained on the surface, and it mirrored the three concerned faces of the party mockingly. It had a gelatinous jiggle, as if it were syrupy and thick—which made it all the more surprising when suddenly the bubble collapsed and the liquid rushed in a quick rivulet over the table's edge and onto the floor below, where it broke into a hundred perfect spheres and disappeared in the grim light of the shop.

For a moment the room was completely silent.

"You must leave today," Cecil Manx spoke finally. "Our errand can no longer wait."

"Today?" Ivy cried. "But I'm not ready!"

"No, your uncle is right. We can't depart soon enough." Axle nodded seriously. "The boat is being readied as we speak."

"But why?" Ivy crossed her arms defiantly.

"Dumbcane has somehow come upon scourge bracken, and it, beyond anything else, must not be allowed to fall into the hands of Vidal Verjouce, or—"

"Or what?

"Or all of Caux's green earth will be reduced to ash. There will be no Prophecy to fulfill, no Doorway to Pimcaux." Cecil walked over to Dumbcane's window and upended the dead potted plants to illustrate. "Just blackness and destruction."

Ivy's heart sank.

"Er—" Rowan called unsteadily from the back of the room, where he'd made slow progress with the filing cabinet. "I think I might have found something important."

The former taster turned to the others, holding a slim packet in shaking hands. "There's a file here with my name on it."

Chapter Fifteen

The Elevator

uddenly Cecil crossed the gloomy shop and flung open the door, exchanging foul air for fair. Looking out at the bridge, he saw that the vultures had retreated, preferring the rooftops and balconies to the cobbled roadway, but he could hear their ugly chatter from above. Ivy's scattered medicines lay abandoned and disheveled beside the old iron elevator. The donkey stood stoically alongside a pillow of hay, chewing vigorously.

"To the *Trindletrip!*" Cecil called, urging them along.

The Knox, in a glorious example of commerce, had in its collection of shops and stalls several taverns. It was the group's misfortune that their way took them by The Deadly Dose, where, bolstered by Mrs. Pulch's tall tales of Ivy's healing powers, a boisterous crowd of earlier would-be patients overflowed into the street, having exhausted their purses inside.

"It's her!" one cried from the throng, pointing at Ivy with a stubby finger. "The healing girl!"

"Stop her! She's getting away!"

Ivy's clientele surged upon the bridge, insisting they be mended. Whereas earlier in the morning their line was somewhat subdued, now, as Ivy emerged from Dumbcane's shop, they were a much more untidy group of unhappy townsfolk. They elbowed each other for prime position, shouting and unruly.

"Er—" Ivy eyed Cecil apologetically.

"Let us pass!" Cecil commanded, his voice booming.

"Cecil Manx, the Steward of Caux, has given you an order!" Axle growled.

For a moment it looked as if the Steward would get his wish, but instead, after a brief delay, the crowd erupted in complaint. They advanced on the foursome, and Ivy and her group found themselves retreating—one step, two steps—and then running as fast as their legs could carry them.

"Over there!" cried Axle, who was beginning to lag behind. "The elevator!"

It was the only way.

Behind them, Mrs. Pulch had joined the fray, her curious nature being one that would never allow an angry mob to go uninvestigated. She stood scolding anyone with two ears—waving her carpetbag menacingly—appalled at the undignified behavior she was witnessing. Spying her wayward pupil retreating on the Knox, she froze in surprise and was lost in the surging crowd.

Cecil wrenched open the rusted cage as the donkey watched indifferently. He ushered first Rowan, then Ivy, and finally Axle into the small enclosure. The thing creaked alarmingly.

"There's only room for three!" Ivy called to her uncle, panicked.

"It's not me they want." His eyes twinkled as the iron gate slammed shut and the small latch caught. The apotheopath looked over his shoulder at the advancing crowd.

"Be well, Ivy." Cecil turned to her. "May you lay your eyes again upon Pimcaux—and may your feet follow this time."

With a resounding clap, he banged his staff against the donkey's hay bin—sending the animal into a clatter of action.

"Uncle Cecil—" Ivy cried.

Down, down they went, lurching and spiraling dizzyingly.

The last thing Ivy would see of the Knox for some time— or of her uncle, for that matter—was a forest of boots, soles worn thin and scuffed with years of wear.

Chapter Sixteen

Departure

The river Marcel—its placid surface betrays none of its deeper secrets. To dredge it would bring up an assortment of collectibles, odd shoes, vials, lost hollow rings. But it is the journey that concerns us here. The waters twist through the heart of the land of Caux, originating from small underground streams in the north, not far from Rowan's family farm, and flow by countless trestles (and over a fair few aqueducts). The river dampens strange woods and fields of verdure alike. There are calm parts, brisk parts—deep eddies and narrow, limestone-edged passages. The Marcel flows by Ivy's childhood home—the Hollow Bettle—and beneath Axle's beloved trestle. And, yes, it winds its way through the capital city, Templar. From there, to the sea.

With one important stop along the way.

The *Trindletrip* made barely a noise upon the water—an un-settling *glug-glug* was all Ivy, Rowan, and Axle heard as they departed the quay. Then, as Trindle, the ship's captain, coaxed the engines into a forward gear, there was nothing but a soft purr. With little fanfare, and as quiet as thieves, they departed for Rocamadour.

"That was close," Rowan admitted as he and Ivy navigated the boat's crowded hallways to their separate quarters.

Ivy agreed. She was feeling a lot of things, none of them relief. Who knew when she would see her uncle Cecil again? The last time they were separated, he had been locked in the Nightshades' dungeons for over a year. Surely Rocamadour—even with its Doorway to Pimcaux—held many more awful possibilities. It seemed she was never to have a proper goodbye with her uncle.

Ivy and Rowan were finding that the houseboat was surprisingly well prepared. It had plenty of rooms and low hallways, but still it was cramped with the many unpacked items from Peps's move—for this was indeed the trestleman's new home. Boxes, wardrobes, and the occasional velvet couch had been placed at odd intervals, making getting around an adventure in itself.

Ivy skirted an overstuffed footstool and came upon an impressive marble bust. It bore the distinct likeness of Peps (although much larger than the original) and somehow even managed to capture the trestleman's haughty smile.

"Rowan—" Ivy remembered. "Peps must be here, somewhere!" Ivy had yet to see her friend since he had taken ill. He would surely be a welcome addition to their travels—he could be counted on to provide them with many distractions. Trindle, she knew, would be busy steering the boat, and Axle would have his nose in a book the entire time.

A cascade of lace doilies fell from somewhere above.

"Yes. But good luck finding him," Rowan grumbled.

There, directly after a teetering stack of polished luggage, Ivy and Rowan finally found their quarters. Each was laid out with their belongings, and their trunks awaited them, but Ivy's spirit of adventure was dampened by their abrupt departure, which in her quiet room now seemed suddenly more absolute. There was a round portal through which the banks of the river drifted by, and Ivy thought to go above and search out Peps.

She found Axle instead, sitting thoughtfully on deck recording observations in a small notebook. Rowan was already there—apparently he, too, did not feel like being alone belowdecks.

"Ah, good." The trestleman adjusted his pince-nez. "You're both here. I was just reviewing my notes."

Ivy sighed, settling in beside Rowan, who was dabbing his nose with a moist hankie.

"Time is, of course, of the essence. Rocamadour exists at the foothills of the Craggy Burls, and, besides its many other defenses—stinging nettles and the usual giant thistles—it is surrounded by an impassable forest of hawthorn trees and impenetrable bramble. Trindle can bring us only as far as the Toad—" At this, Ivy and Rowan exchanged confused looks. "And then he and Peps will return to Templar. But we shall be welcome at the Toad—it has a special place in my heart, and I will be able to sort out the remaining details there. It lies in the shadow of Rocamadour, where, as you know, we will find the surviving Doorway." The trestleman looked at them expectantly. "But know this. The Doorway to Pimcaux is a *Verdigris* door."

"A Verdigris door?" Ivy asked.

Axle was consulting the chaotic stack of papers by his side, and finding the one he wanted, he looked up. "Made of parchment."

Rowan blew his nose and coughed. "I'm sorry. I could have sworn you said the Doorway to Pimcaux was made of parchment."

"Why, of course! Whatever would you expect it to be made of?"

Ivy was about to answer the various materials she might encounter when faced with a door—wood, stone, even the amber-like glass in Underwood. But Axle continued.

"The Doorway is made of parchment because it is in a book! I believe you have some, er, experience with this?"

Indeed, the pair had encountered just such a book in Axle's crowded study, and Ivy's heart leapt at the memory—a dark curtain, and the odd tingling of magic.

"Weren't all the Verdigris books destroyed in the fire?" Rowan asked glumly.

Axle grew serious.

"This one wasn't. It was hidden."

"Hidden! Where?" Ivy asked.

Axle looked suddenly bashful. "That remains to be seen."

"Too bad we can't ask Dumbcane," Ivy said thoughtfully. The scribe seemed to know where all of the Guild's valuable paper was kept.

"Axle, why all this fuss because some calligrapher is making inks from scourge bracken?" Rowan wondered suddenly. "If King Verdigris wrote with these inks, what makes them so dangerous?"

The trestleman narrowed his eyes. "Scourge bracken is not used lightly—in fact, it is not used at all. It uses *you*. It was reckless and negligent of Dumbcane to employ such a potent force for his personal gain. Once King Verdigris realized its true nature, he made it his task to extinguish the very last of it." Axle paused. "And consider, if you will, its other name."

Rowan nodded, mollified.

"What other name?" Ivy asked.

Axle turned to Rowan, who quoted easily.

"'Scourge Bracken—var. Scourge Weed. Avoid at all costs. Easily accomplished by the fortunate fact that the weed is extinct. Obsolete moniker: *Kingmaker.*'"

"Kingmaker?" Ivy frowned. It was probably a good idea to keep a poison called Kingmaker away from a man bent on ruling the world.

Axle reached into his waistcoat and retrieved a small package.

"I had this brought from home for you, Ivy."

Ivy brightened. Opening the simply wrapped package, she found something utterly familiar.

"My *Guide!*" she squealed. Indeed, it was her very own personally inscribed *Field Guide*—the one she had left in her rush as she abandoned her uncle's tavern. It was filled with her curly scrawl and splattered with various spills from her experiments. It smelled like home.

"Thank you, Axle! Now I can give yours back. . . ." She turned to Rowan.

The taster nodded. He was allowing his attention to wander. The fresh air on deck was a relief to his congested head. He had been feeling wheezy and disagreeable and had found it hard to concentrate since boarding the *Trindletrip*. It would not be long before he realized the source of his discomfort. Folded within a coil of greasy rope was a cat of enormous proportions.

A filthy, ink-stained cat.

Chapter Seventeen

Six

ey, that's the cat from Dumbcane's shop!"
Ivy said when Rowan had revealed the animal's napping spot.

The cat slept on, oblivious.

"I'm sure of it. My, he's a big one!" Ivy continued, drawing
nearer. "What is he doing here, I wonder?"

In fact, he was an invited guest.

Trindle had long needed a mouser, and when a cat
appeared—one with a massive appetite—he was relieved.
Houseboats exist in a state of siege; rats and mice and other
uninvited pests were often skittering around the water's edge.
As Trindle searched for a name for his new pet, one soon presented itself. The cat survived both a dip in a dirty oil pan and
twice a fall overboard, and was safely said to be on his sixth
life—if indeed it was true that a cat as large as he was only
granted nine lives. Trindle easily decided upon a name.

He was called Six.

"For the time being," Axle laughed.

"And look—he's got six toes on each of his front paws!" Ivy noticed.

Like his parents and their parents before them, the creature was indeed born with an extra digit on each front foot, and all twelve toes gave him an even more unfair advantage when hunting.

And six gleaming claws on each, Rowan couldn't help but notice. The taster was appalled. He had never once heard of a cat doing anything useful. Here, revealed, was the cause of his intense discomfort! His allergies had never been worse. The monster cat seemed to care nothing for presentation, or any of the usual cat-type pastimes of bathing, cleaning, or preening. There the thing was, its noisy purring punctuated by occasional deep, raspy growls. As he watched the source of his misery through increasingly itchy eyes, the thing perked up a ragged ear and yawned—half its face seemed to disappear in a bountiful row of teeth and gums. It was simply crawling with fleas.

"Humph." Rowan narrowed his eyes at the creature. "The filthy thing has been splashing about in Dumbcane's ink!"

In fact, the cat Six would soon prove to be a large amount of trouble. Here was a cat with no loyalty—or rather, a loyalty of his own design (not much different from any other cat). But, alas, there was no way of foretelling the mischief ahead— even for such a wise man as Axle—for loyalty is only revealed when it is tested.

Rowan resisted the impulse to throw the thing ashore by

his ragged, inky scruff. What a poor substitute for Poppy—his beloved bettle boar! And to his horror, Ivy was currently tickling Six's torn ear with a tentative finger. Worse still, he was soon to find that under no circumstances was Trindle agreeable to deporting Six.

Apparently the trip upriver to the dismal city of Rocamadour was to be made even more disagreeable than the taster originally thought.

Chapter Eighteen
The Cure

Peps D. Roux had quietly taken to bed in his new home on the *Trindletrip*, where he was convalescing alone—dismal and feverish. He vaguely felt the engines come alive and the boat take on a more buoyant quality. He imagined the bed beneath him floating along the Marcel, raftlike, and when he forced open his bloodshot eyes, he was at a momentary loss as to his whereabouts. When he noticed several chatty partridges perched upon the shelf in the upper corner of his cabin, he thought nothing of it and asked them kindly to leave him be. When they became insulted (Peps had tried very hard to be polite) and altered themselves into hideous vultures to demonstrate their displeasure, the trestleman hid beneath his blankets shivering. When the vultures then began swooping about his small cabin, bashing into walls and upsetting furniture, letting their filth spread upon the floor below, Peps cowered deeper. Beneath his bedding, he heard their hissing, which soon became an outright argument as to how best a trestleman tasted—and it was only then that he finally dismissed the birds as delirium. But to be sure, he remained beneath the piles of blankets.

Which was where Ivy found him.

She and Six had been exploring the boat when she came upon Peps's sickroom. At first she mistook the bed as simply unmade, but as she flung open a window to refresh the stale air, she heard a pitiful cry. Its source, apparently, was beneath the bedclothes, which she also threw off. Finding the proud trestleman a mere shadow of himself—pale and drawn—alarmed her, and when he began babbling about mean-spirited birds bent on his destruction, she went at once to find Axle.

It was generally agreed that Peps's ill fortune was brought about by his move to the houseboat. Everyone knew trestlemen did not fare well on water, especially after the disappearance of the alewives who ruled the waterways. It was as if he were thumbing his nose at fortune by relocating away from the natural abode of his kind—that is, beneath a bridge. Since he had chosen to live *upon* water rather than *over* it, well, it should come as no surprise he should end up unwell.

Unwell he was.

"Ivy." His eyes fluttered open; his voice was raspy and hoarse. He was a mere lump in his bed, covers replaced tightly to his chin. "Help me," he cried miserably.

"I will, Peps," she assured him softly at his bedside. The

others aboard the boat—Axle, Rowan, and Trindle—stood somberly behind her, having come when Ivy had raised the alarm.

In her workshop apron were a few odds and ends, a spare river stone that she favored, various-sized corks, Dumbcane's fanciful letter *C*, which she had taken from the shop. In short, nothing of any help. Everything that she needed was strewn about on the Knox.

She looked down at Peps's distorted face and held his cold hand. She parted the few clumps of hair that lay across the trestleman's proud brow and placed her hand upon his forehead. But it was here that her own attempts at relieving Peps's discomfort began and ended, and another, more powerful force made itself known.

An unwelcome smell—the stench from Dumbcane's—briefly filled her nostrils, and her light-headedness returned, while quickly the floor, the boat itself, seemed at once to heave a great sigh. Blinking, she saw not the *Trindletrip,* nor the murky Marcel, but a small, eerie copse of alder trees.

She was somehow wrapped in a shroud of mist and shadow and felt at once larger than the longest river and smaller than the most modest acorn. Wisps of ragged fog caught upon the unfriendly branches of the wood, small, wretched clouds torn from the sky.

Peps was there, but he was not. He was made from the same murk that darkened her vision. He seemed asleep.

Her attention was drawn through the wiry, inhospitable trees to a cloyingly familiar gate. Green serpentine ivy snaked up the poles, brilliant in the bleak landscape. It beckoned in a new breeze. The tall ironwork was splendid, she saw as she drew closer, and was topped with carved figurines. But a strange silence greeted her—an unusual absence of bees or birds, or general garden activity.

"Hello?" she called, pressing her face against the bars. Where had she seen this courtyard before?

She looked around. It was a vast garden, one of great beauty, but kept with a strict and disciplined hand. The manicured rows and trained grapevines stretched on, disappearing into the distance in a thicket of dark fog. A small garden shed—a folly—off to the side. Woven bell-shaped hives for bees.

She tried again. "Anyone home?" Rattling the gates, she found them locked.

Then, a rumble of distant thunder, and Ivy remembered Peps.

The clouds were rolling in quickly and a sudden storm now threatened, and she was overcome again with the acrid smell of Dumbcane's inks. She ran hurriedly through the thrashing trees, which now had grown thicker, more dreary.

She hurried but made no progress. Behind her, the sound of metal on metal—and as she turned, she saw the garden gate hanging open. But the view now through the archway was one of devastation—gone were the manicured rows and ordered vines. In their place only bramble. A thick, knotted spiky growth had overtaken everything. The world then lit up in a pale, shivery blue as she was treated to a bolt of lightning—and Ivy had the uncomfortable sensation that she was due for another.

But before one came, the scene dissolved, accompanied by vague silvery chimes, and the young girl found herself blinking beneath the yellow light of the sun streaming in from a circular portal, aboard the *Trindletrip*. Peps was once again at her side.

The familiar faces around her wore a selection of stunned looks.

"What just happened?" Rowan wondered, astonished.

Ivy blinked.

Six's matted fur stood on end.

"Was that lightning?" Axle asked no one in particular. *"Inside?"*

"I wonder if it's going to rain," replied Trindle, annoyed.

"Er—Ivy?" Rowan frowned. "I could have sworn you—well . . . when the lights flashed, it was like you *vanished*." He laughed nervously.

None of this was of any concern to Ivy, for she was enduring a very potent realization of her own. She suddenly remembered where it was she had seen that particular garden gate before. With a chilling jolt, Ivy Manx recognized the gate

and the garden beyond as the one from Dumbcane's letter
C. She unfurled it to be sure.

All were so astonished that it took them several moments to
notice that the most enthusiastic of the bunch was Peps—
standing, stretching, walking about flush with life.

Chapter Nineteen

The Charm

No one could have been more surprised at the proceedings than Ivy. It was as if Mrs. Pulch had scripted it herself in one of her tall tales. She had vanished from the houseboat, arrived at a mysterious garden, and returned with a clap of lightning to a miraculous curing!

"Inexplicable," Axle concluded.

"Incomprehensible," Trindle added.

"Miraculous," Rowan whispered, and then sneezed. He had seen Ivy's curative abilities but never quite in this way. She had cured him and Shoo, but that had been with a tonic she had made. This was an entirely new occurrence for which there was no explanation.

Peps was the first to celebrate his miraculous recovery at the young girl's hands, standing, his cheeks flooded with color, eyes sparkling.

"Ivy!" he enthused. "I feel a man half my age!"

"Indeed!" Axle nodded in awe. "I've never seen you better—you hardly appear a day over a hundred and fifty!"

Peps flushed with the compliment.

Axle examined his brother again, dumbfounded. But Peps had found one of his trunks and was rummaging inside it, capes, furs, and velvet cloaks flying.

"Ahh!" Peps shouted, his voice muffled by the fine tailoring. He turned, a look of triumph on his face. "And now I am quite ready to present to you, Ivy Manx, a great token of my appreciation."

"Peps!" Ivy was appalled. "I don't even know what I did."

"Nonsense. I'll hear none of that, young lady. Modesty is so overrated!" He dug his pudgy fist into a small pocket of a particularly elaborate morning coat from the trunk, ending his frantic search. "Hmmph." A slight look of worry, then triumph, passed over his smooth face, and soon his fist was an open palm—and upon it a small shiny thing caught the light from the round portal.

"What is it?" Ivy leaned in, curious despite herself.

It was thin and delicate, with a dark oval hole through one side.

"A hatpin?" she asked.

"An embroidery needle?" Rowan suggested.

"Hardly! What are they teaching you these days? It's a birdcall. A silver birdcall. A charm, of sorts. It, er, belonged to

someone quite dear to me. It will bring you good fortune."
Peps smiled, looking remarkably like his marble bust and
treating the room to his gold tooth.

Axle grabbed his brother's hand and peered into it, a look
of surprise and then fury flashing across his bearded face.
"Peps!"

Peps looked momentarily sheepish.

"You never told me you had an alewife's charm!"

"You never asked."

"What do you do with it?" Ivy asked, examining it.

"You mean, besides wear it?" Peps shrugged. He took the
thing, which was threaded upon a silken ribbon, and tied it
around Ivy's neck.

"Well, thank you, Peps. I suppose I could use all the good
fortune I can get."

"It's a potent charm," Axle warned. "I should like very
much to study it—"

Rowan cleared his scratchy throat. "Um, could someone
tell me what an alewife is?"

Chapter Twenty

Troubled Waters

he Field Guide to the Poisons of Caux was the preeminent reference book of the land, containing in its vast pages the antidotes to poisons, the secret meanings of flowers, and even a few magical, hidden passages. But in some ways it was maddeningly incomplete.

The book was written by Axlerod D. Roux in response to the poisonous regime of the Deadly Nightshades and the rise of the Tasters' Guild, and it was used as a tool by those wishing to remain alive in the treacherous land of Caux.

It was also the favorite book of the truly wicked Queen Nightshade. Because it was so widely read by friend and foe alike, Axle wisely chose not to include anything controversial—favoring instead the purely factual—lest he be labeled a heretic and imprisoned in the dungeons for treason. Still, some things were too important to Caux's history to omit, and these he secretly buried within the text. Rowan had discovered such a passage detailing the sad history of King Verdigris.

But the alewives eluded him for a different reason.

Axle did not write of them because there was simply too much heartbreak surrounding their disappearance.

The trestleman cleared his throat and nodded slightly.

"Alewives," Axle began, "rule over troubled water." He appeared to be gathering his thoughts. "They were inhabitants of Caux, and when the Doorway to Pimcaux stood open, they were invited in. But it was an unspeakable trick—and Vidal Verjouce slammed the Doorway shut behind them. . . ." His voice trailed off.

Peps took over.

"They were our wives," he explained simply.

Ivy was wide-eyed. Here was another reason to get to Pimcaux, and she said so. They must hurry to Rocamadour.

But the taster scowled. Rowan somehow could not muster the same urgency to get to Rocamadour as the others did. He was miserable beside Six, who he was sure was menacing him when Ivy wasn't looking. And he missed the bettle boar Poppy greatly—traveling anywhere without her seemed somehow wrong.

In fact, the bleak city of the Tasters' Guild was the last place he wished to find himself. He was a wanted man—an uncollared taster—and his future was grim if he was captured. His head swam and his eyes teared and another fit of sneezing loomed. As Rowan regretted the swift departure, Six was snaking his way around Ivy's shins, coming nearly as high as her waist, leaving clumps of hair and stalky whiskers behind. He was sure the thing was eyeing him as he did so—the large pads of his feet weaving silently along the wooden deck boards.

His misery grew. Here he was, being forced to return to the very place he so feared. The Tasters' Guild severely punished its renegade tasters with a truly awful fate. One meted out by the Guild's own fearsome leader, Vidal Verjouce—the ultimate tragedy for a taster, and one that ensures he might never taste again: the surgical removal of the tongue.

Between Six and Rocamadour, he wanted nothing more than to be alone.

Chapter Twenty-one

Foul Mood

There is little enjoyment in feeling ill. Surely one can forgive, then, the distasteful temper that now settled upon Rowan Truax. He was certain in his gloom that Ivy was *encouraging* the cat—for Six was never far from her side, and he was almost certain the beastly pile of knots and tangles was stalking him.

But moods are just that, moods—often irrational and overpowering. He took no joy in the delicate little filament bulbs that clinked a fine tune, aflame along every available surface of the houseboat. He took no joy in anything, except perhaps solitude, wherein his mood roiled as they began their way along the ancient river, in the fading light, bound for lonesome ruins and low-lying cliffs.

Although the daylight was frail and anemic, Ivy's mood was one of confidence and cheer. Seeing the taster alone, she occasioned to remark upon their method of transport.

"Didn't Axle always say that to travel by houseboat is

simply the very best way to see anything and everything at all?" she enthused.

Rowan, however, was not to be engaged on this topic—or any other, for that matter—and responded in his usual manner of late, with stony silence. Ivy stole a sidelong glance at her friend, noting that he had been uncharacteristically withdrawn since boarding the houseboat, but attributed it to the weight of the approaching Rocamadour.

"Barberry?" Ivy tried, speaking of the flower that symbolizes sourness of temper. "Garden marigold?"

Unfortunately for Ivy, Rowan was not agreeable to having his pout pointed out, and she received a curt reply.

"Lichen," he sniffed, indicating his desire to be left alone.

"Fine." Ivy turned on her heel. But she couldn't resist a parting word. "Orange lily," which she really didn't mean, and "Larkspur," which she did.

The next day was uneventful, considering the circumstances of their departure, with one notable exception.

Rowan had been staring glumly over the railing when the boat slowed its progress somewhat and the river widened into a placid pool. The trees at the edge of the clearing were mostly the leftover yellows of birch and ash—the autumn rarely had much showiness after the ravaging Winds of Caux. Still, this was a small spark of hue, and one made doubly luscious as it was reflected in the mirror-like surface of the Marcel.

Rowan stared, unthinking, at the water. A muskrat was swimming dejectedly through the glassine reflection, a wave of ripples behind him. He headed toward the mud banks of the shore, creeping along a path until he found some safety in the tall grasses. The taster grew tired of waiting for the thing to make a reappearance, and he was just about to rise up from his slump and perhaps search out another form of entertainment when something caught his eye.

A swath of brush grew up from nearby, and it was there that Rowan saw some movement. With only dull yellows and browns in this wood, the patch of brilliant scarlet was conspicuous.

Rowan squinted, just to be sure.

Yes—there. A red-hooded figure retreated into the dusk.

Chapter Twenty-two
A Cautionary Note

The weather had now become a factor, and with the loss of light, a great chill was in the air. Axle was preoccupied with the low-lying clouds—he wanted urgently to consult some of his brass instruments against Caux's night sky. He was forced instead to spend his time muttering and examining old tomes or pulling on his beard and cursing the swollen river.

Ivy found herself happy for her thick woolens—she had discovered them when rummaging in her steamer trunk. She put them on at once. Her *Field Guide* lay open where she had tossed it on her bed. Inspired, she proceeded to dump the entire contents of the trunk onto the floor, taking inventory. Small notebooks—good for cataloging one's experiments with herbs—and lead pencils. Many more of her books. Seed packets. (Whoever packed her trunk must have known her quite well.) A waxen bag of violet-infused gumdrops. At the bottom she found it—a small leather satchel containing her poison kit.

Upon it, there was a letter.

My dearest Ivy,

This is a cautionary note.

What we know of the Prophecy are mislaid fragments; much of it was lost to the fire. But what we do know is that there are great and potent forces determined to see you fail. Your path as a healer is your salvation. You will need to remember this to combat what lies ahead of you.

You will practice your own brand of healing. Not mine. Since your knowledge is of these potent herbs, I would be remiss in sending you to Rocamadour——and Pimeaux——without them. But exercise the utmost restraint. Your beloved assistant Shoo might not be by your side, but he is never very far away in spirit.

Have faith in the ancient writings, my child:

Those Who Seek
Look to the Crows
For Crows Never Lie

Your loving uncle,
Cecil Manx

She realized she had been holding her breath as she read, and, exhaling sharply, she donned her stiff apron.

And set about tinkering.

Interestingly, Ivy knew a few recipes for the alleviation of allergy symptoms, but many more for causing them. Her old ways—the ways of Poison Ivy—had produced for her an impressive profit from the sale of itching powders, and dreary potions and tonics that could mimic Rowan's current state—or worse (much worse!). But she set to work now—with a sprinkle of pussy willow and a soupçon of ragweed—to help Rowan return to the sunny side of health. And temperament.

She normally felt very much at home with the poufs of odd smoke and choking wafts of powdered charcoal, but today she found there was a new thought intruding upon her concentration. She was unusually distracted, forgetting to turn over the small hourglass that timed her distillations. Annoyed, she blew a stray hair from her face and began again.

Her mind was not on her work. If only Shoo were here, he might gently guide her in the right direction.

She thought of the dark, mysterious garden she had seen. What lay beyond the gates? Whose garden was it—and why had Dumbcane drawn it, rendering it quite expertly with his strange inks alongside the image of her own face?

And, most of all, she wondered what grew there.

Her own potion needed something, she realized, and walking over to her messy bed, she plucked a few hairs from Six's backside and added them to the brew before her. The cat eyed her uncivilly and then, with a swish of his tail, turned away.

Scourge bracken.

She found herself fascinated with the potent plant.

At her uncle's tavern, with Shoo by her side, she had concocted a true panacea for poisons, a helpful cure-all for anything. But she could not duplicate the recipe no matter how hard she tried. It was the greatest disappointment. With scourge bracken, she found herself thinking, what other potions were possible? Surely she, Poison Ivy, would be knowledgeable enough to use it with the proper restraint—to overcome its domination? Queen Ivy, she found herself thinking. Princess of Potions.

With a shudder, she realized her error in thought. Surely this type of reasoning was what got Hemsen Dumbcane in trouble to begin with! And, worse, she found that it reminded her of someone. Someone quite close to her.

Her mother.

Hadn't Clothilde wished for herself the very glory of curing the King? Wasn't she quite troubled that this was not her destiny?

Ivy stood up in disgust, disturbing the vials and scales before her, her experiment upended.

It was a fine thing that Ivy abandoned her tinkering then, for Rowan would not have been persuaded to ingest it. Rowan would not be persuaded to do much of anything—especially reveal the mysterious scarlet figure he had glimpsed that day. Such was his misery that he was determined to keep the incident to himself.

Chapter Twenty-three

Fog

he last thing they saw before the thick, rolling fog set in was a small iron trestle some ways above them, spanning the cliffs that now drew high on either side. It was a comforting sight. Even from below, Ivy could see the amber light of a fire dancing on the ceiling, and she thought of Axle's lovely trestle beside her childhood home. And then, quite suddenly, there was only gray.

This was a fog of some proportion. It had heft and body to its billowing wisps—and a smell of damp basements. It was, in fact, emanating from the Marcel, as the early cold snap pressed against the warmer river. It made Ivy tired, and finally, she went to bed.

Stretching out upon the cot, and fighting Six for space, she opened the *Guide*. She found herself at a page at the rear of the reference work—a densely annotated section entitled "Appendix IVb: Dictionary of Symbols." Upon it, the image of a snake consuming its own tail.

Ivy read, thinking of the strange imagery from Dumbcane's shop, the fantastical creatures. The golden door with this very same symbol.

Ouroboros:

A serpent consuming its tail. An obvious symbol for Caste, adopted by the Casters' Guild as their own, but harking back to a much earlier time.

She had a feeling that there was more to this. She made a

note to discuss the ouroboros with the *Field Guide*'s author at the very next opportunity.

In the morning, Ivy awoke with the edge of the book imprinted upon her face. Something was different. The engines had ceased.

Chapter Twenty-four

The Snodgrass Toad

There was nothing at first, just the fog. Ivy was huddled on deck now with Axle and Peps when Rowan joined them. Trindle had slowed the boat to a near crawl and was forced to blare his foghorn dully.

Then, as if a giant's breath blew through, the fog shifted and rolled. It lay still listless on the earth and river, but above, enormous, hulking stanchions of heavy iron materialized as if from the ether. They dwarfed the *Trindletrip*. The passengers craned their necks at the black vertical trusses—the thick metal emerged from a cloud above only to return to it below, disappearing into the impenetrable fog. They were disembodied legs, eerie and immense.

"The Toad," Axle called to Trindle in the steerage compartment.

Trindle cut the engines entirely and the boat bobbed along as if in a cloud, until in another breath the trestle's supports were gone.

Ivy heard herself gasp.

From somewhere above, a clanging of metal against metal, and then silence.

They were thankfully treated to another break in the fog, and as the shroud slowly lifted again, here and there blackness replaced the gray. There was now a body to those legs—a body of a trestle on a grim cloud, ghostly and ungrounded. It was completely unreachable.

"It's enormous!" she whispered.

"Shh!" Axle held his finger to his lips and listened.

Indeed, as Ivy waited, there came a clinking sound—at first very far off, but then definitely on approach.

"Ah. You are in for a treat!" Axle was saying to Ivy and Rowan. "First-class service. Simply spectacular! The Toad is the pinnacle against which all others are judged."

After what seemed to Ivy like an absurdly long time, a dark object was lowered beside the stern. It was an elevator of sorts, she realized. On it was a note.

It read:

No Vacancy.
Go Away!

"*Go away?*" Peps was incredulous.

Axle was still holding the offending note—written on

impeccable stationery with a fine script atop confirming the sender to be the Snodgrass Toad.

"Who do they think they are?" Peps was working himself up into a froth of insult.

"I suppose it is their right." Axle shrugged.

"They are a *hotel*, Axlerod. A hotel, no less, for *trestlemen*."

At this, Ivy looked upward with renewed interest.

Axle was feeling around in an inside pocket of his great-coat for a pen, thinking perhaps a polite missive would gain their entry. A simple misunderstanding, he felt sure, and he would right it by explaining himself. He set about composing.

Peps adjusted a flashy orange scarf, throwing it casually about his shoulders, and polished his signet ring. "Don't bother! I will investigate this further."

And with that the small man hopped aboard the elevator.

"No you don't—not without me!" Axle admonished, joining his brother.

Ivy, too, would not be left behind, and Rowan—Rowan under no circumstances wanted to be left anywhere with Six.

Peps flipped an ancient-looking control, and the entire thing lurched upward.

"Humph," Peps complained, inspecting the drab inside. "Seems we've been relegated to the freight elevator."

Chapter Twenty-five

No Vacancy

The Snodgrass Toad was a majestic and ornate trestle that harked back to an earlier time in Caux, a time when great things were built to last, if not to look at. A trestle hotel, it was big and grand, made from stone and wood and iron. A fancy place— inside. But from the exterior, the stone and wood and iron made up a hulking bridge, which spanned two sheer limestone cliffs in an ungraceful arc. The Toad threatened to either leap up and away or fall into the waters below, depending on the time of day you looked at it.

The architects were baffled. Their designs—all seven hundred pages of them—called for elegant lines and graceful bends, but what they got was a place that would, when completed, look remarkably like a crouching toad straddling the waters below. They tore it down and began again, only to be rewarded with the same vision, only beastlier. It was plain that there was some sort of magic responsible—a spell, perhaps from a disgruntled alewife.

Indeed, since alewives ruled over waterways, everyone knew their blessing was necessary to successfully complete any bridge or crossing. And the builders had neglected this one very important act: obtaining the alewives' approval.

Upon the trestle's completion, wild snodgrass grew up in tufts atop its bulging roof, untamable, filling in every last detail of the toad's silhouette. The sheer cliffs to either side and the waters below formed at this point in the river's geology a sort of wind tunnel, and the Toad at times was even made to sound as if it groaned. But no matter—if indeed there was a curse from an unhappy alewife, she was thwarted in the end. The Snodgrass Toad became instantly famous and a wildly popular attraction, and soon all the people involved in the execution of the remarkable trestle would imagine that they had never meant it to appear any other way.

As the lift made its slow, incremental progress up the underside of the expansive trestle, the group was silent. The trip was punctuated with worrying pauses, when the elevator would stop its ascent and hang aloft, twisting lazily—and then lurching back downward. Ivy gripped the worn brass rail that ran along the side of the interior, but that did little to alleviate the distress of the ride. There was some sort of thick green moss clinging to the underbelly of the trestle, and their journey seemed to be disrupting it. Large clumps of it dislodged from the damp beams and rained down upon them like sludgy wet beards.

"I see they've fallen behind on the upkeep," Peps sniffed, watching a trail of green slime slide down the old window.

They did arrive, finally—the elevator's topside alighting with a thud upon a set of spring-loaded trapdoors, and then, in a final crescendo of metal against metal, through the underside of the hotel. With a pop, the old thing reached the lobby, bobbing perkily.

The doors opened to a chamber devoted to stone and mirror. Yet it seemed that at some time previous, light and mirror had quarreled, and light had retreated in a sulk. What remained was mirror and polished stone with little sparkle. It was a remarkable room in that the visitor expected to encounter his reflection at every turn but never did—imparting the odd sensation of wonder at one's own existence.

Ivy stepped forward onto a rich red rug, and the rest followed. Before them, a desk.

Peps was the first to ring the small attendant bell, which he did impatiently as he looked around the lobby.

"What kind of greeting is this?" he asked to no one in particular, ringing the bell again for good measure. He ran a gloved finger along the tabletop and inspected for dust.

"You know," Axle began, "I don't like to think about how long it's been since I was here last."

As if to illustrate the passage of time, they were now joined by an impossibly old and brittle trestleman whose uniform had been laundered with entirely too much starch. He looked

as if he wished very dearly to stoop but was being suppo…
his upright position by the sheer crispness of his attire. This
man was the concierge, who, like the hotel, had surely seen
better days.

"The card said 'No Vacancy,'" the old man whispered in a
creaky voice. He cleared his throat and, with great effort, repeated himself, but only managed it slightly louder.

"We can read," Peps replied dryly. "So every one of the
hundreds of rooms here is filled?"

"Excuse me." Axle stepped forward. "Surely there is some
place for us? We will take whatever you have. A storeroom,
even? We've traveled from Templar. Our errand is urgent."

"Master D. Roux," the concierge, a trestleman named
Crump, began wearily. He knew the face of every guest who
had ever stayed at the Toad.

Axle nodded happily.

"Your errand is of no concern to us."

This was a surprise indeed, and Axle's smile stalled upon
his face.

"If I m-might respectfully disagree," Axle stammered. "It
is of *great concern* to you, and the others, and in fact all of
Caux."

Crump paused. His uniform was losing the battle with his
posture, and he seemed to be distracted by his shoe.

"The winds of change have blown, old friend. The
Deadly Nightshades no longer rule! The great Master

Apotheopath Manx is now Steward of Caux while his niece Ivy—here—journeys to Pimcaux to restore the Good King Verdigris to full health!" Axle's enthusiastic speech now stalled.

A strange look filled the entirety of Crump's sagging features, but not exactly one of relief or liberation.

"Forgive me, sir. But you are wrong."

"Oh, I think you will soon see—" Axle began. But Crump was not finished.

"You have made it decidedly, horribly, worse."

There was a stunned silence. Finally, when it became quite clear that Crump had nothing further to say, Axle drew himself up and produced from his waistcoat a small card of thick stock upon which, in raised oxblood ink, was written his name. He thrust the calling card at Crump.

"Announce our presence to Rhustaphustian. Now."

Chapter Twenty-six

Rhustaphustian

Crump shuffled away holding Axle's card, leaving the mood in the lobby distinctly darker than he had found it.

"How have *we* made it worse?" Peps scoffed.

Axle was frowning, and Ivy began to notice she had an awful feeling in her stomach.

She turned to examine the nearby wall and was introduced to numerous panoramic, sepia-toned photographs. It seemed to be a catalog of Caux's many trestles and their various occupants. The images populated nearly all available wall space, except where there were obvious absences—ghostly rectangles and lonely nails indicated that several had been removed.

The trestlemen within the dark frames were frozen in an earlier, more innocent time. Ivy peered at the blurred visages, some faces shy and coy, others caught in a moment of exuberant delight. The river beneath them was ever calm; the sun behind them threw a pleasant shadow upon all the gridiron and scaffolding that formed each overpass.

As Ivy wondered at this, she came upon a small picture. This one was somewhat different, she noticed at once—the trestle was of a very simple design, and the photographer seemed to feel the need to enliven the shot. The camera had been placed further away; the woods beside the small arched bridge were more wild, the stream (for it was not a river here but a shallow, rock-studded waterway) more frothy beneath the camera, as if the presence of so much nature would deliver the tiny trestle from its own coarseness. Ivy inspected it closely.

To her great surprise, of the two figures depicted upon the trestle, one was not a trestleman. It was a *lady*—a striking and refined lady, who complemented the trestleman in size quite accordingly. Although she was dressed in a fashion from long ago, she seemed to be well acquainted with good shoes and impressive tailoring, possessing, Ivy noted, a distinct proclivity for pearl buttons. From a ribbon around her neck, Ivy noticed, hung a small, glinting charm. Her hair was a blur in the old print, as if it were made of the same stuff as the stream below.

"Rowan!" Ivy whispered, standing still before the small photo.

The taster turned to investigate.

"I think that's an alewife!" She pointed, feeling for her own alewife charm around her neck.

"Where?" Rowan peered in.

"There—she's a bit blurry, but I'd swear it's so!"

It was then that Crump made what for him was a speedy

return. The concierge addressed Axle, completely disregarding Peps. "Rhustaphustian will see you now."

The group followed him into the adjoining hallway and eventually to a low, squat door.

"Everyone is gathered," Crump informed them.

Axle stole a look at his brother, who, for once, was silent—his hand frozen on the threshold. Over the years, Peps had made no secret of his disappointment in nearly all his fellow trestlemen—while profiting from their absence. It would be an uncomfortable reunion.

They entered what at one time was the Toad's grand ballroom. Currently it was populated with rocking chairs, the preferred seating of the trestlemen of the Toad. The chairs were everywhere, willy-nilly upon the scuffed wood floor. The room's walls were a dim, mushroomy beige, that is, until they were not—when dramatic red polka dots prevailed. And atop the red-spotted walls was a ceiling of finely carved balsa wood—like a folded fan. Or gills. In fact, Ivy and Rowan were now realizing, the entire room was made to evoke an enormous toadstool.

"Axlerod D. Roux," spoke a barrel-chested trestleman who sat in the middle of the room on a high-back rocker. "It must be dark days indeed that have made you abandon the comfort and solitude of your own trestle."

"It's been some time, Rhustaphustian," Axle acknowledged uncomfortably.

Ivy stole a glance at the rest of the room. Many of the weathered chairs sat empty, but those that were full were occupied by ancient-looking trestlemen of similar temperament and discouraging expressions. Their only audible contribution to the conversation was a ceaseless creaking of each rocker. Behind them on one wall, the round windows revealed that the fog had lifted.

There was a pained silence punctuated with the elder trestleman clearing his throat.

"To what, then, do we owe this . . . honor?" He held Axle's card uncomfortably by its corner.

"Surely news of our travels has reached you here?" Axle smiled ingratiatingly.

"It has." Rhustaphustian turned to look now at Ivy Manx.

"Ah. Allow me to introduce—" Axle began excitedly.

"Poison Ivy," Rhustaphustian interrupted. "We have heard of Poison Ivy, yes." He nodded, appraising the girl. "Particularly, of late, some incredible feats of healing."

Ivy blushed heartily under his gaze. She wished again that Mrs. Pulch had tamed her penchant for exaggeration.

"Um . . ." She stepped forward and found herself falling into a curtsey. "Sir, if I may. Don't believe everything you hear." Ivy was about to launch into a pithy explanation of her tutor's gossiping habits but stopped abruptly. The old trestleman's cold gaze froze her in place.

"We don't." The elder trestleman looked her up and down. "How *well* the child looks," he added, turning to Axle.

Ivy wondered at this.

A worried look flitted across Axle's face. "Yes. No—but—"

"To truly heal, one must know grave illness," Rhustaphustian quoted, eyes narrow. "Or are we picking and choosing our ancient wisdoms?"

Rowan shot Ivy a worried look.

"The actions of Ivy Manx—one girl—ended the torturous regime of the Deadly Nightshades," Axle reminded the room defensively.

"Perhaps. But in that we see no reason to celebrate."

Axle could not disguise his surprise. His eyes opened so wide they evicted the spectacles from his nose.

"The Deadly Nightshades were villainous," the elder trestleman allowed. "But the Tasters' Guild is worse—much worse! Was it not Vidal Verjouce who whispered poison into the Good King's ear, spreading his awful brand of betrayal from behind the dark curtain of the Tasters' Guild? For so long, Verjouce was preoccupied with his puppet king, but now he casts about in search of his enemies. The Snodgrass Toad exists in the shadow of Rocamadour—we cannot risk attracting the Tasters' Guild's attention."

"I assure you, we have not been followed," Axle insisted.

"Verjouce employs a new breed of spies." Rhustaphustian's voice was scornful. "They are his Watchmen. Literally—his eyes. You would know them, for they wear the robes of the Tasters' Guild, only scarlet."

With a lurch in his stomach, Rowan remembered the red-hooded figure from the riverside. "Um . . ."

But Axle's surprise had turned to anger, his face now fierce and flushed.

"Do you refuse us, then?" he demanded.

"You should not have come. You have endangered us all," Rhustaphustian said softly.

From his place of relative hiding behind Rowan, Peps burst forth.

"You cowards!" Peps squeaked. "The lot of you! How *dare* you speak to him that way! If Axlerod D. Roux desires your aid, you will provide it. Do you forget the debt you owe him? And do you dismiss so easily the ancient Prophecy and, in turn, the girl—the Prophesied One?"

This colorful outburst, while causing Ivy some embarrassment, was oddly received. There was no reaction at all—it was as if the entire roomful of trestlemen did not hear Peps's tirade, in fact did not see him, either.

"What did I tell you, Axle? They are just tired, feeble old men," Peps muttered.

When, after a moment's time, it became clear that their hosts were not going to respond, Ivy looked around the room, catching Rowan's eye. The taster seemed just as confused as she was. Peps had begun to sulk and had resumed an angry silence.

Axle finally spoke, and when he did, he began with two things dear to all trestlemen's hearts. "I am afraid the time for sitting idly by has passed. Beneath us the river flows dark and sickly. If you cannot muster the needed courage for yourselves, then you must find it for the alewives."

Chapter Twenty-seven
Tribunal

Deep in the misery of the Nightshade regime, at a deadly time in Caux's recent history, a secret trestleman tribunal was called to order. Such were the times when Caux's elders were in hiding, and this tribunal, unfairly or not, was made up of former residents of the Knox and various injured parties that Peps had amassed over the long years. These were all old men, from an ancient race, but the majority of the trestlemen who gathered undercover at the Toad had never been a part of such an assembly. Axlerod D. Roux was not alerted, for the topic of the arcane assembly was none other than his flamboyant brother, Peps. For many years, Peps had been impersonating Axle for his personal gain, but this was not the reason for the hearing. Actually, *hearing* was the reason for the hearing—for this was a secret trestleman selective-hearing tribunal.

There it was decided that Peps D. Roux, having appropriated their living quarters as he stayed behind enriching himself on the Knox, tearing down walls and hiring expensive decorators, was to no longer be heard from again. Various documents were produced and signed, and some ancient words spoken in turn, and then, indeed, Peps—the small, enthusiastic, slightly high-pitched voice of Peps—was to be heard by them no more.

At the Toad, once it became clear that Peps had been the victim of a selective-hearing tribunal, he actually perked up. The role of persona non grata agreed with him. He began taking pleasure in shouting loudly, even into Rhustaphustian's polished ear horn. He placed spiders in the trestlemen's boots as they dozed. He took to shrilly complaining at the state of the grand hotel. At other times, he practiced stealth and would sneak up behind napping residents of the Toad and attempt to startle them from sleep. He stomped his feet; he abandoned all dignity and sneezed without covering his nose.

Yet none of this attracted any attention, and he quite soon tired of the game. The magic that the trestlemen had spoken at the conclusion of their tribunal was of a potent sort—one from the earliest times of their collective memories, from the times when enchanted manuscripts were being composed into scrolls with the aid of powerful ink, and the first threads of the seven panels of the ancient tapestries were being woven into a pictorial.

Axle offered to approach the tribunal in Peps's defense,

claiming there was no precedent for such a decree against one of their own kind, but Peps merely scoffed.

"The sooner Trindle and I are off, the better." Peps scowled. "You're as close to the Guild as we can get you by boat. The rest is up to you."

He instructed Trindle to be ready to depart come morning and satisfied himself by creating mischief until then.

here was, Ivy and Rowan noticed, a fairly starkly lit room off the hallway in which they currently found themselves. While Axle saw to preparations for their departure, they had been left alone for the remainder of the afternoon—a happy event in such a seemingly endless structure as the Toad. The pair wandered the maze of halls with distraction as their only real goal. Most doors had numbers and were guest rooms of various designs. Some had fireplaces.

A few of the doors opened to broom or linen closets. There was a reading room with plush couches and a crackling fire. A game room with shelves of all manner of entertainment, a selection of contemplative games with which the men whiled away their time in exile. Ivy saw a puzzle or two and an abandoned card game. A table held an intricate board upon which stood carved stone pieces with an air of royalty and intrigue, of war making.

But it was the room off of the game room before which

the pair now stood. Two glass-paneled doors opened inward, revealing a selection of display cases of assorted sizes, some freestanding, some mounted, museum-style, upon the walls.

In fact, it was an exhibit of sorts.

It was apparently devoted to the innumerable trestlemen contributions to Cauvian society throughout their long years, but as trestlemen were not an ostentatious race, it was assembled and displayed without any fanfare in simple glass boxes. Rowan was enthralled and began walking the center aisle eagerly. Ivy, however, was distracted by an open book upon a podium at the entrance. Peering at the ruled pages, it took her but a moment to realize what it was.

"A guest book!" she called to Rowan as she began paging through.

There were columns for the date and the visitors' names and a small space for comments, and the last entry was some time ago.

"No one's been here in ages!" she called.

Rowan was standing before a weather-themed display, reading the small cards beside each object.

"Snowtwirlers," he exclaimed. "Sleetbeaters. Rainmakers. Windticklers. Ivy, this is amazing!"

Ivy nodded, holding the registry now, paging through quickly to the middle.

"And here"—Rowan had moved on—"charting tools of some sort. I think I've seen Axle with something similar.

'Constellation Calibrator,' it says. 'Starwhistles.' A 'Night-harness,' whatever that is."

The next display box was an impressive collection of knots and an unlikely array of twisted barbed wire, but Rowan glossed over it in favor of the last exhibit in the row. This one, he was realizing, was devoted to air travel.

"Windwhipper," the first card read.

Indeed, the umbrella-like flying machine was behind a dusty glass door, with several other mysterious oddities. Rowan was unimpressed. His memories of flying the thing over the waters of the Lake District were poor ones at best—less about flying and more about swimming.

Beside the windwhipper there was some sort of wheeled cart with a large sail and a canvas balloon; a faded card beside it implied the device worked in tandem with the rails of a train track. But the next contraption—now that looked like something interesting. It was a thing of beauty, and Rowan stopped to examine it fully.

It was a set of wings, and the curator had chosen to show it off with one appendage folded neatly, as if in rest, and the other extended in flight—broad and proud. They were of masterful construction, millions of scalloped petals—scalelike—sewn out of some sort of lightweight linen. The fabric had a sheen to it, and Rowan longed to be able to feel it. The label read, "Springform Wings."

Ivy was reading something of her own.

She had thumbed to the middle of the guest book, reviewing the last entries, some more legible than others. Turning the page, she came to an entry so surprising—and horrifying—it rendered her speechless.

In jagged letters, many times the size of other signatures, was a name.

Vidal Verjouce

And if that weren't enough, beneath it, smaller, but just as lavish and seemingly from the same pen, was another. Her mother's.

Chapter Twenty-nine

The Cafeteria

hey are untested." Ivy realized a creaky voice was speaking beside her. She slammed the book closed in surprise but soon saw that Crump was looking in Rowan's direction.

"The wings," the concierge explained. "They have never been tested. Who knows if they work."

Rowan looked at Crump as if in a daze. He had been miles away, floating on the rim of a sunset in his mind.

"It's all speculation. Grig could never find anyone who wanted to risk life and limb to fly them."

"Grig?" Rowan asked dumbly, and Ivy scowled. She was not fond of being interrupted, especially by stealth concierges. They should put a bell on him, she thought darkly.

"The inventor. He could make anything out of wire and canvas. Didn't always work as he intended, though." Crump reverted to an uncomfortable silence but after a moment seemed to remember the reason behind his errand. "Master Axle is awaiting you in the cafeteria," he announced.

This was good news indeed, as the pair now realized their hunger, and they set off at an idle pace behind Crump. This gave Ivy the opportunity to discuss her findings.

"They were here together!" She was appalled.

"Who?"

"My mother and Verjouce!"

"When?"

"Twelve years ago."

"Ugh. Ivy, I don't know."

"Rowan, you don't think—" She had been avoiding an awful thought for a while now, ever since Sorrel Flux had taunted her in Templar.

"It doesn't matter what I think. Ivy, you need to take this up with Axle. Or Clothilde. Or both."

They joined the trestleman in the brightly lit cafeteria. The room was alive with the usual buzzes and clinks, but Ivy and Rowan had never before seen a cafeteria such as this.

First, the food came to you.

Crump stopped abruptly beside a counter lined with metal stools and, after pressing a big red button, departed.

A shiny conveyor belt came alive before the diners as the counter buzzed with activity. Little oiled wheels turned and metal links worked in consort to meander about the entire room. Soon a feast of choices paraded by slowly, rambling from the kitchen through the serpentine path the conveyor belt followed. Small plates at first: a jiggling glass of cider, a slice of hot buttered toast, a tin of plum jam, rumbling puddings with clouds of thick cream.

Separated from Six, Rowan's sinuses were clearing, and with it, his appetite returned. Rowan thought of his only other experience with institutional food: the Tasters' Guild had many classrooms set for meal consumption—courses such as Edibility and the dreaded Irresistible Meals—and then there was the vast student dining hall. There, the apprentice tasters waited in long lines and were served palate-cleansing broth alongside plain, uninspired fare.

The threesome sat down as a selection of fresh, plump doughnuts clinked by—bursting with jam and dusted with cheery powdered sugar.

Outside, a storm was settling in, and the joy of the meal would be short-lived. Just as Ivy was preparing to ask Axle (with a mouth full of apricot scone) about the guest register, Rowan sheepishly remembered a confession. He had something of great, newfound import to disclose.

Chapter Thirty

Farewell

"atchmen!" Axle was muttering to himself, contemplating this new and potent danger. "As if Outriders were not enough . . ."

"Don't forget the vultures," Ivy chimed in, happy to point out that the Guild's surplus of deadly obstacles was staggering.

In the icy light of the storage closet, Axle was frantic to depart. He had abruptly ended their supper at the mention of Rowan's Watchman sighting.

"Here," he said as he tore into his satchel. "Put these on." He hastily threw a mass of dark wool at Ivy and Rowan.

"Tasters' robes?" Ivy asked, holding hers up first one way, then another. They smelled nice. "Why aren't they black?"

But Rowan knew. The boiled wool and myriad pockets were once a source of great pride for him. The robes of the Tasters' Guild, students' robes. A strict olive drab, they were eventually to be exchanged for the true black tasters' attire after the Epistle ceremony.

"Apprentice robes," Rowan informed Ivy dully. But Ivy was already throwing hers over her head and, with an excited twist, maneuvering the hood to its proper placement.

"I love all these little pockets!" she replied, delighted. She busied herself transferring the contents of her cherished workshop apron into the inner lining of the robe. Her *Guide*, her leather-wrapped poison kit, and an odd cork or two all fit quite nicely inside, with room for more.

The robes were a heady souvenir of Rowan's former life, and they felt heavy now in his hands. His mind flashed to his least favorite classes—Irresistible Meals and Devouring I, II, and III—and then to his most thrilling of all courses, Advanced Taste Theory. This was taught by a very old Professor named Breaux, and if there was one person Rowan still admired at the Guild it was he.

"Right." Axle pulled his beard, and Rowan finished dressing. "A pair of waders for each of you."

"Waders?" they asked.

"Crump has advised me that there is a small stream not far from here."

"A stream?" Rowan was aghast.

"You'll hardly notice your wet feet, my young friend, with all that rain slashing down on you. It could be worse. We could have the Winds of Caux at our backs!"

The weather was indeed to prove an impeding factor in their travels. Thunder, lightning, and a miserable rain awaited them for their departure. The thin metallic rails of the train tracks upon the trestle were slick with runoff. The ties were overgrown with bristly grass and necessitated a careful passage. But they weren't for long on the Toad's topside, and once they made land, they began trudging along the tracks with a wary eye at the distance.

Thunderheads curdled the sky above them, occasionally dropping a bolt of barbed lightning nearby. Rowan began to consider the scope of his science education, in particular his studies in Terrestrial Disciplines, and he wondered whether the metallic rails were indeed a smart place to be in such a weather condition.

Axle, on surprisingly nimble legs, led the children forward

as he searched around
the tracks nervously
for any signs of
the small stream.
On either side of them, the low
menace of the forest began, a thick and dark
black in which thousands of gleaming needles and knotted
branches reverberated with each flash of lightning. He considered continuing along the tracks but knew how exposed they were upon them—exposed not only to the elements but also to the many eyes of the Tasters' Guild.

"No bearing stones to mark our way this time," he yelled. "Just fortune."

Another streak lit up the sky, and with that he gave a loud shout. He had found the small stream. He urged the children on.

But Rowan did not see Axle's small triumph. For with the same slash of blue light, his eyes were drawn to the area just behind the trestleman. Upon a ruined Royal Cauvian Rail sign, in an evil illusion that seemed to perch upon the jagged edge of the lightning bolt itself, was a vulture. A Rocamadour vulture. The taster was certain he saw it—its eyes eagerly regarding the threesome, its beak pulled back in a gruesome hiss. They were plunged again into the blackness, and the next time the lightning came, the giant bird was gone.

Chapter Thirty-one

Springforms

With a splash, Axle plodded into the stream. It cut a small path through the otherwise impenetrable forest, one that they might use to traverse the dense bramble. The way was far from easy, as the travelers had to navigate rocks slick with viscous algae and clumps of phosphorescent slime. They were forced to travel single file, with Axle leading and Rowan bringing up the rear.

Overhead grew a canopy of dark vines and interlocking limbs, blotting out much of the driving rain, so as they made their way, they were at least thankful to escape the worst of the downpour. The thick black lace of barbs and needles from the forest of hawthorns left their spirits downcast and somber.

"Hawthorns"—Axle looked apprehensively over the rim of his spectacles at the surrounding woods—"are quite treacherous. In ancient times, it was said that they bound people, entrapped them. They are thought to contain imprisoned souls."

The threesome shivered at the thought of the vivid enchantment.

Decomposing leaves sat in piles beside the fetid stream, washed-up detritus from the forest floor. They walked on for some time in a sloshy silence. There was no place to rest—the water's edge was an inconvenient sheer of mud from which brambles grew up as soon as they might find some earth to cling to—until they met with a large, stout rock. Its tip was flat enough to offer seating and it was, as rocks are, implacable in its position—some giant had long ago placed it in the stream's midst. The roiling water coursed around it and rejoined downstream.

Axle clambered on top and offered his hand to Ivy and Rowan in turn. Once the group was huddled together, the trestleman set about producing some lunch. Rowan held some special memories of Axle's picnic baskets—trestlemen are known for their cooking prowess, and during his various travels with Ivy, he had been introduced to some of Axle's specialties. And even here, in the gloomy shadow of the Tasters' Guild, the former taster was to enjoy a delicious—albeit hastily collected—meal from the Toad's cafeteria's conveyor belt.

Besides the loaves of hearty, pillow-soft bread, wax-coated wheels of cheese, chicken potpies, and chocolate fudge, something else was stuffed within Axle's sack. Ivy spied the curious things as they finished eating in silence. Reaching in, she retrieved a small package, part of a larger collection of identical packets. Each was tied with drab canvas strapping, about the size of a young girl's palm. After she asked her friend what they might be, Axle responded with a word.

"Springforms!"

"Springforms?" Rowan perked up.

"Yes, various springforms. A gift from Rhustaphustian."

"What do they do?" Ivy wondered.

"It depends, of course."

"Well, what does this one do?" Ivy indicated the one in her hand.

"Oh, I couldn't tell you."

"Well, shouldn't we find out?" Ivy stared at the small canvas objects with renewed enthusiasm. "Did they come with instructions?"

"When Rhustaphustian gave them to you, didn't he tell you what they do?" Rowan asked.

Axle looked suddenly sheepish.

"Axle?" Ivy asked suspiciously.

"Well, no. You see, he didn't technically *give* them to me. . . ."

"You took them?" Ivy laughed out loud—an odd happy sound in the midst of such a forlorn wood. "Well, let's see these springforms, then." She pulled upon the secure bands.

"Be careful!" Axle warned. "They must be opened with great caution!"

"Hardly. It seems simple enough—"

With an enormous *whoosh*, Ivy untied the strapping and released a tensed coil of wire sewn into the seams of the fabric within. The force of the springform opening very nearly threw Rowan from his perch on the rock back into the syrupy murk, but the taster hardly cared. His thoughts returned him to the gallery at the Toad and the small card beside the set of wings he had admired.

"Springforms!" he repeated excitedly.

An enormous sucking sound filled the air between them, and quite suddenly in their midst a sizable balloon appeared. The canvas sacking was interlaced with a hemp net, and as the thing began to inflate, it hung suspended in the gloom. Quite quickly it had completed its transformation. A perfectly round, elegant balloon bobbed before the surprised group. At its base there was a paddle—more like a large pinwheel— which appeared to be its driving force. It turned lazily with a *click click* noise. And then, to the great surprise of the three travelers, it began to slowly rise.

"A weather balloon!" Axle gasped. How he had wanted one of these on board the *Trindletrip* when dealing with the impenetrable clouds!

"Wow," Ivy added appreciatively.

"Oh," Axle cooed, reaching up fondly, but it was already out of reach.

"Oh!" Rowan echoed, this time with dread, as the balloon

met the eventual ceiling of the forest, snagging on a fierce branch of thorns.

With a sad hiss—a noise that could really mean only one thing when in the presence of a balloon—it was over very quickly. It was soon shredded by the brambles and became an unrecognizable clump of fabric and wires.

Looking quite helpless, Axle turned to Ivy.

"I think we might practice a bit more prudence when opening another one," he suggested quietly.

But before Axle knew it, Ivy had a new springform in her hand, and although he shouted at her to wait, she untied the binding and let it go. It instantly revealed itself to be a sturdy coatrack, and Ivy heedlessly jettisoned it downstream. She reached for a third and opened it.

What next lay between the three upon the boulder was, in fact, a most welcome sight.

"A raft, Axle!" Ivy happily proclaimed.

"Not a raft," Axle corrected. "A skimmer!"

A skimmer is a lovely flat boat with a fan-type motor mounted behind the passenger seats. It is a craft primarily used by trestlemen and is therefore apportioned for their smaller size.

"A springform skimmer! I wonder what else you have in there—"

But the trestleman managed this time to stay her hand.

"I think we should wait to open any of the others until we

know what they are—or at least until we have more space." Axle pointed to either end of the skimmer, which, like the weather balloon, was being menaced by the dark, needle-like barbs. After wrestling with the thing, and setting it in the water finally, Ivy, still quite pleased with herself, reluctantly agreed, which left Rowan to peer through the trestleman's curious sack alone.

"And these?" Rowan asked, holding up a handful of tiny packets he had found at the bottom. "Are these more spring-forms?"

"Ah!" Axle clapped his hands excitedly. "Those! I'd forgotten! I'd packed them before we left."

Ivy turned to look, grabbing several. "Flintroot sachets!" she said happily. "Perfect!"

"Careful—that's all there is, and we've just begun—" the trestleman protested as Ivy passed out the small silken squares. She had already squeezed hers, and the soft pillow was beginning to glow with a cheery warmth. After showing Rowan what to do, she settled a pair of them in her socks and, replacing her boots and waders, stood on warm feet for the first time all day.

The skimmer was designed to ride along in troubled waters just deep enough for the small set of rear paddles to propel the raft forward. Conceived by trestlemen, it was of course fastidiously made but was, Rowan was soon reminded, of miniature scale. It was intended to carry the standard crew of seven trestlemen and a captain, which made it just spacious enough for the two children, Axle, and their various packs. Rowan was finding the small bench to be an uncomfortable fit.

It was a delicate affair to avoid the thorns that threatened the canvas raft from every angle. As the whirring of the paddles commenced with a swift yank from Axle on a pull cord, Rowan huddled down, keeping warm. The stream had widened a bit. Casting a dark eye about the wood, rain drenching his face and robes, he found himself wistful for the perilous windwhipper ride over the Lake District he had endured with Ivy at the beginning of their adventure.

Despite her warm toes, Ivy noticed that the temperature seemed to have dropped, and her teeth began chattering. Axle, too, felt the cold despite his thick greatcoat. The rain had varnished each sinister barb of the hawthorns into a crystal spear. He began to imagine a fire, a place to make camp, and looking at the children—and seeing two pale faces—it suddenly became imperative to get them warm.

Shortly, Axle's heart surged to see a break in the overgrowth. There was one particularly enormous tree root that grew up and over itself, before plunging into the earth beside the stream. It was a natural foothold, and there was a small place to make shore beside the muddy bank. Behind the gnarled root, a space above the stream beckoned—Axle was sure he saw a soft inlet of green moss.

Axle tied up the skimmer—there was no hope of manipulating it back into its tight packet with frozen hands. Hopping through a gap beside the mud-caked tree root, Axle helped Ivy disembark, and the pair turned to assist Rowan.

By now the gnarled root upon which they stood was quite slick, and Rowan was having trouble finding his balance. The stream had exposed the old tree's root system, and its bare tendrils clawed at the eroding bank in gruesome shapes. Fistfuls of earth rained down on the travelers as more of the ledge gave way. Rowan was forced to crawl his way up the unforgiving wall, and came finally to lean against the old hawthorn trunk. Amid the heaving, muttering, and splashing, no one heard the strange creaking (and then splintering) from somewhere deep within the ancient tree. A thorny branch suddenly snaked itself around the former taster, pulling him tight.

"OWW!" Rowan shouted, struggling against the barbs that pricked his skin, and then standing quite still.

Which was worse? The taster could not decide if it was better to be soaked to the bone—and freeze to death—or to be trapped by a wicked, mean-spirited tree. Somehow they both seemed preferable to landing at the dark gates of Rocamadour. Either way, as he lazily turned the topic over in his mind, it became clear to him that he was stuck.

Chapter Thirty-two

The True Nature of Plants

s every apotheopath in Caux knew, some plants are good, some bad, but all are powerful when harnessed. It was this harnessing of Caux's forests and glens that apotheopaths practiced, for healing and ultimately good purposes. And it was another truth that these natures—indeed, plants themselves—were again awakening, after a long, and at times fitful, sleep.

Two things happened simultaneously.

First, Rowan recalled Axle's earlier statement that the hawthorn tree binds people and imprisons their unfortunate souls, and in the vague recesses of his brain, he remembered some of his lessons concerning lost travelers in these very woods. And, second, he began to feel quite unfortunate himself, as several more spiky branches advanced upon him, encircling his chest, compressing.

"Axle . . . Ivy . . . ," he wheezed. "The tree—I can't breathe!"

The pair watched in horror as the tree flexed with an ancient strength, maneuvering the unfortunate taster toward a new and terrifying opening that had materialized within a hollow in its mighty trunk.

"Hawthorns!" Axle spat bitterly, casting about the skimmer for his sack. He emerged with a shout, brandishing a steely ax.

Quickly he set about chopping.

It was quite a fortunate thing that Axle's ax had been carefully sharpened, for the first few strikes found their mark and left bitter gashes in the ancient wood, and the tree seemed to loosen its grip on Rowan. But the ax was a small one; a few more swings and the trusted tool soon dulled.

"Ivy—" Axle called. "Pull!"

The ax left less and less of a mark, but Ivy managed to help free Rowan—and as the taster shrugged off the final lasso of barbs, a bitter creaking accompanied the tree's retreat. With great effort, and emerging scratched and tattered, Axle and Ivy managed to half-drag Rowan to the grassy area, an inexplicable oasis in the tangle of the wood. Around them the wet of the bark made the forest a dirty brown, dark slashes of damp upon the thick hawthorn trunks. From everywhere, the smell of earthy decay.

Yet—above, through the crisscrossing branches, a sliver of moon, and with this, Ivy realized that it had stopped raining, and the storm had passed.

Chapter Thirty-three

The Uninvited Visitor

The ground was crisp and even imparted a slight crunch as the threesome set up camp in the darkness. Beneath a tarp, Axle unpacked the remnants of their lunch and started to contemplate dinner, while Ivy was overjoyed to discover several springform cots with the Toad's crest upon them. Soon Rowan was resting comfortably upon one.

Ivy offered to examine the tired taster, but Rowan was already drifting off.

"Ivy, I'm fine—I just need to rest," he assured her.

Axle had built a small fire after some deliberation and was happily burnishing his iron pan after producing a length of plump sausages.

"Do we dare have a fire?" Ivy asked, happy in the moment to warm her hands over the coals. Ivy thought of the Tasters' Guild, its tall spire. Surely someone would be on lookout, and she said so.

"I think we must." Axle nodded at Rowan. "It's more

important to be dry. Besides, I've dug it deep enough where it won't be easy to spot."

Axle fell silent, a dark thought upon him. It wasn't the subrectors at the Tasters' Guild that troubled the trestleman currently. It was their spies and assassins.

"Axle, why would Vidal Verjouce meet my mother at the Snodgrass Toad?" Ivy wondered softly. Sitting quietly, waiting to get warm, had brought her back to this underlying question—and a sinking feeling.

Axle stopped tending his potatoes and spoke carefully.

"Ivy, your mother was—is—a woman of untested loyalties. She traveled easily in both the realms of the light and dark. We were told she was a spy, for us. But I do believe it was more complex."

Ivy nodded. She found herself holding the charm she had received from Peps, the ribbon knotted about her neck.

"Your destiny is quite different from hers," the trestleman said kindly.

In the silence, Ivy peered about the woods—so very menacing now, after what she'd seen with Rowan and the ancient tree. Axle continued, warmed by the fire.

"Ivy, I have been wrong about something."

Ivy waited. It wasn't often that Axle was wrong.

"*Whosoever speaks to the trees speaks to the King.* There is much unwritten in the Prophecy, but I now see that *you*—and not the tapestries—are the source of the plantworld's awakening. And that is both a blessing and a curse."

"How?" she wondered.

"Some plants are helpful, and these you can harness and use for the good of all. They will come to your aid in a time of need and gladly do your bidding."

Ivy thought of King Verdigris. There was an old saying that he led with an army of flowers. "And the others?"

"The others—well, let's just say some are controlling, mean-spirited, and bent on destruction. They are better off forgotten."

"Scourge bracken?" Ivy guessed. By Axle's silence she knew that she was right.

Ivy looked at the sleeping form of Rowan. A hawthorn had nearly enslaved and strangled him today. Could this have been her fault? Is this what she should expect when Axle spoke of the awakening of the deeper natures of the plantworld? She liked it better when such behavior was blamed on the tapestries. She would have to be very careful from here on out.

The cessation of the bleak rain brought with it two things: freezing cold and a new, discomforting silence. Ivy now realized that their entire trip had been one of much noise: the slashing rain and tumbling waters, the tearing hawthorns, and the slapping of the paddles of the skimmer. As she lay down to rest, there was nothing but the muffled brook at the end of the small clearing.

Still, she fell quickly into fitful dreams, ones of knotty

trees and hairy vines encircling their camp. Ugly, mocking birds shouted down at her awful things, and although she could not understand them, she knew they were singing of her destiny of failure.

She wrenched herself awake.

The wood was silent, the clearing desolate. Her companions slept, unmenaced. There, in the dark, she thought of Cecil. She longed for their old life at the tavern, a simpler time, when—after a nightmare—she could scurry down the low hall to take comfort in her uncle's calming words. Occasionally she would find him still in his workshop, poring over notes or wrestling with his messy bookshelf. Together they might throw open the window and contemplate the stars, or he'd distract her with stories of the more colorful regulars. Always in these moments he would tell her to never be afraid— that in her dreams nothing could harm her.

But, as she contemplated just this, Ivy heard something. A small something, but in the new silence of the forest, it was magnified. Ivy strained to hear it again.

It was a *crunch,* followed by another tentative one, and Ivy was now certain she was hearing footsteps.

"Axle!" Ivy whispered urgently in the darkness, but a trestleman can sleep the sleep of the ages, as Axle was currently demonstrating.

The footfalls were quickening now as she turned instead to wake Rowan, and she had little time to shake her friend before the unwelcome arrival was upon them. She felt about her side for anything with which to defend herself, finding nothing more than a long fork that had previously been used to toast Axle's dinner.

"Who's there?" she shouted in a voice she hardly recognized, waving the dinner fork. It was, however, enough to wake Axle, and so it was that in the dim light of the morning, the three travelers faced a startling sight.

For an odd moment, Ivy thought she was still sleeping. In the way of dreams, she knew Axle to be by her side—but also there he was, standing, cut and bleeding from a crosshatch of deep scratches, at the edge of the clearing. She was seeing double.

"Peps!" Axle sputtered. His brother stood before them, a living statue, as pale as his marble bust.

Axle sprang from bed stammering a litany of questions at the mute trestleman, none of which expressed much pleasure at the reunion.

"Did I not tell you to under no circumstances attempt to follow us?" He stamped a little foot. "What were you thinking? You might have been discovered!" Axle looked around for any signs of such, finally gazing uneasily at the stark sky through the knit of thorns. "There are eyes everywhere," he said with a scowl.

Rowan sneezed, and the noise of it reverberated in the uneasy silence that followed. Indeed, it seemed that Peps was not alone. Quite silently, stepping out on twelve front toes, came Peps's companion.

"Six!" Ivy cried.

The tomcat settled himself before the smoking fire pit, while together Rowan and Ivy brought Peps one of the cots. Axle attended to a small enameled teapot while muttering under his breath.

"I don't know what you were thinking—you have endangered us all!"

After a moment in which Six began an awkward preen, Peps finally spoke. "Trindle's dead!" he whispered. "Poisoned! While he slept!" He fell again into a bitter silence as Ivy looked nervously around.

"Poisoned?" Rowan asked, alarmed.

"There, there." Axle's voice took on a note of kindness. He handed his brother something that smelled suspiciously like brandy. "A nice cup of tea."

"And the rest of them—Rhustaphustian, everyone—all gone!" Peps took a long swig from the delicate cup and held it out for more. "Poisoned, every last one!" he howled.

"Who did this?" Axle asked sharply.

Peps paused miserably. "They wore the robes of the Tasters' Guild, but red," he squeaked. "They were Watchmen."

Chapter Thirty-four

Peps's Story

The storm in which the three had left had prevented Trindle's houseboat from departing—much to Peps's disappointment. After a brief moment of despair, the trestleman resolved to make the most of the delay and create as much of a nuisance of himself as possible at the Toad, a task into which he delved with characteristic aplomb.

Finally tired from his mischief, he made his way below the hotel to the houseboat, where, because of the late hour, he retired without seeing Trindle. As Peps tried to sleep, the enormous cat crept up on the bed—as was his habit. As Peps drifted off, he was vaguely aware of losing the battle for space with Six but was too tired to care. He rescued a pillow from Six's clutches and crept down off the mattress, falling into a deep sleep beneath the bed.

"That cat saved my life!" he said, and after a short pause, he indicated he would enjoy some more of Axle's brandied tea.

The Guild's assassins had boarded the boat and fanned out

to quickly dispatch the captain and crew. Seeing only a mangy cat in Peps's quarters, they continued on their appalling errand.

"Assassins?" Ivy was horrified.

Peps continued. He had listened until he was quite sure they were gone, and only then did he emerge from beneath Six. He rushed to the captain's quarters, but he was too late for Trindle. Dismayed, the trestleman scrambled to the elevator in the pitch black, feeling about desperately for the lift switch.

At the Snodgrass Toad, he shouted until he was hoarse, but no one answered.

"The selective-hearing tribunal!" Ivy gasped. "They couldn't hear you!"

Peps nodded. "But the assassins could—and I was nearly captured!" He looked around dramatically. "I ran to the grand hall with Six and up the stairs—the ghastly Watchmen right behind us. I never thought I'd long for the time of Outriders, but these were dreadful men. Sinister, calculating—completely organized. They would have had me, too, had I not earlier in the day—in a stroke of genius—untacked the entire stairway carpet. As the Watchmen pursued us up the marble steps, the rug slipped out from under them, and they landed in a heap at the bottom! Six and I escaped to the roof tracks."

The cat swished his ragged tail as Ivy scratched him behind the ear.

"And so you see," Peps said somberly, "there was nothing left to do but follow you."

"It's awful news," Ivy said sadly. "Trindle. The others. So many poisoned."

"A moment of silence, please, for Trindle. A fine ferryman, chef, and friend. Let his death not be in vain," Axle said somberly.

Silence did follow in the small clearing—with the exception of Six, whose raspy purr was either a fine tribute (thought Ivy) or deeply insensitive (thought Rowan).

"If you ask me," Peps resumed, "those worthless old men were of little help to us, and they got what they deserved."

Quietly, Axle looked at the fire. Finally, he spoke. "There are things more enduring than grudges to be upheld, Peps. There are traditions."

"I suppose."

"Soon we will return to the Toad. But for now we must keep moving on." Axle poured the remains of the tea on the embers.

"Where to?"

"This stream should take us right to Rocamadour, and the Tasters' Guild," he replied. "It won't be pretty, but it will suffice."

"How so?" Peps wondered.

"Oh, well." Axle cleared his throat uncomfortably. "It has its beginnings beneath the city. Specifically, in the sewers."

Part 11

Rocamadour

To truly heal, one must know grave illness.

—An ancient apotheopathic truth

Chapter Thirty-five
Red

Vidal Verjouce sat behind his stone table, quite still, musing—oddly, for a blind man—on the color red. It had been his favorite. At once the color of life (a delicate flush in a maiden's cheek) as well as death. Here, in his self-imposed world of darkness, Verjouce was proud to still be capable of imagining the brilliant color, producing it in the black palette of his mind.

He ruminated on a cardinal, its red wing, its fearless disadvantage. He saw the intrepid bird, blood-red, on a snow-white plain, a streak of black a mask across its face.

"Director," hissed a small, potbellied man in scarlet robes, a man with an odd scrunch to his posture that marked him as impish and pitiable. It was the subrector named Snaith, who could at any given moment be found at the dark Director's side.

·The cardinal vanished, and in its place—in the void of color—was a stab of anger, a dark hunger for more. A black hunger. A blind man lives with a gnawing wish to return to the world of light and hue, but within Verjouce this wish was magnified and distilled into something akin to ferociousness.

He turned his fierce face—with its deep pits where his eyes had been plucked from their sockets by his own hand—to the exact place where the hunched Snaith stood.

"We have him," Snaith said proudly. "We have the calligrapher. Hemsen Dumbcane."

"Ah, yes." Vidal Verjouce mused on the weaselly scribe. For years their relationship had been one of discretion. Dumbcane had been retained to perform the work of a scholar—searching out and cataloging various manuscripts. The Director had entrusted Dumbcane with the ancient works under great pains of secrecy and for this had been repaid with deception and thievery—the scribe had replaced the stolen works with nearly perfect fakes, polluting the Guild's collection with his forgeries. And worse yet, a truly precious document—one that the Guild's leader valued above all others—was now missing from the secret drawer in his private desk.

Well, Dumbcane was about to discover what treachery would buy him. Verjouce sat back, lacing his long, pale fingers together, and ordered Snaith to show the scribe in.

Dumbcane soon made his appearance, trembling before the fearsome leader of the Tasters' Guild. He had been caught by Snaith's red-cloaked Watchmen as he made his way over dusty highways, stooped from the burden of his stained canvas sack. Today he stood with the iron grip of Snaith's men on either side, a collection of flies gathered about his head.

With an imperceptible nod, Vidal Verjouce indicated that his trusted servant should relieve the prisoner of his bag, and Snaith, shuffling over with his crablike gait, snatched the tattered sack and emptied its contents upon the stone floor.

"It's not here, Director." Snaith leered at Dumbcane.

"Not there?" Verjouce murmured.

"No." The subrector unrolled and tossed aside the various contents of Dumbcane's bag, unfurling parchment after parchment. "Just worthless maps and charts, nothing else. Oh—"

"Yes?" the Guild's Director sat forward, eagerly.

"There are a few tins here. Four. Appear to be ink of some sort." Snaith waved his billowing sleeve over the gathering of flies that had suddenly, greedily, moved from the calligrapher to the small canisters.

Verjouce sat back, disappointed.

He turned his grimace to his guest.

"You know what it is that I seek, Hemsen?" His voice was smooth, oiled, and coldly polite. It breathed a bitter chill into the calligrapher's very soul.

Dumbcane paused, torn. If he admitted to knowing about yet somehow not having the thing his captor so eagerly sought, would it be worse than if he denied any memory of their last, secret transaction? He finally settled on the first option and found himself nodding—then, in a swift reversal, violently shaking his head. This silent indecision continued for some time, to the amusement of Snaith, who finally broke the dizzying display with the following question.

"Well, which is it?" he hissed. "Do you have the scroll, or don't you?"

Verjouce leveled his empty gaze at him, the dark pits of his eyes emptying the prisoner of any last resistance.

"I—I do not," squeaked the tortured man.

"How disappointing," concluded the gruesome Director. "How terribly disappointing, Hemsen. Disappointing for me, yes. But mostly for you."

And with an offhanded wave of his arm, Vidal Verjouce signaled the Watchmen to take him away.

"Wait!"

The scarlet-clad Watchmen—the Guild's assassins and, in every way, Verjouce's eyes—paused in the doorway.

"I know where it is! I am certain!"

"Yesss?"

"I was recently visited by two members of the Taxus Estate. They came searching for the Epistle of a graduate of yours, a taster called Truax. Rowan Truax, if memory serves. I must have given them the scroll in error—in my haste!"

"Taxus, you say?" Snaith demanded.

"Yes, Taxus. I am sure. This Truax taster broke his sacred Oath, and the Estate demanded the Epistle. Please—with the

Guild's resources, it shall be easy to discover them. They surely know not what it is they possess—"

"Thank you, Hemsen," Verjouce interrupted.

And if the scribe thought that he had bought himself a pardon, his hopes were soon dashed.

"Hemlock." Verjouce flashed his gravestone teeth. "The weed grows wild by riversides. An efficient poison. It begins as a heavy coldness on the soles of your feet, moving upward, in numbing stages. To your knees. Your thighs. You will feel it keenly, but you are helpless against the creeping paralysis. Your mind is clear to the very end. By the time it reaches your heart, you are dead."

Chapter Thirty-six

Gripe

It was not long after Hemsen Dumbcane was escorted away, sobs reverberating throughout the dark stone halls, that Verjouce's henchman Snaith decided to take a closer look at the contents of the calligrapher's bag. He had, after all, gone out of his way to depart the Knox with these scrolls in hand, these rolls of flimsy parchment and thick, sticky inks.

For his efforts, Snaith enlisted a subrector named Gripe, a man whose position was beneath his own, a favored colleague. Snaith and Gripe had worked together over the years; it had been Gripe, after all, who came up with the idea of experimenting on the poor and indigent in many of Caux's hospitals, and Snaith found the man quite like-minded and discreet.

"Why don't you begin with those," Snaith suggested, indicating the dented tins of Dumbcane's ink.

Gripe nodded and rolled his red robes up to his elbows. Selecting one—he began with a deep, shocking blue—he wrestled with the closure. Like the others, it was crusted with dried, flaking sediment, and Gripe had particular trouble moving the lid at all. A lazy cluster of fruit flies settled upon his hands as he worked. Gripe was a man of much strength and also much patience—a deadly combination in an assassin. Trying the tin several more times, he moved on to another, this one black. Still, no movement. Spots swam about the strong man's eyes—or were they insects?—and he found himself gasping for breath.

Across the room, Snaith was oblivious to his colleague's difficulties. He was thoroughly engrossed in the selection of scrolls before him. Examining the documents more fully, he was realizing that Dumbcane's treachery was far greater than he had previously thought. There were hundreds of scrolls here, each apparently belonging to the Guild. His eyes narrowed at the enormity of the transgression. He knew that the calligrapher had been associated with the Tasters' Guild long before his own personal rise within the subrector ranks— he had only recently won the complete trust of the Director; for years the man had exclusively associated himself with that bitter, loathsome assistant called Flux. And that could mean that the damage the forger might have done would be incalculable.

He looked then at his associate.

Gripe had finally decided that he would pry off the lid with his penknife and was in the process of doing just this as Snaith peered over. The subrector Gripe was in the prime of

his life, so, understandably, he had never given any considera-
tion as to what his last words might be. (He had inspired plenty
of others' throughout the course of his career.) The penknife
loosened the lid easily, releasing it with a loud *pop*. The room
filled with the odor of Dumbcane's ink.

"What is that *appalling* smell?" gasped Gripe. He looked
to Snaith, his face curiously helpless.

That would be the last thing the scarlet-robed Watchman
said in this land, or any other, as the potent ink—ink made
from the deadly scourge bracken, a weed dedicated to destruction and dominance—spilled upon the subrector's hands, and
across his broad chest a deep black stain rolled in, a shadow so
dark, so entirely pitch-black, that it seemed as if it swallowed
up the very sun.

Snaith donned his scarlet leather gloves and rushed to cap the
offending container. He was not sentimental—what assassin
is?—at the loss of Gripe; instead, a surge of excitement swept
over him. He would wrap up and present this curious new
toxin, this mysterious danger that the forger had somehow
come upon, and deliver it to the Guild's Director. He knew if
there was ever a man to appreciate a deadly poison, it was
Vidal Verjouce.

Chapter Thirty-seven

The Wall

There was still in the sky a pale smudge of moon—covered with an odd cushion of nightcloud. But it was enough to light what stood before them: the thick-cut stone of the fortifying walls of the ancient city of Rocamadour, an impossible amount of sleek, dark rock and perfect, polished mortar. The stream was but a rivulet now, emerging at its source, a rusted circular grate as old as the stone itself.

Rocamadour, like many ancient cities, had been expertly executed with a series of underground channels. The freshwater circulated throughout the city in coils of thick pipe, within the mouths of gargoyles and blank-eyed statues, eventually terminating at the Guild's dark pools and bleak fountains. On the way, the freshwater channels passed along cobblestone streets and through tight, twisting paths, occasionally quenching the thirst of the city's rat population or watering the slippery creeping moss that coated most of the walled city's interior.

The wastewater was an underground affair. Evacuated from the various components of the academy—the lavatories, the laboratories, the Infirmary—it snaked its way beneath the streets in a series of mystifying tunnels. So it was that one was never far from the sound of running water, or seeping water, or the dank smell emanating from the grates that barricaded the sewer below.

There is no need to detail the components of the soiled debris that made up the city's sewage; it is enough simply to state that the bleak passages beneath the Tasters' Guild were a place that very few dared to go. Yet here the group stood, before the terminus of one such underground waste channel. Upon inspection, Ivy noticed a thick slime caught up in the ravaged iron bars, and she did not relish the idea of entering the yawning blackness of the tunnel behind.

Axle was fishing around for a tool in his sack, and Rowan stood apart from the group, neck craned upward in a vain attempt to see to the top of the thick wall.

"There are Outriders posted up there," he whispered. Ivy motioned for him to be quiet.

It had been a harrowing trip up the remainder of the stream—they were forced to walk the final leg, for the oilcloth of the skimmer had at last become waterlogged. They took turns pulling it—with Six inside, as the cat firmly refused to get his feet wet again. As they approached the stream's source, the weight of their errand grew heavier. The

air was thick with the smell of the greasy water and swamp gas, making breathing—and conversation—an unpleasant task.

"Nearly there!" Axle called as they plodded through the mucky shallows while pockets of mist floated above the surface.

Stink cabbages dwarfed the girl, and strange ebony-colored lily pads with long, prowling tentacles floated in Ivy's way—she shuddered involuntarily as she felt them waft along her leg. The slime was more substantial here, too; whole chunks of it slooshed like gelatin as she shook it free from her waders. Thick, dense algae covered the perimeter of the bog like pudding skin.

Axle produced a favorite tool of his, one with telescoping odds and ends and an extraordinary amount of pincers. Energized, he nodded at his brother and turned to Rowan.

"You are the tallest. Loosen the top of the grate—but by all means, be quiet!"

Rowan waded over and took the complex tool. The grate was an old, massive thing, but no one expected what came next. The years of corrosive waste had been hard on the ironwork, and almost as soon as Rowan began prying at the seam, the thing gave way—followed by an explosively loud splash. The splash was itself followed by a dreadful gurgling and bubbling, and finally, as the last *glub* subsided, the group stood frozen in place before the dark passage.

What they heard next made Ivy's heart sink. From above, along the thick walls patrolled by the Guild's Outriders, came a bellow, followed by an incomprehensible command. A rough clanging of the alarm—they had been discovered.

Chapter Thirty-eight

Mind Garden

idal Verjouce sat perfectly still in his room atop the black spire of the Tasters' Guild. A shaft of pale moonlight from a diamond-shaped window cut a jagged line across his face, laying dark his absent eyes. This was his moment for meditation, the night, the time when the Guild's Director withdrew from the challenges of tyranny and domination, and went instead to a very private place within his mind.

This place was born from a childhood memory, and from his desires to remember light and color. Over the years, he had tended it, and it grew with his attention into a vast and impressive garden. A Mind Garden. He carefully imagined each planting and carefully disciplined each shoot and limb into a scene of personal perfection. He had chosen and cultivated a spectacular selection of deadly plants, upon which he willed the sun to shine and the rain to fall. He had fashioned a magnificent folly and envisioned it complete with rare peacocks, the color of shadow, their chilling cries punctuating the silence.

It was to his Mind Garden he would retire at the end of the day, for the Guild's Director never slept.

Yet today his garden was troubled by a darkness. Never before had he seen such roiling clouds—and since it was a garden of his own imagination, he was quite understandably shocked to discover that he was powerless to send them away. The folly stood empty and ravished, a few ruined feathers of the last birds scattered beneath a broken window. The normally pleasing horizon was vague with chill and cloud, and Verjouce was completely unable to think them into oblivion.

His disturbing meditation was disrupted on the temporal plane by a slight yet insistent knock at the chamber's doors.

With a flash of anger, Verjouce was forced to leave his garden—and the mysterious encroaching clouds. His attention returned to his body, where it sat straight and still, behind the old King Verdigris's former table, within the old King's chambers, inside the very halls King Verdigris had built.

"Enter," he commanded.

"Forgive the intrusion," Snaith begged. "But this couldn't wait."

Snaith had in his hands the ink. He had been conflicted earlier as to how to report Dumbcane's seemingly vast treason and had settled on the solution most advantageous for himself: to simply not mention it. Instead, he explained the colorful demise of the subrector Gripe and presented—ever so carefully—his master with the curious tins.

The moment Verjouce touched them, he was struck with a dreadful surge of desire, and for an odd moment, the vision of the churning clouds returned to him. His long, pale fingers easily released the lid of one, and even before it was loosened entirely, the smell of its contents surged out, spilling forth in a choking gas. Verjouce did not flinch. Instead, as his heart began to quicken, its deep, thunderous beat now rocketing and erratic with an implacable dark joy, he inhaled deeply.

Scourge bracken.

The scribe had brought him scourge bracken.

The only place he knew of that it still grew was in his mind.

Snaith had been prepared this time and had covered his face with his robe against the ink's stench. He observed with an ugly fascination as his master drew in more of the ink's scent, feasting on the malevolent odor. Then, to his great surprise, he watched as a cloud of sleek wasps, black as night, descended upon the head of Vidal Verjouce, from nowhere, darting about angrily, each hoping for a chance to drink from the deadly ink in the open tin.

"Shall I test his inks in the usual way?" Snaith asked.

"Yes, by all means. And"—the Director's nostrils flared—"find the fugitive Truax, this fool of a taster. Initiate the return of my paper."

Deep within the bowels of the Guild's catacombs—bordered by the dank tunnels of the sewers—Hemsen Dumbcane let loose a scream of agonizing proportions. He had long worked with—no, worked *for*—the destructive weed. It had seeped into his pores, crusted his cuticles, and made him rich. Now, as he felt its power leave him, he looked about his prison. The strange, lazy fruit flies that accompanied his daily machinations, the very flies that had shadowed the inks he toiled over, had evaporated. He was now truly alone.

Chapter Thirty-nine
The Sewer

A shrill, heart-stopping scream greeted the travelers as they bounded into the dark opening, a howl so desolate, so piercing, none could possibly have guessed it to be Dumbcane's. It was a scream of one destined not to die but to *live*—to live a horrible life when death would be ever so much preferable. The pitch and volume finally ebbed, but the echo remained for a few more moments as the group huddled, pressed against the inner brick tunnel of Rocamadour's sewer.

"Wh-what was that?" managed Peps, who was the last into the passage and was certainly contemplating a swift exit.

For some reason, everyone looked to Rowan.

"I don't know." He tried hard not to let his voice crack.

"A trick of the wind?" Axle offered unconvincingly.

"What wind?" Ivy asked.

"Where are we?" Peps demanded, looking around with disbelief. Six bounded on ahead, at home in the underground territory of rodents.

"The sewer," Ivy offered helpfully.

"The sewer?" Peps was horrified. "Surely not?"

The passage was not entirely unlit—and Ivy had a hard time deciding if this was a fortunate thing. Bare crooked pipes emerged from the brick-and-mortar walls at uneven intervals, belching out thin, wicked flames. The dingy walls were slick with moisture, and every so often a dark hole opened up above them, a hole from which rats—among other things—emerged. And there was, of course, the smell—one that defined the sewer as a place not meant for lingering.

"We should probably begin walking," Rowan said, and cleared his throat tentatively. "Because if there's one thing I'm sure of, it's that those Outriders will be here momentarily."

"Yes, but which way?" Peps prodded.

There was a brief section ahead where the tunnel continued, but quite evidently thereafter a decision would be needed—the sewer branched out in various directions as it serviced the city above.

"Axle, surely there's a map in that book of yours?" Peps demanded.

For a moment everyone looked at the author expectantly. Ivy felt around for her *Field Guide* in an inner pocket of her robes.

"There's no time," Rowan whispered urgently, casting a fearful look over his shoulder at the entrance. But Ivy was already paging through the midsection, folding out various charts and almanacs, finally pointing and nodding to one lonely section in a far corner.

"This will do." Axle joined Ivy. Together, the author and the girl peered at the shadowy page of his masterwork. In the brief moment of silence that followed, the two conferred over the unfolded page.

"I can't make heads or tails of it, Axle," Ivy admitted. The map before her was dense with squiggles, and the light was too low. With a lurch in the pit of her stomach, she heard the dull clang of an alarm, which spread along the rooftops and outer walls of the city, reverberating throughout the tunnel.

"Patience." The trestleman looked—oddly—not at the map but around the dark tunnel. "Any moment now."

And then, very faintly, Ivy saw it.

Upon the slick ceiling of the tunnel was a golden arrow, long and feathery, but growing ever more distinct. It emanated from the book in her hands and pointed—quite decisively—to the tunnel to the left.

"Oh!"

"Indeed." Axle looked quite proud.

"Shall we?" Peps asked in a tone that very much hoped they should not.

"Yes," Ivy agreed, gathering her wet robes around her with one hand and cradling the open *Guide* in the other.

Thankfully, they heard no more of the gruesome screaming

as they inched forward against all instinct. Having Axle's map was a fortunate thing, and they followed its projection unfailingly—sometimes the arrow appeared upon a wall, sometimes on the slick floor, even sometimes rounding a bend. Finally, they came to a junction.

One passageway was neatly cobbled and appeared to gradually lead up. The other tunnel was of a grimmer sort. It began with an iron gate of some menacing design and only got worse from there. It twisted and turned and seemed to be headed down, very much down, as if the result of the stroke of a madman's pen.

"That's the one." Axle nodded at the arrow, which indicated the more pleasant of the two.

It seemed a natural choice to everyone but Six, who froze at the opening and for no amount of encouraging would budge. Rowan would have been happy to leave him behind—and just as he thought to suggest this possibility, a strange noise issued forth from the passage. It was a small sound—at first. A sort of rumble, or a scratching, or maybe—and this odd thought occurred to Ivy—the sound a million marbles might make if released down a cobbled hill. Soon the rumble grew, and the group looked around nervously.

Six was a cat transformed. He spat into the darkness, and his hair stood in electric clumps, his tail alive. Ivy leaned in to comfort him but pulled away as he turned upon her, eyes

unrecognizing. They stared at each other for a moment, the grumbling sewer punctuated with a steady drip from somewhere nearby.

Then, spilling forth from the passage they came: thousands—no, tens of thousands—of dark and slick rats, a sea of them, in which each drop was a gnashing, unblinking, stinking rodent. Their claws clicked against the floor. Their squeaks assaulted the ear. The walls were instantly blackened with their greasy hides, the floor a series of waves.

In the nick of time, the group fled, following Six. For his escape, the cat took the only passage available to him: he sprinted through the creaking gate beside them, into the yawning, decrepit downward tunnel. The rats flowed onward in the direction of their unknown errand, but a few stragglers followed the group, and these now faced the heel of Rowan's boot. He stamped his foot menacingly, and effectively, but there was one awful, unforeseen consequence. The barbed iron gate of the battered portal creaked uneasily on its hinges and, with a surprising amount of force, swung shut. The explorers—while rid of the rats—were left to stare at their newest misfortune.

With a click, the gate had locked.

Chapter Forty

Down

ismally, they turned into the darkness. "Axle?" Rowan asked hopefully.

"It appears this, er, passageway is not on the map," the trestleman replied.

"I see."

"It must let out somewhere, though," Ivy offered. "I mean, it *is* a sewer. . . ."

Similar in construction to the other tunnels they had traveled, this one was made of stone, but by perhaps a more careless hand. The rocks were chipped and jagged and variously shaped. Periodically, portals of iron grid were rammed into crooked side openings that veered off into an uneasy darkness. The slope downward was unapologetic and perilous—with each step there was a very real danger of sliding away into the pitch black.

Axle felt around in his satchel and finally retrieved a telescoping torch; its dull filament was flickery and pale, but a welcome addition to the group.

With one clanging and dejected attempt to unfasten the gate behind them, Rowan turned and sighed. Six was on ahead. Apparently, he muttered, he was now at the mercy of the creature.

The tunnel plunged downward for quite some time, and the travelers were quiet with their own cheerless thoughts. Occasionally a foul wind would blow from a rusted opening, and the group would be forced to fend off waves of queasiness. As their path finally leveled out, the tunnel opened upon an intersection of sorts, where four similar channels met at a deep, brick-lined pit. There was a ladder leading down, although the nature of the business that might take a person into the dark hole was one not lightly contemplated.

A distant roar came from somewhere far below, and a dank wind blew past and, with it, a horrible, mildewy odor.

Some long-ago traveler had placed a board across the pit, reaching treacherously to the other side. This was fortunate since the channels were designed not for foot traffic, but for the steady flow of wastewater, and without the plank, this would have been an impasse. Yet the board was a weathered one, sagging in the middle, and it seemed unlikely to support the weight of a trestleman, let alone the others.

"I shall be first," Axle announced, as he threw his satchel over to the other side.

"Hardly," Peps argued. "That will leave us stranded here should you fall!"

"Stranded, but safe." Axle was feeling about in his pockets in an attempt to balance out his load.

"Safe? What sort of safety is this? We will be stuck here forever!" Peps continued.

"I think"—Rowan's voice was shaky—"since I'm the biggest, I should go. We'll know for certain if I am able to cross."

"I'll go first," Ivy announced.

Here the other three finally agreed. "No!" they bellowed at once.

Ivy blinked.

"We can hardly spare you! A hard time you'd have curing the King from the bottom of this stinking pit!"

And thus began a lengthy discussion, and since everyone had quite a strong opinion, it was with great diplomacy that the order of the crossing was finally established. Peps would go first—with his bountiful waistline, his successful passage would almost guarantee that everyone, with the exception of Rowan, the largest, would be light enough to cross.

"Where's Six?" Ivy asked, looking around for the cat.

The cat had vanished—only to appear on the opposite end of the pit. He had crossed the plank during the debate and sat, quite lazily, scratching his scruff.

They began their meek parade across the old board. Putting one foot in front of the next, Peps nearly ran. Ivy's years upon Axle's trestle had instilled in her an enviable sense of balance, and she walked quite easily to where Peps was waiting. Axle, too, had an uneventful crossing.

And Rowan? Rowan would have been fine, had he not looked down.

Chapter Forty-one

Bitter Swill

Actually, falling in the dark is probably the best way to fall.

There is no scenery racing by to distract you. There is no view of where it is you are falling *to*. There is only the mad rush of wind. That, and the occasional bump as your body collides against the confines of the brick pit—and the ancient, broken ladder.

The ladder! Rowan realized, as it struck the side of his cheek in passing. The next time he bounced against it, he was prepared. Somewhat. He managed to catch hold of it, but, like the rest of the sewer, it was slick and wet, and he lost it soon enough.

It did eventually interrupt his fall.

An old and rusted rung had come loose and stuck out, like a broken and dead branch. It was upon this that his robes caught, and the former taster had a moment in which to reflect upon the fact it was his robes that very well might have saved his life. But this thought was followed by a terrific *rip,* and Rowan found himself again falling, downward, ever downward—and into the river below.

No more troubled waters had he seen than these. But *see* he did, for there was some sort of dull light now in the gaping opening into which he had fallen—a cavern that served mainly as a housing for a vast underground river, mostly storm runoff. A bitter swill, indeed.

As he surfaced, spitting and gasping for breath, he saw what lay ahead. The waterway opened up somewhat into a wide underground lake. It flowed steadily against the sheer walls of rock and then bottlenecked in a mad rush of falling water. Beyond the drop-off—for that's what Rowan was heading toward—was nothing but darkness.

Chapter Forty-two

The King's Flower

he roaring grew much louder as Rowan was swept along in the sturdy current toward the cascading, falling water. With a sickening feeling, he saw that what followed was a sheer, wet drop into nothingness. In desperation—and cursing the fact that he was not the most athletic of swimmers—he cast about the cavern looking for something to grab on to. Made from the rock of the mountains above, the walls were a sheer, smooth stone. Then, he saw it. A large, cluttered mound of debris to one side. With his last strength, he battled toward it.

His robes clung to him heavily and he gasped for air, but aided by the current and utter strength of will, he made it to the perimeter. There Rowan clung to a maze of tangled waste. It was a watery web of clotted and decaying matter—branches, soggy term papers, a twisted and ruined tail feather of a vulture. The river surged by quickly, and it was hard to gain a foothold on the shifting matter, or anything of substance. His face was pressed roughly against an old shoe.

As he contemplated his predicament, somewhere deep within him was born the urge to simply let go. Perhaps, this new voice reasoned, it would be easier to face the rapids than to continue on a journey certain to bring him further indignities. How impossible this task he had embarked upon! How utterly foolhardy to return here, to the Tasters' Guild, delivering himself to his enemies. He allowed this thought to blossom in his mind like an invasive weed—and, as is the nature of such thoughts, it quickly grew, offering its defeating reasonings up to his tired mind.

Verjouce, his distorted face, swam before him, a vision of ruin. He felt his fingers letting go of the web of deadwood.

But something caught his eye. It was something quite impossible, and just atop the pile of debris in which he was tangled.

A splash of green—of life. And from the thin green stem, more color, this time five petals of golden yellow.

A cinquefoil!

The King's flower was growing very much as if for Rowan himself, growing against all odds in the bowels of the Tasters' Guild. Somehow he found the strength to reach for it—and beyond. He pulled himself up, tired and dripping from the dark underground river, and heaving deep, grateful breaths, he lay beside the flower, and slept.

Chapter Forty-three

Malapert

The Field Guide to the Poisons of Caux contains but a passage on the great and tragic loss of the contents of the Library at Rocamadour. Axlerod D. Roux did not dwell too long upon this sad part of Caux's history, for his hand trembled and his heart ached too much as he wrote the text.

The ancient fire of Rocamadour that even Hemsen Dumbcane cursed was ordered by the new and evil King Nightshade—but, like many other things, was actually the sinister idea of Vidal Verjouce. It destroyed nearly all the books in the famed Library, and the ancient knowledge that those magical books contained within. It doomed Caux to a fate of sorrow, for without knowledge, one is left only with folly.

The fire was fashioned by Outriders: in their menacing silence, they gathered armfuls of the enormous tomes and threw them in a growing pile. But the flame was cast by the trembling hand of the Librarian.

Oh, to go against one's character in such an evil act as that! To be charged, as a librarian is, with the caretaking of knowledge—only to be the cause of its demise! It is a betrayal of one's very nature—a poisoning of the soul.

Deeply ashamed, the Librarian of Rocamadour, a man named Malapert but for whom names had now become obsolete, came to live in the cesspit beneath the city. He sought for himself the most miserable of existences—a penance for his evil deed. He built a small shack from a pile of nearby stones and took up a wet residence beside an underground gulch—finding a certain irony in his proximity to the antidote to fire.

Fire and water. Doomed to this watery existence, the wretched soul of Malapert. The soul of the Librarian.

The soggy tip of Malapert's cane was poking at a suspicious lump of boiled wool. It hadn't been there yesterday—nor even that very morning—and he wanted it away. But the Librarian was realizing now that things were more complicated than he had first thought. The boiled lump was moving about—and moaning. The boiled lump was a boy.

"You there—" He continued his poking. He idly wondered what fate had brought the wretched creature down here, but this was not a compassionate thought. He was too soaked in misery for compassion. "Rise at once!" he ordered.

Rowan was in fact dreaming.

In his dream, Ivy was there, her eyes searching for him. But as he drew closer, they withered into distant knots—her skin was now a wrinkled brown. Ivy, Rowan dreamed, was becoming a tree. A great and wild one. And the tree struggled with him—pulling him rudely with her branches. Poking him repeatedly in the ribs. The tree, oddly, smelled of fire—of smoke.

It was this smell that finally awoke Rowan, and it was Malapert who was the source of it.

Rowan blinked at the strange and pathetic specter he now saw. The creature was stooped and clothed in the remnants of a robe, but one so ruined by fire that it was a miracle it stayed together at all. At regular intervals, his scalp showed through in places where his long gray hair refused to grow. And his skin—it possessed a particular sheen to it, and the texture was of melted wax.

Rowan received another poke in the ribs and this time cried out.

"Oww! What are you doing?"

"None shall pass!" The Librarian leaned on his weapon and tried to stand tall.

"Pass? I'm hardly moving!" Rowan pointed out.

"I am the guardian of this waterway, and you are but a trespasser. I say again: None shall pass!"

After one more prod, Rowan struggled to his feet. His side ached horribly.

"Very well," he said, looking about him. An uneven set of steps carved a jagged path in the rock wall, leading up to a dubious overhang. There, upon the precipice, Rowan now saw that the pile of stones he had glimpsed from the river was in fact a home of sorts, built haphazardly and threatening to fall down at any moment on top of their heads. "If you'll just show me the way out . . ."

Malapert blinked.

"I don't mean to trouble you, Mr. . . . ? If you would just show me another way out. I can hardly go back the way I came, now can I?"

Malapert opened his ruined mouth and snapped it shut again. He cocked his ear. A look of disbelief passed over his shiny face.

"No—this is not possible," he muttered, and crossly he escorted Rowan up the remaining pile of refuse, along the precarious stairs, to terra firma.

There, a second source of dismay awaited the Librarian.

For countless years he had lived a life of lonely exile, and not once had he had the trouble and bother of visitors. Yet, incredibly, twice in one day he had faced trespassers.

"None shall pass!" he repeated a bit incredulously.

But his warning was not to Rowan this time. Ahead, the lonely precipice of the Librarian's home met the stone wall at a tunnel. In the opening stood Ivy, an enormous cat, and two trestlemen.

Chapter Forty-four

The Riddle

Rowan!" Ivy ran across the bridge to where the taster and the Librarian were standing. "Rowan! I was sure—" She dared not finish her sad thought but instead rushed to hug her friend.

"None shall pass!" Malapert's cane stopped her in her tracks.

"I—I'm not trying to pass. I just want to see my friend!"

Malapert looked momentarily flustered but soon regained his menacing composure.

"Back off, child!" He waved his ragged arms in his burnt cloak.

Ivy ignored him.

"How did you ever—?" She was trying to peek around the bothersome man, but with each attempt she was matched by him. This dance continued for a moment, until Rowan merely sidestepped Malapert, to the Librarian's great chagrin. There was a great hug, followed by a painful gasp. Rowan's side was bruised, and each breath seemed somehow incomplete.

"Let me see." His robes were torn on one side, and she examined this. "Deep breath—good. Nothing's broken. You're pretty banged up, though. Scrapes and scratches—and quite a splinter, I think." She looked at it closer. "That's probably a thorn from the hawthorn forest. I can get it out if you want. And you could use a bath."

"No kidding."

Axle and Peps had advanced along with the tattered cat, and everyone began chatting happily—talking over each other and embracing.

The Librarian suddenly felt uneasy.

Such joy disgusted him. Better to get them out of here as fast as possible.

He cleared his throat.

"None shall pass," he tried again weakly.

"Yes, yes, we know!" Ivy said.

"Unless . . ."

"Unless, what?" She was curious.

"Unless you first answer my riddle."

Chapter Forty-five

The Reply

Ah! He had gotten their attention, he saw. Malapert looked around the bridge carefully and
asked, "Are we agreed, then?"

The Librarian took a step forward, toward the group,
and for his efforts received a warning hiss from the
mangy cat. Malapert hissed right back.

"We are agreed," Axle spoke.

Had Malapert been a more perceptive sort (he had lived a
life entirely devoted to literature, until his undoing), he would
have seen a strange look pass over the trestleman's face. But
the Librarian was currently enjoying a dramatic pause before
his challenge, and in this pause he congratulated himself upon
the insoluble nature of his special riddle, one that he had carefully composed over his many lonely years. No one had ever
before answered it.

"Is that *you*—Malapert?" Axle asked, incredulously wiping
away the grime from his pince-nez and replacing it. "You
are alive!"

The riddle stalled upon the burnt man's tongue.

"It *is* you! I knew it!" Axle stepped forward and clapped the old man upon the back. A puff of disintegrating cloth swirled about the gesture, smelling fiercely of fire, and was gone.

It had been countless years since the Librarian had thought his own name, let alone heard it spoken. Nevertheless, he was not one to let a good riddle go unasked. Stepping away from the small trestleman, the Librarian raised his head high.

"What is never hungry but always eating?" Malapert asked, voice loud and obstinate. He directed his gaze at the girl before him.

Ivy had been watching the curious exchange between Axle and the stranger and was caught off guard.

"Er— Could you repeat the question, please?"

The Librarian obliged.

"What is never hungry but always eating?" Ivy reiterated thoughtfully. She turned to Rowan, conferring.

"Pigs eat a lot," Rowan, the son of a pig farmer, offered. "Even when they're not hungry."

"I think it's something less obvious. It *is* a riddle, after all."

"Let me think." Rowan stalled. He tried to recall his years of taster training.

"Malapert—" Axle would not be put off. He tapped the Librarian on the backside again insistently. "Certainly you must remember me—Axlerod D. Roux? You were always so thorough and knowledgeable—a great help in my research. A true professional. I owe you a debt of gratitude—I always intended to thank you—but, well, in light of the events, I never could make it back to Rocamadour. Pray tell me, how did you come to be . . . *here*?"

Malapert sighed. It seemed there was no discouraging this tiny man. He looked about the group. The water passing below them gurgled. And in that inexplicable way that enlightenment arrives, as if offered down from above, delivered intact, whole and at once, Ivy suddenly realized she knew the answer to Malapert's riddle.

"A serpent—devouring its own tail!" she said brightly. "The ouroboros is the answer to your riddle!"

Chapter Forty-six
Tea and Sympathy

he fact that the girl had cracked his riddle so quickly, combined with the insistent small man repeatedly saying his old name, finally brought Malapert to tears. He broke down swiftly, soot and ash streaking his ruined face. He cried bitterly. He cried for so much loss, so long ago.

And then, with a great sob, he invited the visitors to tea.

Malapert's hut was not designed for guests—it was, in fact, not designed for human habitation—and luckily the small, smoke-stained pile of rocks upon which he brewed his tea lay scattered before the wrecked entrance. In a dented old basin, the Librarian poured some foul water and settled it atop a few burning coals.

Except for the occasional Outrider, the Librarian had seen no one from the world above for the entire Nightshade regime, and since Outriders were not conversationalists, Malapert knew nothing but his own misery. He found now that there was room in his broken heart for wonder, and he was happy—or, to be more precise, he was not unhappy—to hear what events he had missed after the fire. As Axle and Peps caught him up, Ivy and Rowan had time for a quiet word.

"There—you see it?" Rowan pointed down the awful steps to the small, delicate cinquefoil.

Ivy squinted into the gloom.

"Yes!" Ivy gasped. "Yes, I do! It's a sign, surely. They grow only in the presence of magic."

Uplifted, she turned again, examining the haphazard construction of Malapert's home behind her. It was a teetering disaster, made from unusually fine stone blocks. The Librarian had, inexplicably, hung some dirty rags to dry along a frayed line, and these drooped depressingly to one side of the shack. A vague chill ran up her arms as she realized the stones of the hut were distinctly familiar.

"Rowan!" she cried, grabbing her friend's arm. "Look! Malapert's house! It's made from—"

The pair moved forward quickly, Ivy nearly pulling Rowan along.

"Bearing stones!" the taster realized.

"Yes! I am sure!"

Racing over to the shack as best she could, she ran her hands along the enchanted Verdigris stones. Once everywhere, they were a beacon to those who found themselves lost, pointing the weary traveler in the direction of home. Ivy had come across several forgotten ones in her travels to Templar, and they had been just as uplifting. She knew the evil King Nightshade had had most of them impounded, feeling anything from the previous King to be contemptible, and Malapert was the inadvertent benefactor of this roundup.

But Ivy knew one thing that King Nightshade did not. It was the magical nature of the stones that as they were moved, so, too, changed the information etched across their smooth sides. Written in a fine script, a scrawl repeated a thousandfold on each and every stone of the Librarian's hut, was this:

½ knarl to Pimcaux

Pimcaux.

Such is the power of a single word. It was written on some stones in small letters and on others quite grandly—here in a dazzling font, and there in plain, practical letters—sideways, upward, and then on the diagonal (for Malapert's home was not one to follow a clean line). Seeing it now as they did, announcing itself over and over again, the two weary travelers burst into broad smiles.

The visit to Malapert produced one other thing of note.

Axle and Peps listened with wide eyes as the Librarian described his last minutes beside the vast fire—engulfing so many enchanted and irreplaceable books from the Good King's reign. As Malapert saw them all succumb to the flames, saw ribbons of angry orange slither across the illuminated pages, he felt in his very soul the wrongness of this act. He saw the dense, magical texts he had guarded for so long turn a sinister, inky black before finally drifting off to ash. And that was when he found his feet working seemingly without his knowledge, for he was suddenly within the awful burning mass, frantically saving what he could and suffering greatly for his regret.

"What little I managed to save I hid in the catacombs," Malapert confessed. "In the oldest crypt beneath the city. The Book of the Ouroboros is there."

Chapter Forty-seven

Professor Breaux's Moonlit Garden

heir murky tea was drunk and the group said their quiet goodbyes. Through another brief tunnel, just as Malapert had promised, they soon came to an iron-rung ladder—not unusual in the sewers, but this one was different. It was splashed with a weak shaft of silvery light.

Rowan was still feeling quite bruised and battered, and a sharp, searing pain was now stabbing at his ribs where the splinter was. As he peered up the hole, it seemed the passage went on forever. This climb would be a challenge, he thought miserably, and he dreaded where it would take them. Suddenly his apprentice robes made him feel wretched and heavy, and he was struck by a memory. It was of the very day it became clear to him that, as a taster, he would never amount to much.

This daunting realization came to him in a theoretical class on taste, taught by an elderly subrector named Professor Breaux. The class, Advanced Taste Theory, was meant for much more adept students—or at least those with better grades—but somehow Rowan's application had been approved. Breaux was quite old and stooped, but his voice could reach to the very end of the lecture hall and sound more vigorous than it did in the front row.

The course over the years had not deviated from its curriculum and had thus fallen out of favor with the newer tasters—who dismissed it as old-fashioned and difficult. For this reason, Rowan sat almost alone—his only companion in the back row was a petulant girl named Rue. Rowan knew her as having a reputation for being somewhat thorny, and since she was a year behind him, their paths at first crossed only at Breaux's lectures.

Rue took no notes that he could see, while Professor Breaux expounded upon the subtler sides of taste and appetite. Rowan, however, knowing quite rightly that he was no natural-born scholar, attempted to fill sheaths and sheaths with scribbled notes, but somehow his talent at note taking never translated into deep knowledge. It seemed more often than not, later, when he was reviewing his work, that the words on the page were not at all right, that he had somehow failed to capture the essence of the lecture entirely. Still he persevered, oftentimes more to prove to Rue that he could succeed—for in his own mind he had invented a competition with a girl who barely seemed to notice him.

While it was the rest of the subrectors' duties to teach taste in terms of various combinations of sweet, sour, salt, and bitter—the flavors the tongue is capable of detecting—it was Professor Breaux's idea to teach taste in a very different way. Breaux added to the list savory—a fifth and controversial taste—and from there, things got even more confusing. Rowan struggled to learn taste as an entire *experience*, as a whole, and this class in particular put him at odds with the rest of the Guild's teachings. It was as if he were trying to learn two separate but confusingly similar languages at the same time, and the result was a particularly bad mess.

And so Rowan could pinpoint where in his training he knew he would never amount to much of a taster, and it was here, in Breaux's worn lecture hall, with the afternoon sun catching dust motes in its muted rays. In one way, Breaux's class planted the seed in Rowan that made him a good companion for Ivy, and an enemy of the Tasters' Guild. But in another, more practical way, it muddled him up so that he was a danger to himself and anyone he tasted for—and that, of course, had proved fatal to Turner Taxus.

It was well known that Professor Breaux grew a garden of which he was quite proud. It was a moonlit garden, an uninteresting garden in the daytime, but as darkness descended, it came alive with pale blooms, delicate, sweet scents, and glittery surprises. He would host gatherings here in the evening, and when Rowan was invited to attend one—quite an honor—he was surprised to see Rue at home there.

Rowan sat shyly beside the stone fountain and watched as the older students offered up discourse on taste. He hoped he would not be asked his opinion on anything and fretted the entire evening. And, to his great dismay, as his senses wandered to the moonflower and night phlox beside him, he realized his name had been called. Turning, he saw Rue there, holding out her arm.

"More dandelion wine?" she asked again.

"Huh? Oh, yes, please," Rowan answered, and smiled sheepishly.

"Your first time here?" Rue asked, and Rowan nodded. "I love his class. Don't you?"

Rowan said that he did.

"I never see you taking any notes," Rowan mentioned, curious.

"Yeah." Rue nodded. "I get enough of it at home."

"At home?"

"He's my grandfather." She indicated the Professor. "Didn't you know?"

"No!"

Rue shrugged.

Rowan looked at her now, her brown hair tied back carelessly with a ribbon.

"I'm glad you came," she added. "I've been working up the courage to invite you for some time."

Chapter Forty-eight

The Ladder

It was the memory of Rue and her grandfather that finally gave Rowan the strength to begin climbing. For the ascent was to be indeed a long one—Malapert had chosen for himself the very depths of the city as his penance—but all in the group were bolstered by the wedge of moonlight that fell upon their worn and dirty backs. Periodically, Six—strung in a canvas sack, a matted clump of angry fur poking out—would yowl an eerie complaint that echoed down the passage endlessly, as if a thousand forlorn and imprisoned cats had formed a cruel symphony.

The ladder was of an impossible length, uneven rungs that twisted about the tunnel in a maddening way. Still, they noticed a gradual shift—the silvery light grew stronger, until, after many long steps, it shone itself through a long horizontal slit where the tunnel terminated.

"Not long now," Axle called down to the rest.

After several grunts, he succeeded in moving the heavy

grate at the ladder's end. He climbed out, and then there was nothing.

The nothing was excruciating, but not nearly as excruciating as what came next. There was a shout—followed by several muffled comments, and then again they were left with the sound of the slow seepage of water upon the clammy wall.

Ivy clung to the cold rung in horror.

But Rowan was next up the ladder, and he went freely, without time to contemplate what dangers might possibly await him. In this recklessness, too, was a slight glimmer of a homecoming—Rowan found a rush of emotion at seeing his old campus. He was followed by Ivy and Peps. But what greeted them was not the sinister visage of an Outrider—or Vidal Verjouce himself—but a calm, midnight, moonlit garden, one filled with silver blossoms and nocturnal scents, with twittering nightjars calling in throaty delight.

And, having emerged from beneath a drainage grate beside a tumbling fountain, Peps—small fists swinging and ready for a fight—was completely startled by the sight of his brother and a strangely cloaked man clapping each other on the back like old friends.

Rowan knew at once exactly where he was. He felt an odd surge of happiness—odd, because he was here at the dreaded Tasters' Guild, but they had somehow emerged within the delicate confines of Professor Breaux's moonlit garden. There stood the Professor—and beside him, Rue.

"Rowan!" Rue cried, and rushed to give him a welcoming hug—only to be stopped in her tracks by his smell. "How did you ever get here?"

Ivy, who thought it was quite evident how they had arrived, and that anyone who would ask such a question was either foolish or blind, scowled at the girl.

Rue was clad, like them, in the drab robes of an apprentice—she was a student still, having not yet undergone her Epistle ceremony, during which, among other things, she would receive her taster's robes. But something was different about her, Rowan noticed at once. Her hair—it was chopped short in the brutally cropped fashion of the subrectors at the Guild. And it was shaved in a receding arc, making her forehead more pronounced and broadening her face into a full moon in an off-putting demonstration of devotion.

Rowan's eyes widened, and he took a step back.

"Y-you're tonsured!" he stammered.

A frown flitted across Rue's brow and was gone.

"Yes!" She laughed. "I always planned on continuing my studies after commencement."

"You— You want to be a *subrector*?" Since meeting Ivy, his opinion of the Tasters' Guild had changed drastically, but even he would never have considered becoming a Guild scholar.

"And why not? Can you think of any greater honor?"

Rowan was silent.

"Who's this, Rowan?" Peps asked, looking between the two.

Rowan, remembering his manners, turned to make introductions.

"Ivy, Peps, this is my friend Rue. Rue, this is Ivy Manx and Peps D. Roux. Oh, and over there is—"

"Axlerod D. Roux!" Rue nodded enthusiastically. Like most of Caux, Rue possessed a great respect for the *Field Guide,* and its author, who was currently filling in his old friend on news of Cecil and Templar. Rue turned again to Ivy, who had so far failed at any attempt to make herself appear more friendly.

"I am named after him," she confided with a wink.

Ivy scoffed. "After Axle?"

"Yes—my parents were great fans of his work."

Ivy narrowed her eyes. She suddenly felt proprietary of her lifelong friend.

"Really. How nice." She glared unpleasantly at the strange girl and found a spark of her old self return—wouldn't it be nice to test Rue's tasting abilities? Ivy was certain she could easily get the better of the would-be scholar with a few drops of her famous toadstool tonic. Six's yellow eyes gleamed encouragingly.

Rowan, glancing anxiously from one girl to the other, interrupted the stalemate.

"Ivy grew up beside Axle's trestle. They are old friends," he revealed. His words relaxed Ivy some, and she found herself smiling in satisfaction. Rowan, quick to change the subject, demanded news from inside the Tasters' Guild and soon found Rue was quite happy to oblige.

As the two classmates caught up, Ivy's attention drifted.

"Ivy Manx," came a low baritone, a voice that made children learn complicated theories easily by the mere melody of its rich tones. "What errand brings the Child of the Prophecy, the Noble Child, here, to the Tasters' Guild? In this uneasy realm, surely this can be no social visit."

She was joined then by Axle and the Professor—his silver hair gleaming a rich hue against his black robes in the low light. The old friends looked serious, and the Professor bent down to inspect her.

"Um—" Ivy found herself suddenly unable to answer. But, as it turned out, this was a question more directed at Axle, for, indeed, Professor Breaux knew that Axle was the one to answer it.

Axle looked around the dark night, and Breaux at once understood.

"We are safe here, in my garden, for the time being," the Professor said. "Verjouce has not seen fit to bother an old, doddering lecturer. Yet."

"But . . ." Axle grew quiet as he studied Rowan and Rue from afar.

"Oh, yes. Rue," sighed the professor. "She is young. This is the only life she's known, within the Guild's walls. But she can be trusted—she is my granddaughter, my blood."

"Yes, of course," Axle said quickly. For a moment it seemed as if there was something more, but the trestleman shook his head and was quiet.

They gathered at the fountainside, where Peps was happy for the chance to dip his kerchief in the water and begin the impossible process of becoming presentable.

"Surely, old friend, it must not surprise you that we are here?" Axle asked.

Breaux's eyes twinkled a moment, and then a stillness settled into them, a sadness. He shook his head. "I only wish it was not necessary."

"We search for the Doorway here at Rocamadour. The Doorway to Pimcaux."

Breaux was silent for a moment. "Of course," he said finally. "I am at your disposal."

"Have you any news?"

"So I do. None of it good."

Chapter Forty-nine

The Plan

rofessor Breaux sat, with the help of his granddaughter, upon a smooth stone bench. He was
assisted in this chore by a gnarled walking
stick, but all the same a look of pain swept across his face,
and Rowan was stricken to behold just how old he had
become in the few short years since he'd last seen him. Settled
now, the Professor took a deep breath.

"You say you have seen the Librarian, Malapert?"

"Indeed," Axle replied. "I have seen him."

"Well, that *is* something." The Professor looked around, his
eyes settling on Ivy. "I must pay my old friend a visit."

"Malapert hid some Verdigris books in a crypt beneath the
city," Axle said excitedly. "Maybe the Doorway to Pimcaux is
there?"

Ivy thought of the time—it seemed so long ago—in Axle's
study, when she and Rowan had together seen such a doorway in
a book. She knew the power of the great and ancient magic, and

at the memory of the strange vision there in the trestle, her stomach leapt.

But the old man shook his head sadly.

"Perhaps it was at some point. But the page was torn from its binding long before Malapert could salvage it, and is now the subject of much speculation."

"Then it might still be here!" Rowan said.

"I am afraid not," Breaux said sadly. "It was thought the paper found its way to Vidal Verjouce, who hid it well."

Rowan cast a dark look about him. It would be impossible to breach the Director's chambers.

"And now there are whispers it is gone again." Breaux sighed.

"What did this parchment look like?" Ivy suddenly asked. Valuable missing scrolls reminded her of someone, and a realization was dawning on her.

"It was said to be a door, drawn simply, but one adorned with the ancient symbol of regeneration, of healing. The ouroboros."

"The ouroboros!" the travelers said in unison. The golden serpent from Dumbcane's shop.

"What is never hungry but always eating?" Ivy cried.

"Verjouce has apprehended the thief," Breaux continued. "He is a scribe. But he is also a forger and has apparently been stealing valuable papers from the Guild for many years."

"He is called Hemsen Dumbcane," Axle announced, to the surprise of his host.

"You know of him?"

Axle nodded. "A neighbor of sorts."

Peps scowled at the thought.

"He awaits his sentence, a prisoner in the catacombs." Rue now spoke.

"Sentence? What sort of sentence?" Axle demanded.

"Conium maculatum."

"Poison hemlock," Ivy whispered. As a poison, it was perfection. Swift and deadly.

Breaux turned his wise face to Ivy again.

"Ivy, I knew your uncle Cecil at a gentler time. How is he? He must be quite proud of you."

Ivy mumbled that Cecil was well.

"Do you like my garden?" he asked. "I hear you are quite a gardener yourself."

"Yes, I'd love to look around," she replied shyly.

"Nothing would make me happier." He gestured. "Be sure to smell the elderberry," he said casually.

Ivy nodded.

"Elderberry and, of course, arrowroot."

Odd requests, she thought, since neither had a particularly pleasing scent, but she nodded again politely.

"Elderberry, arrowroot—and sourbush."

Ivy peeked at Axle, who wore a look of amusement.

"I will be sure to, Professor."

"How do the forkedtongue and spittlesap grow here?" Axle asked casually.

Sourbush, she thought quickly, in its most general sense meant *captive, a prisoner.* And forkedtongue, a spiky reed with seed pods filled with fluffy thistledown and gooey sap, meant *to decipher.* The Professor and Axle were speaking in Flower Code! She was realizing how instantly fond she was of this old man, Rowan's favorite teacher. She listened gleefully as Professor Breaux and Axle suggested that a visit to the catacombs was necessary, to find Dumbcane.

It was too dangerous, Axle continued in Code, for Ivy to leave the Professor's compound. She wasn't instantly recognizable, but still, there was too much at stake. The Professor agreed, and it was decided that Rowan as well was to stay within the moonlit walls. He was known here, as a former student, and known to be uncollared, an Oath breaker. If Verjouce found Rowan . . . Ivy knew what future awaited him and did not need the Professor to continue.

Ivy reached for a dry inner pocket in her borrowed robe and, fishing out her beloved copy of Axle's book, quickly turned to a dog-eared page.

"Stinkhorn?" she asked, after finding the plant she was looking for. "Because crimped gill and thick-footed saddle weed."

The Professor laughed.

"Yes, of course! The sewers of Rocamadour are as dismal a place as I can think of. Let's see what we can do about getting you cleaned up!"

Chapter Fifty

Something That Grows

It was not long before the travelers were re-united again before the fountain, this time bearing the more pleasant scents of bath salts and fresh soap along with new robes. Ivy smiled at the sight of Peps, who was so relieved to be done with the sewers, he cared not at all about his borrowed, ill-fitting clothes. His gold tooth flashed as he grinned at her. Axle and Professor Breaux were still conferring in low voices, and Ivy waited for Rowan to appear.

There was a table set in the garden, and Rue was seeing to various delicacies and small dishes. Ivy's appetite was still absent—the smell of a sewer is one that does not diminish easily—but she looked on with a vague sense of happiness, tempered by the very real fact that she was now an uninvited guest of Rocamadour. She must somehow navigate this terrible city and find her way to Pimcaux. But for now, the garden around her was magnificent, and its delights beckoned.

She walked, grateful for the time alone—quickly, the low

conversations about her faded into the background of insect trills and toad calls, and the ever-present bubbling of the fountain. The living, growing things around her rejoiced at her presence—as they had done since she was born—and as she followed a pebbled pathway, flowers upon stalks upon root-stems strained to be nearer to her. Yet, no matter where she went in the oasis of Breaux's garden, there was no escaping the steep black spire of the Guild's tower blotting out the peaceful night sky, and when she looked upon it, a palpable shadow crossed her heart.

Ivy rounded a showy tuft of silvery grass and was surprised to find her host alone in the moonlight, sitting beside his staff in a forgotten corner of the garden.

"Professor Breaux?" she asked, approaching.

He put a finger to his lips, quieting her.

Even though his was a residence—one acquired in advanced age and seniority in the subrector ranks, a safe house of sorts for the travelers—it was, after all, a part of the larger Tasters' Guild, and the walled ramparts of the city weren't that far off. From here the two watched as several guards patrolled it. On the other side of the high stone wall that encompassed Breaux's home and garden was a cobbled walkway, and on this Ivy now heard footsteps plainly receding.

"Join me?" he asked in the silence that followed.

Ivy nodded and did so.

"I envy your travels. Pimcaux! Although it is not in my

future to see it again, I do so wish I might." He paused. "There is something I must tell you, though. It is of grave importance to your return."

Ivy glanced at the Professor quickly and nodded.

He reached beside him and plucked a night lily from its stalk. She smelled its thick perfume, the rare flower a small joy to her beside him. His fingers were crooked and lumpy with age, but he had no trouble crushing the beautiful blossom. The air smelled bruised and thick. He opened Ivy's hand and placed the ruined thing within, closing her fingers over it.

"We are a land born of the earth, of things that grow—both good and bad. Great wisdom is found in the forests—great power is there for those who seek it. But plants must be used wisely, not against their natures, or they will turn upon us. They will harm instead of heal. They will poison. You speak the Language of Flowers, Ivy. In this lies your destiny. *Whosoever speaks to the trees speaks to the King.*" The Professor was silent for some time.

Then he said, "Getting to Pimcaux—that is but half the journey. To return, that requires something else. In order to leave Pimcaux, you must bring with you something of the earth, something that grows from the soil of Caux. Otherwise, there is no way back."

Ivy nodded and the Professor relaxed, as if a weight had been lifted from his shoulders. She bent forward and opened her hand, curious, peering down in the moonlight. Within her small fist, the fragile night lily was reborn—with not a sign of trauma at the old man's hand.

She slipped the lily behind her ear.

"So it is true." He nodded. "I have now seen it for myself—plants are awakening again. Your uncle worked some ancient magic when he roused the Verdigris tapestries. But what is more potent is your own effect upon that which grows."

Ivy thought of the hawthorn tree, of its evil desire to imprison her friend. She shuddered. Apparently all plants were awakening—not just the good. How many people must suffer because of her?

There was a crunching nearby, a dried leaf underfoot again on the walkway, and Ivy froze. Through a veil of creeper, thin iron bars faced the narrow street, a vertical peephole, and it was here that Ivy thought she saw something move. Looking out again on the sliver of dark cobblestones, she was certain now. A splash of scarlet—but then there was nothing.

Since Snaith had given his master Dumbcane's notorious inks, Verjouce had become ever more bitterly empowered with wrath—a cold, omnipotent wrath that seemed to consume him. His master's new intensity was disconcerting, even for the assassin, and the furious black wasps that now haloed his master's head were vicious things, bent on guarding the inks that Verjouce toyed with and—it seemed to the subrector—keeping him at bay.

At all times of day, the Guild's Director could be found behind the great stone slab of his desk, the burnished surface covered in a stenciled leather, drip- and splatter-stained. Ink crusted the great man's nostrils, and Snaith found the thick air foul and unbreathable.

The Director had given him a task, though, and that was to discover the errant taster Truax. With Truax they could barter with the Taxus Estate for the missing document. This would be an easy enough task, and he began to doggedly pursue it. The Guild's meticulous records had him placed with

Turner Taxus shortly after completing his studies. He worked in Templar and then, interestingly, took a small trip north to a tiny tavern where Taxus was to issue a commonplace repossession notice. It was there that Truax had failed his charge—and, worse yet, broken his solemn Oath to stay by him until representatives of the dead man's Estate could claim him, as, according to Guild law, the taster was now their property to do with as they wished. Such disregard for the Oath was punishable. And it was here that the trail of the taster went cold.

But what Snaith found to be most interesting was the name of the pitiful tavern. He found it written in the meticulous scrawl common to the Guild's many dossiers: the Hollow Bettle. The Hollow Bettle. He knew it to be the tavern wherein Vidal Verjouce's former assistant, Sorrel Flux, had stayed at the Director's insistence, and the very tavern where the Noble Child was hiding. And the taster Truax had disappeared along with the Prophesied One.

And then Snaith had a marvelous thought—one that sent a shiver of excitement up his hunched and ruined spine. Perhaps, Snaith reasoned, they traveled together. A prize indeed it would be to discover the two of them.

Chapter Fifty-two

Kingmaker

ot since Axle had holed up in the famed Library, researching and composing his masterwork, had the city seen any of his ancient race. Now there were tollhouses and guarded gateways, and, for that matter, a hawthorn forest more thick and impassable than any moat.

Rocamadour, fashioned by the great hand of King Verdigris, was built as a place of learning, a place where all matters might drop away before the earnest desire for knowledge. Only it was never the Good King's intention that what would be taught was the dark and shifty subject of poisons, nor that the teachers would all answer to his former and traitorous advisor. The Tasters' Guild, like the tasters it produced, was a symptom of a sickness, a lawlessness in the state of the natural kingdom.

The city was built into the side of the mountain, and the stone that made up every brick, every pillar, every keystone, was as black as pitch. Blanketing this stone was a glaze of fine moss, growing nearly everywhere along the damp passageways and carpeting the fine cloisters. At its base there were cobbled streets and a few shops, all Guild-run, providing the student tasters with supplies. The lecture halls, the offices, and the Library, a former pinnacle of learning now mostly empty, were above. But the catacombs—and Dumbcane— were below. Far below.

It was decided that Axle and Peps would make the trip to these catacombs, and while this sort of outing had none of the flavors that might inspire Peps D. Roux, he was eager to redeem himself for being an uninvited stowaway on the larger excursion. Together they donned the drab robes of the students, Peps's fancy shoes peeping out from beneath the rolled hem.

"Scourge bracken," Peps was whispering as he and his brother shuffled along in the shadows of a twisty cobbled street. "What is all this talk of scourge bracken?"

"Shh!" Axle admonished, stopping. "Do not be careless again with that name." His eyes flashed. "Especially here."

"Well!" Peps was taken aback. "A fine way to speak to your brother, that is."

Axle stopped peering about for the moment and looked at Peps, softening.

"I'm sorry. You're right, of course."

"I just meant, before, when I was asking about scou—"

"Peps!" Axle menaced.

"I, er, when I was asking about that *thing*. I just meant that it seems like there's a whole lot of fuss over this one particular *thing*. A *weed*, no less."

"Indeed. There was a time it was known not by that name but by another. Before King Verdigris banished it, it used to be called Kingmaker."

"Kingmaker?"

"Yes."

"That hardly sounds like a bad thing."

"Until you realize that it will stop at nothing, it will exhaust all resources. Kingmaker will leave the fields burnt and smoldering, the forests blighted and crumbling, the rivers, well, the rivers poisonous and black, and then—as you stand amid the rubble—only then will you be king."

"Oh. I see," Peps said. "However did that Hemsen Dumbcane get his hands on any?"

"That, my dear brother, is what we're going to ask him ourselves."

The pair set off again, discreetly maneuvering through the dim streets and taking cover at the sound of any footfalls. Axle had concealed his blunt beard, and from afar the undersized pair could be mistaken for any first years.

Above them was the bleak tower wherein lay Vidal Verjouce's awful, inky chambers, but the trestlemen were headed in a different direction. Down. Very much down, through the Warming Room, past its great fire and chimney, and beneath a series of archways, each a little less extravagant, as if even their ancient sculptor had given up all hope.

Finally the passage deteriorated into a simple tunnel, living rock chipped away with trembling hands. Here began the land of shadows. At the end, a wooden trapdoor. There was no lock—for why would they need to lock away the dead?

Chapter Fifty-three

The Catacombs

idal Verjouce was alone with his thoughts—always alone. Well, not entirely. If truth be told, he hosted a vast array of sleek black wasps, and just the other morning he was vaguely surprised to feel beside his hands—how distant they seemed to him these days—an army of leeches slithering upon his stone table, slowly circling the last of Dumbcane's ink. But alone or not, his thoughts were of one thing only: scourge bracken.

If he were a person of sight, and cared to present himself before a mirror, he would feast his eyes upon a man transformed. The furious buzzing in his ears was taking form—the wasps huddled in thin air around the blind man's head in the shape of a spiked crown—an extraordinary, living, angry crown. From the inks, the skin upon Verjouce's hands had darkened to a deep black, and his face was streaked and filthy. He had abandoned his strict attention to outward appearances and began instead to look within, to consult his most dark places. To cultivate his Mind Garden.

Yet, with the entrance of Kingmaker into his lurid existence, Verjouce's Mind Garden had become overgrown. The threatening clouds he witnessed upon the horizon had indeed moved in, and with them a storm of such ferocity that most of what was lovely was ripped from the earth and stamped out as if beneath a giant's heel. In its place grew dark, wiry things—black, scabby leaves that cast enormous shadows. Strange nubbly fungi, like bat wings.

Only in his Mind Garden did scourge bracken flourish, and as far as he knew, the weed grew nowhere in Caux. And this was the very root of the trouble in which the Guild's Director currently found himself. For Dumbcane's inks were perilously low, and Vidal Verjouce needed to feed his desire for more.

So, driven by his appetite, Verjouce rose suddenly—a large albino bird in his corner cage hissed with displeasure but settled back down as the Director felt for his walking staff. It was dark, but the blind man did not need light.

The catacombs were home to the Guild's outcasts: the Outriders. Axle knew this—Axle knew most everything there was to know, after all, about Caux. Peps did not. In the interest of not alarming his brother until truly necessary, Axle had avoided this topic. Until now, that is, as they pulled back the heavy trapdoor and stared at the dusty stone steps that greeted them.

Peps was satisfactorily alarmed.

"The thing about Outriders," Axle continued matter-of-factly, "is that without their sense of taste, their sight has adapted. They see quite well in the dark."

Peps's eyes grew even wider.

"But," Axle continued, "we have an advantage. They tend to rely on their remaining senses and not their intellect."

Peps looked as if he had tasted something sour. Finally, he shrugged. "Fine. What's your plan?"

"The catacombs were built over many years, each generation of subrectors leaving their mark. If I am correct, Dumbcane is being held in the deepest, oldest part."

"Of course," Peps muttered. "I suppose you have a map?" Peps thought of the sewers earlier, and the *Guide*'s illuminated arrows.

"The catacombs are uncharted," Axle said brightly. "I've been waiting for this chance for many years."

Peps groaned while Axle produced a long line of gloamwort twine—a fine silken cord that was vaguely luminescent—along with a jingling sack. "We'll need to leave a trail of thread as we go. That way, there'll be no getting lost."

Peps stood mutely as Axle outfitted him in a leather belt with several brass rings upon it and, from his clinking sack, removed a carabiner—an oval-shaped clip that clicked on to the belt neatly and disengaged just as quickly. Axle donned a similar belt and looked about, satisfied.

"All right!" Axle rubbed his hands enthusiastically. "Off we go!"

Peps wondered if he should remind his brother that they were headed into the Guild's burial ground.

The narrow steps down twisted about on themselves, and the pair's small footfalls echoed uncomfortably in the dark. When the ground leveled out, Axle felt about the wall for a chink in the mortar, and quickly and expertly nailed the frayed end of the gloamwort thread to the wall with a brass tack. After attaching his own belt, and then his brother's, to the gloamwort, he began feeling his way forward, with the intention of stopping every so often and securing their line to the wall behind them.

They went on like this for some time, in the dark, against the cold, smooth wall. But eventually the wall gave way to an open chamber, and Axle paused to record his progress on paper. He did this quickly and quietly, as it was a great risk to light his small lantern.

But as Axle lit his lamp, the flickering light caused wild shadows to play about the chamber, and with mute horror Peps saw that they were in a crypt of sorts, a burial ground for the Tasters' Guild. Ordered stone plaques depicting various names, ranks, and achievements adorned the wall, seemingly forever. Signs in the old tongue announced elaborate lineages. Puddles of oily water reflected Peps back upon himself—his pale look of fear mirrored about the death chamber in ghostly pools and lent the illusion that the ground was quite thin and insubstantial, and at any moment might give itself over to this watery existence. He thought of drowning.

In the very center of the room, atop a mound of stones, was a large statue—an enormous hooded figure of a man, arms spread wide, a champion for the dead.

Peps shrank into the corner, trembling.

Across the vault, ordered bones were perched along the length of a high shelf.

"This way." Axle pointed, to Peps's disgust, in the very direction of the bones. "Just through here—I'm almost certain."

He then extinguished the light.

"Almost?" Peps squeaked.

"We've been walking due east—I'm pretty sure. . . . It is hard to tell in the dark."

"Well, leave the light on, then!"

"Shh!" Axle was suddenly alert.

A breeze blew the faint gloamwort thread in the dark.

"Someone's coming!" Axle whispered urgently.

The two trestlemen pressed themselves—just in time—against the wall, like dead leaves. In the dark they heard them. Quiet, still, deadly. A grouping of Outriders passed them by—swiftly. Mercifully, the Outriders were on an errand of the utmost importance and were not aware of the unlikely pair of tiny men cowering in the dark. They accompanied their master, their blind master, to visit the newest prisoner.

Chapter Fifty-four

Hallowed Ground

Hemsen Dumbcane sat in his squalid cell in the bowels of the catacombs wishing with all his might that he'd be given the chance to steal away his past—not refute his misdeeds but reclaim his inks and scrolls and make a swift exit to anonymity. He had been on his way to a quiet retirement when he was apprehended, and he now cursed that fact, too. The years of working with the deadly plant had taken their toll on the prisoner, who, accustomed to the uplifting effects of the bracken, could now barely muster the energy to scratch the lice from his brow. He sat in a clump of dried swampgrass, in a swoon, and it was only after much prodding that Vidal Verjouce managed to convince Dumbcane he was indeed not a specter of the dead. Behind him, a row of Outriders glared wordlessly, eyes gleaming in the semi-darkness.

The Director stood tall and frightening while Dumbcane rubbed the grit from his eyes.

"Hemsen Dumbcane. Do you know why I've come?"

Verjouce addressed the scribe, his voice hollow and commanding.

Dumbcane grunted. A flash of envy curdled his spirits further. Verjouce had appeared heralded by his crown of sleek wasps, which pulsed with a mean purple glow—a bitter reminder of what the calligrapher had lost.

"Kingmaker. Tell me all," Verjouce ordered.

Dumbcane swallowed. Plainly, this was a dilemma. If he admitted all, then his worth to the Director was diminished and his life practically forfeit. Yet, under the threat of the barbed cane currently being brandished before his temple, it hardly seemed intelligent to be casual with the truth.

"I— Er. Perhaps I could show you?"

Verjouce thought. "You will tell me," he commanded after a minute. "And if you speak the truth, then I shall reward you." The wasps whipped about his head in a frenzy.

"Reward, kind Director?" Dumbcane inquired. He thought of feeling the sun on his back again, drawing sweet water from a deep well.

"I will reward you with your life," he stated flatly.

Dumbcane was quick to see the merits in this proposition.

"Of course. I understand completely. What, exactly, do you want to know?"

And here Verjouce was to learn how Dumbcane came upon the recipe for his treacherous inks, in the margin of an ancient text. And how, one late night after much searching, he found a single small shoot of the weed in a dark forgotten wood, growing beside an old slab of granite with ancient carvings written on its face. It was an eerie graveyard, even by Caux's standards.

"Kingmaker grows only on hallowed ground," Dumbcane sobbed.

"Then that is where I search." Vidal Verjouce gathered his Outriders about him. Their instructions were simple. Find a specimen of the bracken, find it alive, and find it now.

He turned back to Dumbcane.

"You will soon be in the business of ink-making again."

Chapter Fifty-five

Capture

Axle and Peps, with their thin and faintly illuminated line between them, had only just recovered from their fright when they were again spooked—this time by a less organized group of the same servants of the Tasters' Guild. The Outriders were fanning out, muttering to themselves in an incomprehensible guttural language, one that rendered any last feelings of brightness and optimism extinct. Peps threw his cloak over his face in a vain attempt at hiding, terror-stricken.

They were overlooked, but the spirit of adventure within them had departed, and they made their way with supreme caution through the remainder of the route, arriving finally—and without further incident—before the cell door.

Hemsen Dumbcane was there, imprisoned in a sad crypt, lying on the floor beside a pile of old bones.

"You there . . . ," Peps whispered. "Hemsen Dumbcane."

Dumbcane did not bother to look up. His eyes skittered about to the sound of his name, and then quickly back to where they were contemplating the curve of what appeared to be a finger bone. His was a place of such dejection that he thought it entirely possible that his mind might be manifesting visions of further torment. Didn't that small man belong back on the Knox? Hadn't he been a regular—and annoying—presence on the bridge for all of Dumbcane's long years performing his illicit activities? Certainly he was not here, in this hellish prison, then, but a vision manufactured to remind him of his previous life.

"Away, you dull spirits! How perfectly tedious to be bothered by a pair of nosy trestlemen of my own imaginings!"

Axle cleared his throat as loudly as he dared. "Dumbcane. Pull yourself together. You are not dreaming! We are here just as you are—the only thing that separates us is these bars. If you help us, we will do our best to see that they are opened."

Dumbcane raised himself enough to lean upon a worn elbow. Indeed, they were persistent, these small, make-believe visitors.

"What do you want?" He humored them.

"You were, er, entrusted with a document. . . ."

Hemsen sighed audibly. This was beginning to sound familiar.

"A very ancient document, one that you recently . . . lost."

Hemsen knew the one. He sagged. It was the reason for his current incarceration, and suddenly he felt a wave of anger course through him.

"The bounty hunters!"

"Who?" Peps asked. "What bounty hunters?"

"The ones who came for the taster."

"Bounty hunters came to your shop? Were they by any chance called Taxus?"

Hemsen nodded dully. "They came for an Epistle. I gave it to them—but . . ." Dumbcane was reliving the hurried exchange in his shop and becoming more and more agitated. "I just wanted them to leave! I gave them the ouroboros scroll by accident."

"The Estate of Turner Taxus has the scroll?" Axle asked.

"This—all this is because of that horrid taster! Everything I've lost is because of him. Truax, they called him. Rowan Truax!" He spat. His voice was escalating, echoing against the dank walls.

"Shh—" Axle advised, to no avail. Dumbcane was lost in his realization.

"Truax! Wait until I get my hands on him! *He* is the source of my demise! I will make him suffer as surely as I have been made to suffer."

It was an impossible task to console the scribe—he was mad with his years of scourge bracken and suddenly deeply offended at his current situation—for all of which he found not himself to blame, but Rowan. His voice took on a tone of great injury, the volume rising quickly. Peps looked at Axle helplessly; neither knew what to do or say that might soothe

Dumbcane, and quite soon they were certain to be discovered.

"Shut your terrible racket!" Peps hissed.

By now Dumbcane's pronunciation had pulled the name out to two very long and plaintive syllables, and it was all he would say, over and over into the dark passages, where the name took an echo on, becoming even louder.

"Tru-ax! Tru-ax! Tru-ax!" he sobbed.

They were there silently, before either trestleman knew it. The Outriders, a pair of them from earlier who were busy searching the burial grounds beneath Rocamadour for their master's desire. Quite quickly, they had settled their terrible and cold grasp upon the tiny shoulders of Axlerod D. Roux, and as Peps drew further back into the shadow, he watched in horror as they ushered his brother away to the rhythm of Dumbcane's lament.

Chapter Fifty-six
Gloamwort

eps felt himself unable to breathe as panic began to overtake him. His arms flailed about in the dark—he had backed himself into a small vestibule, or so it seemed, for it was utterly and completely black. When an impossible amount of time had gone by and he had not been discovered, and that traitor Dumbcane had fallen again into a stupor, Peps finally allowed himself a moment of hope. This small sparkle, though, was immediately extinguished upon recollecting that his brother was now in the hands of the Tasters' Guild—in the hands of Vidal Verjouce.

Peps realized that for his brother he must find his way back aboveground. He must warn Rowan. He must report on the missing scroll. It's what Axle would want him to do. He took what he hoped would be a deep, calming breath, and his hand alighted upon his unfamiliar belt. There was the brass fastener, he realized. They had unclipped themselves as they made their way to Dumbcane, leaving the gloamwort tacked to the wall before his cell. He merely needed to creep forward and find it, and follow it out.

And so with great courage—for some are born with this glorious trait, and still others, like Peps, seem to manufacture it just when they need it the most—the lone trestleman tiptoed by the open bars of the sleeping Dumbcane's cell, freezing when it seemed at first that he might have roused him, freezing again when the forger's eyes fluttered open in a fit of delirium, and finally grasping with his cold, clammy hands the languishing roll of thread from the wall where Axle had tacked it.

Its faint phosphorescence somehow calmed him—or perhaps it was touching something with origins aboveground. For it was now that Peps realized just how draining the utter depth of the darkness was down here, devoid of life and light. Of course, Peps thought nothing now of scourge bracken, nor would he have guessed its very nature thrived away from the life-giving sun.

He reeled in the twine, carefully, and as quickly as he could, and at each mount where Axle had attached it to the crumbling wall, he clinked off his carabiner and, heart racing to be detached from his lifeline, reattached it on the next lead. Thus it was that he did eventually return to the light—the stone steps that before seemed foreboding were now a most welcome sight.

He sunk down to his knees and kissed the ground.

Trestlemen no longer walked the cobbled streets of Roca-madour, and those who lived nearby lived in fear. The rising dawn brought with it the dangers of being noticed, and Peps felt more conspicuous on his own. He scurried along the cobbled streets, avoiding any that looked busy or required him to pass by the menacing iron grilles that encased most windows in the city. Cacophonous bells rang at intervals, announcing classes and lab-oratory sessions for the students. He passed a small group of younger pupils who huddled together eyeing him, and he ducked further beneath his hood.

"First years, this way!" a voice commanded, and the nearby crowd jumped to attention.

Peps hurried his pace.

"You there!" the voice called, and to his dismay, Peps realized it was directed at him. "Where do you think you're off to?"

Peps turned, keeping his face lowered, and mumbled some-thing about being on an errand for Professor Breaux.

"Breaux? He should know better than to send a first year out without a badge. Come with me, then. I am forced to report you."

Peps opened his mouth in protest but remembered his hurry. His brother needed him. He turned and ran, breathless, his short legs carrying him to Breaux's large stone gate, the indignity of being mistaken for a mere child stinging a crimson color in his proud cheeks.

Chapter Fifty-seven

The Final Exam

I t had occurred to Ivy that she hadn't seen Six in a while. Indeed, Rowan had noticed his sneezing was better, but Ivy hadn't thought to inquire after the cat. When she stopped to think about it, she hadn't seen him since they deposited him at the foot of Breaux's fountain after the horrors of the sewer. Now she had looked up and down the entire compound and, with growing concern, still could not find him.

But at hearing the muffled knock on the old wooden door, her spirits lifted. Axle would surely know just what to do! But Peps's face told her at once of trouble. She rushed over.

"Peps! You look awful!" Ivy glanced around. "Where is Axle?"

Peps found his knees buckling with the general relief of being back safely beside Ivy, and she half held him and marched him to a nearby bench, where they were joined by the rest of the group, eager for news.

Peps had never delivered so much bad news at one time,

and the severity of it threatened to strike him mute. Where to begin? He took a deep breath and told them of Dumbcane, and that the scroll of the ouroboros was now with the Estate of Turner Taxus. He told them that the Taxus kin were pursuing Rowan and had obtained his Epistle. And then—words tumbling out of his mouth lest his courage fail him—he announced that the Outriders had captured Axle.

Ivy was silent for a moment, contemplating Axle's fate.

"Well, we'll just have to rescue him!" she decided, looking about the gathering in the garden.

No one would meet her eye except Professor Breaux.

"I'm afraid that's an impossibility, Ivy," he said softly.

"Hardly!" She looked to Rowan. "If the situation were reversed—"

"Let's all be glad it isn't," Breaux replied. "But Axle is equipped for his arrest. His vast knowledge of his . . . captor will be helpful."

Ivy felt her face redden. "You expect me to sit around and do nothing while Axle is . . . is . . ." She realized she couldn't bring herself to finish. She straightened. "Well, I'm afraid that's an *impossibility!*"

Ivy turned on her heel, and, throwing the hood of her robes over her golden hair, she heaved open the very same door through which Peps had entered, and stepped out into the dark alley.

"Ivy!" Rowan called, but she was gone.

Ivy was unprepared for the bleakness of the Guild's design, and departing through the small arched gateway onto the cobbled streets of Rocamadour, she sagged suddenly with regret. If melancholia had a weather system, this was it: a dampness that crept into your very spirit and made you move as if underwater. Stepping through the portal from Breaux's garden into the heart of the lower city, the pleasant scents within the Professor's compound were instantly replaced with the overriding smell of decay. The patches of creeping moss that covered most of the Guild's stone surfaces were a tatty, unhealthy brown. Ivy pulled her robes closer to her face.

She had little knowledge of the twisting streets and even less of where she might find Axle. Soon she came to a small square—congregating around the once-lovely fountain were the baleful forms of Rocamadour vultures, their untidy roosts making piles of filth. At the sight of the birds, she took a step back, unconsciously, and found herself against something soft, something that wasn't there a second ago—not some*thing*, she realized as she turned, startled.

Some*one*.

Snaith's hunched spine and protruding belly made him an appalling sight indeed, but his scarlet robes—the robes of the Watchmen—caused the young girl's blood to run cold.

He regarded Ivy with interest, his eyes shining from beneath his jutting forehead and odd, paunchy cheeks.

"You're late," he assessed. As if to demonstrate this, a discordant bell chimed nearby. He glared at her. "Well?"

Ivy's heart was in her throat, but she managed to nod.

The subrector held out his arm—at the end of his red cloak, one blunt, pudgy finger pointed to the nearby door. On it, Ivy noticed as she swallowed hard, was a peculiar symbol. An ox head—a swarm of bees flying forth from its mouth. Pulling her cloak about her tightly, she ducked as she passed him by, entering the lecture hall.

And oh, what a hall this was! It was long and narrow, with a ceiling as high as the cliffs around her, tiered with balconies and velvet chairs. In the center was an extraordinarily long dinner table. It was hung with low chandeliers and set with the most alluring of golden flatware, and laid with a meal like no other. Running along its great length was a supper of such splendid proportions as Ivy had never seen—not at any trestleman's table, not in the royal halls of Templar at the queen's table. Attending to the feast was a long row of impeccably dressed waiters, poised and ready.

Every type of food was represented in its most alluring form. Tarts burst with sweet fillings and were kissed with crystals of sugar. Buttery rolls nearly popped with their own plumpness, beside carved pats of butter. Roasts glistened, each outshining the last in delectability. The gravy steamed and puddled invitingly. Fowl and beast were arranged in a fashion of utter temptablity, and it was all Ivy could do not to rush to the table and begin eating. It had been some time since her last hot meal—she had left Breaux's compound before her breakfast.

The long table was assembled in front of receding stone benches, and here the students waited. Ivy joined them.

Snaith advanced on the lectern and faced the group.

"Let us begin."

He eyed the assembly, his body swiveling as his ruined neck could no longer turn.

"I am sure you are all well prepared for today's final exam."

Ivy looked about as the Guild's pupils, in varying states of preparedness, all awaited their examination. A few were reviewing their notes, paging through for any last glimmer of knowledge. Ivy's nearest neighbor was muttering to himself, arranging his Guild-issued utensils and brushing up on the *Field Guide*.

With mounting horror, Ivy returned her attention to the front of the lecture hall, where Snaith was now seated at the head of the impossibly long dinner table, snapping a taster's collar about his drooping chin. His thick lips were unusually wet as he leaned over a silver-domed credenza and, with practiced authority, flicked the polished lid open. Inside, a selection of bone-handled carving knives, the smallest about the size of a trestleman's pinkie, the largest—a broad knife meant for both hacking and carving—suitable for an entire steer. But the one that brought a wave of revulsion over Ivy was a modest one, off to the side, with a particularly nasty-looking hook blade, not polished like the rest of the subrector's collection. His fingers fidgeted over the tool, pausing to lovingly thumb the crooked teeth of the instrument—and Ivy felt her flesh crawl. His attentions finally alighted upon something in the middling range, something polished and sleek, meant for carving food, and once chosen, he brandished it—gleaming—to the crowd. Beside the knives awaited a long, thick emery, and he took this now and began artfully running it up and down the sharp edge of the blade, producing an uncomfortable noise.

"Let us not delay any further. You—" He pointed his steely spear directly at her. "Last in, first up."

The room of tasters turned to her expectantly, and Ivy noticed among the foreign faces a few smirks. She looked behind her, hoping to find someone rising in her stead, but the benches merely carried on upward, seemingly forever. With great reluctance, she stood.

"Yesss," Snaith coaxed.

Ivy arrived at the staged table.

"Your three?" he asked.

Ivy blinked. "My three?"

"Choose your three." Snaith's voice was tinged with impatience. "The three dishes you wish to taste for the final exam in Irresistible Meals."

She looked at the table again from this closer vantage

point. A heaping bowl of fruit beckoned her, dewy and great, like a living still life. It was all she could do to not reach out and pluck a pomegranate from the platter. In fact, there wasn't a thing within reach—within sight—that she wouldn't eat readily. Her stomach grumbled.

Ivy looked about—all thoughts of the many eyes upon her forgotten in her hunger. She walked along the endless display, past large roasts and savory side dishes, until she came to the desserts. In the very center, a majestic chocolate cake iced with little white flowerbuds sat upon a crystal plate. How was she to choose only three?

Somehow she pointed, and quite soon before her a place was set, and she sat down to a meal of buttery, crisp fried chicken, a savory corn pudding, and the cake. For each, Snaith served her himself, fastidious with the presentation, dismissing the waiters who stepped forward eagerly.

Of course, Ivy knew she was eating at a table of the Tasters' Guild, in a class designed to test its tasters' abilities to detect poisons. And she knew also that she was better equipped than most at poison detection because she was better than most at making poisons. But she was no match for the Guild's most dreaded course—it was mandatory, after all, to take Irresistible Meals, and not uncommon for a student to repeat it several times until receiving a passing grade. Or die trying.

This was to be the end of her inner debate. The food before her smelled like nothing else. And seeing as there

was no one there to tell her otherwise, she began with the
dessert.

Ivy took a small, delicate forkful of the cake, a rich, deep
chocolate—so very dark and fluffy. Superb and irresistible, it
was almost an inky black.

Chapter Fifty-eight
The Dose

The nature of scourge bracken is so very unpredictable, and so very little is known about it in a land where so much is known about plants in general. Indeed, it grows in hallowed ground far away from the sun and was rescued from extinction by Hemsen Dumbcane. It holds its user captive while it searches for yet another, more powerful victim to transport into its dark realm. It attracts insects—and other creatures—to its unwilling host as it assumes power. It lulls and whispers kingly promises while laying waste to all around it—and would have probably overtaken all of Caux had not the Good King Verdigris banished it just in time.

But why it strikes down some while elevating others is a mystery.

Snaith had reserved for himself a small portion of Dumbcane's inks and set about his plans to test this new, intriguing poison. He regretted instantly that there weren't any orphanages in the immediate vicinity—it was a wonderfully anonymous place to try out new and deadly wares. The next best thing: his loathsomely tedious class of untested tasters. The final exam featured a year's worth of pernicious poisons in a tempting and distracting environment—a realistic enough occurrence in life outside the Guild's walls. But none had learned of scourge bracken before, so no student could possibly be prepared.

Did this worry the subrector? Not at all. He plotted the exam, one that would feature this new inky toxin, and prepared to catalog his observations as carefully as he would in any hospital for the indigent or home for wayward youth.

Ivy Manx swallowed a second mouthful of velvety chocolate cake and suddenly began to feel entirely peculiar. Immediately, wavy shapes floated before her eyes, thick spots of ink—or were they insects? She waved her hands before her eyes to shoo them away, only the spots returned, this time more vigorously. Her stomach lurched in fear.

Then, inexplicably, she was far, far away from the lecture hall, in a dark and ruined garden. Clouds circled the perilous sky. Barbed wire ran along a ravaged iron fence, and beneath her feet lay nothing but charred earthen remains. It was a garden transformed, but she still knew it. She had been there before. Once prosperous and now a wasteland, this was the garden she had seen when curing Peps.

In his silent chamber high atop the Library, Vidal Verjouce

suddenly, horribly, stood. He had been in a Kingmaker reverie, blank dreams of ultimate power and burnt ground. He readied his cane.

There was an intruder in his Mind Garden.

He knew at once of Ivy.

Ivy had been standing quite vacantly, Snaith looking on with a curious expression upon his paunchy face. The girl did not clutch her sides or cry out in despair, he noted. Nor did she scream and grip her chest, as did Gripe, while a deadly stain of scourge bracken spread across her vital organs. Was there some antidote of which he was unaware? He looked about the table. He was certain he had served her an enormous dose. Yet she defied him, standing there unblinking. A rage surged within him.

The Guild's students, unaware of his treacherous experimentation, were readying themselves for their inevitable turn at the table, and those not busy whispering were silently spraying their mouths with distilled water or using their tongue scrapers to earnestly clear their palates.

Snaith clapped his hands for his assistant—he was tiring of the impasse—and immediately she was there. Ivy watched wordlessly as Rue stood before her, speaking quite familiarly with the awful subrector.

"Failing grade!" Snaith pronounced loudly as Rue made a note.

"The Infirmary, sir?" Rue then asked. Her face was inscrutable as she reached for Ivy's arm.

But Snaith waved the question away. He was already scanning the seating greedily for a new subject. Rue began to guide Ivy away from the curious eyes of the class, into the shadows of the large hall.

"You!" He pointed at a thin, frightened boy. "Dinner's served!"

As the student made his way haltingly down the stone steps, Snaith turned. He watched the pair go, his assistant guiding the stiff-legged creature away from him. An evil surge of excitement swept through his belly. Fresh with the memory of the subrector Gripe, he knew she was doomed. Clearing his throat, he looked around him, and sharpened a knife.

There are beings that rule over fire and beings that rule over shadow, much in the same way alewives rule over troubled waters, but these creatures are mercurial, dangerous, and should not concern us here—except that Ivy now straddled these two worlds, one of light and the other of dark. The world of shadow is a suspect one, and one unused to tourists.

As Rue led her by the elbow into the dingy courtyard, Ivy saw a glimmer of these two worlds—fierce, shifting black shapes, small, insistent sparks of fire. The ox and the plaque upon the door had undergone a transformation—the bees were now dark, sleek wasps and appeared on the verge of a swarm. Upon another, a brass salamander writhed in agony as fire consumed its hide. In fact, the small courtyard seemed to hold an extraordinary amount of doors suddenly—all repellant, fierce, and glimmering with life.

Ivy stumbled on a loose stone, and Rue caught her beneath

the arms. Propping her upright again, and stealing a look back toward the lecture hall, Rue continued in the direction of the Infirmary.

They came upon a twisting alley, and with a look behind her, Rue quickly ducked into its damp mouth—their shoes dripping at once from the sluice of water that ran along the path. It was here, over the calming tones that water can bring, that Rue whispered to Ivy.

"I will take you back to Grandfather's, but I do not know what will become of me for this," she said.

Ivy watched Rue's face twist and glow.

"This way." Rue ushered Ivy home as best she could, the young subrector guiding Ivy's stiff form through the backward alleys.

But how strange it was that Ivy's trip home differed so entirely from Rue's—although their path was the same! For Ivy was not walking in the sunshine, the light of day—or even within the gloom of the city's tall spire. She walked the land of shadows—the very blackness where the walls met the street were thick, fertile places where they bred, a sweeping swath of the darkest velvet. Her own shadow towered over her and seemed to possess a distinct dislike for Rue. She began noticing strange insects that darted around her and was forced on several occasions to wave her hand about in a vain effort to dispel the pests.

They had reached Breaux's garden wall.

"Quickly," Rue urged. A noise in the distance startled her, and she gripped Ivy's arm tightly.

Finally, the doorway swung inward, and the pair entered into what was previously an oasis but now brought Ivy no relief. The world was reduced to light and shadow, with no middle tones. Brightness burned into her pupils; blackness brought a deep, wrathful peril. Spiky weeds had invaded Breaux's paradise, unseen by all but her. They menaced the silvery blooms and tugged mercilessly at their roots.

Suddenly, before her in a sea of phosphorescence, the figure of Breaux—his robes aswirl with moonlight and shadow—a pattern like ancient writing upon them.

"Ivy?" he asked, as he knelt down to inspect her.

"Two parts crabgrass, a pinch of saltgrit, and a suspicion of seadew," Ivy answered, reciting the recipe for an obscure tea.

"Hmmm." The Professor bent forward holding her chin, turning her face this way and that, inspecting. "Rue?" he asked. "What happened here?"

"Snaith," Rue whispered. "Irresistible Meals."

"Not enough can be said about the necessity of a good mortar and pestle!" Ivy added inexplicably.

"She *looks* well enough," Breaux assessed finally.

"I told him I was taking her to the Infirmary," Rue added. What person in Caux might say they were spared the effects of poison? Not many. But Ivy was unable to speak of her experience directly, for every time she opened her mouth to complain, she found herself speaking a strange litany of recipes, unguents, and obscure inks. Her mind was completely aware of her odd behavior but powerless to intercede.

"Snarewood!" Ivy cried. Her doom settled heavily upon her shoulders. The Prophecy—Pimcaux—what would become of them now?

Rowan and Peps were there suddenly, battling the shadows of the garden as Ivy watched, appalled. As the foursome exchanged a meaningful, worried look, Ivy tried again to explain herself but was capable only of reciting an elemental table from her apotheopathic studies.

She finally gave up speech and agreed to be led by Rowan to the relative comfort of a back room, where she sat dully, ignoring a cup of tea beside her.

The Field Guide to the Poisons of Caux does not attempt to offer advice to those who have been poisoned by scourge bracken. Indeed, because the plant was believed to be extinct, very little was known about its lethal legacy. The book, however, did offer the girl a certain measure of comfort, and as she held it close to her, she wondered what its author would say about her current predicament.

Before her tea had even cooled, Snaith's Watchmen

appeared at Breaux's door, banging with confident authority. They acquainted themselves with the idiosyncrasies of the garden ramble, and thereafter the house, swept past the flustered Rue, and soon enough, the scarlet-clad group found both Ivy and Rowan.

They took the outlaw pair into swift custody.

Chapter Sixty

Arrivals

It was with great expectation that Vidal Ver-jouce prepared his playground—the Guild and the city of Rocamadour—for the production of Dumbcane's scourge-bracken inks. The Warming Room had been given over entirely to this new venture, and even the massive round firepit was not enough for the bed of coals the Director wished ready. He had ordered his subrectors and many of the advanced students to forage for all burnables—nothing was sacred.

All that was needed was the weed.

The vast iron-studded portals of the old city were flung open to the hawthorn wood beyond, the impenetrable over-growth hacked away at, revealing an old, ghostly road. Great axes clanged against cobble and the thorny path, and the bramble was gathered and hastened to ash. Outriders poured from the city, searching every grave.

Dumbcane was given a leather apron and a reprieve, and allowed to supervise the preparations. The stinging scent of char replaced the damp, and from his chambers high atop the city, Vidal Verjouce sat and waited.

He was not alone.

Upon his lap, matted and ink-stained, a set of large claws gathered the boiled wool of his cassock. They drew in the stiff threads, snapping a few, finally piercing the thick fabric effortlessly—and releasing. Purring haughtily sat Six, and Six and Verjouce were waiting for word from the Outriders that their beloved scourge bracken had been found.

A different sort of word came, however.

"Director." A subrector named Mimp cleared his throat. Mimp's duties were few that led him to personally set eyes upon the Director, but here he was now. He couldn't bring himself to look at Verjouce, the horrible wasps that circled his head, his posture of tense expectation. That cat.

"You have visitors, master. I explained that you are not receiving anyone at present, but, well, they will not go away. They insist—"

Verjouce fixed his potent stare on the nervous man.

"Have Snaith see to them."

"Snaith, er, cannot be located currently, Director."

There was a moment of silence in which Mimp wished to be anywhere—even overseeing the enormous bellows that fired the cauldron's scorched air—other than here.

"Who are they?" asked Verjouce, stroking the matted cat.

"They are called Taxus. They wish to file a petition."

"Taxus?" Verjouce intoned in a throaty voice, one not often used to ponder the unknown.

To the subrector's great surprise, the Director stood, not menacingly but hungrily, eagerly, the awful feline falling ungracefully from his lap with a hiss. Mimp wondered fleetingly whether he should mention the discarded clumps of cat hair that occupied the blind man's lap—but thought better of it.

"Yes. Show them in." The Director gestured to the door, the wasps shifting lazily and instantly regrouping.

The subrector bowed and departed quickly, and quite soon there was another knock.

"Enter," came Verjouce's voice, and if given a choice, most would do well not to obey.

Chapter Sixty-one

Caged Reverie

xlerod D. Roux, famed trestleman and guardian of apotheopathy, sat, very cramped, in a filthy gilt cage. The cage's owner, a surly albino vulture Verjouce had raised as a hatchling, knew no other home—and since he was displaced, he crouched atop a nearby urn. He directed an evil grimace at his unlikely usurper and occasionally pulled his head back, emitting a low hiss at the small man, shaking his feathers into spikes and spreading his wings wide.

For the trestleman, this room held a great many memories. Ignoring the bird, Axle drifted off into a quiet, caged reverie.

The walls were lit with mirrors and crystals, and the shadows had yet to take up residence. Rocamadour was still the school King Verdigris intended it to be—an academy for healing, for apotheopaths. Axle saw before his eyes the chamber transformed into the welcoming beacon it once was. Years of misuse peeled away in his mind's eye. The floors were scrubbed of the recent ink stains, the black splashes upon the walls and ceiling vanishing in a mist to be replaced with rich carpets and woven tapestries. Sumptuously pigmented murals returned to their rightful place within the paneling. Only the stone table and diamond-shaped window remained the same. The bare, pitted walls had been replaced with ornately carved shelving. Huge and impressive as the cabinetry was, it was of no comparison to what it held. For lined along the room's four walls were glorious, leather-bound books, the Good King's own writings, and they were currently being attended to by a tall and quiet man—a man who, it was quite obvious, possessed in him great respect for the books he handled.

Malapert.

Axle remembered him now as a somber, learned man in his youth, before the fires had ravaged his body and mind. He paged through one enormous tome, lovingly, eagerly. Finding finally that which he sought, he turned, revealing a companion, and with great satisfaction displayed the page to this cloaked figure, a man in a long robe of silver, and one well known to the trestleman. He nodded, reading. And Axle was strengthened by the vision of his old friend and Master Apotheopath, Cecil Manx, as a younger man.

A new scene materialized.

The room shifted to shadow, but Cecil was still there. Behind the stone table sat Vidal Verjouce, his face vague in the dimness. Smoke filled the air. Ash drifted across the floor. Cecil gestured angrily, arms wide, staff midair, as the moon, battling smoke and flame from outside, made its abrupt appearance through the angled window above. The weak light now splashed across the Director's face—revealing a new, terrible feature. His face was freshly bruised, and where his eyes had been that morning, there was nothing.

Cecil Manx grew quiet—appalled. Verjouce said something, but Axle was distracted by a door opening. In the square of yellow light, there was framed the slight figure of the Director's new servant. Although a younger incarnation, Axle recognized at once the particular stoop to the man's silhouette—the long and haughty nose, and tatty, unkempt robes.

Sorrel Flux neglected to bow—for who needs to bow before a master who is blind?—and, with fresh bandages in his arms, made his way over to where Verjouce waited.

With a jerk, Axle awoke from his vision.

The jerk was delivered by a velvet rope that attached Axle's housing to the Director's wrist.

It was fortuitous timing. The Director was preparing to greet the Taxus Estate.

Chapter Sixty-two
The Petition

The Taxuses were a pair of stout fellows, one tall, one not, and as they entered the room, they carried themselves—even in this devastatingly grim environment—with confident swaggers. Yet as the elder, Quarles, greeted the Guild's Director and looked into Verjouce's pitted face, his voice faltered and failed him. When he realized that the man wore a crown of what seemed to be vicious stinging insects, he stopped dead in his tracks.

"What is your errand here?" Verjouce asked in the silence, leaning forward on ink-stained hands. The meager daylight from the diamond-shaped window found his face now, and the Taxuses took an involuntary step back.

"I—uh—we are here with an Epistle."

"An Epistle."

"W-we wish the taster Rowan Truax—as is our r-right."

"So it is." His crown droned loudly.

The elder of the two Taxuses stammered his appreciation.

"A petition. For a graduate named Truax. So . . . *disappointing* to hear the Tasters' Oath has been broken. We have such severe deterrents, you see." The Director turned to the silent subrector without the aid of vision.

"Have you examined their paperwork?"

Mimp held a tidy ribbon-clad scroll. "The Epistle is here, Director, and all appears in order."

"Is there, perhaps, any other paper there, besides the Epistle?"

The Taxuses exchanged a tense look.

"No, Director. Just the Epistle."

Verjouce contemplated.

"Should Truax make an appearance here, I would prefer to carry out my own form of justice upon him," he began. "I assure you—it is very effective." Verjouce paused, thinking terrible thoughts.

"Um, there is the small matter of a reward, Director."

"Ah. A reward. Still—I feel this matter should be concluded . . . internally."

The Estate sagged. Their business did not seem to be concluding in their favor.

Scraping footfalls could be heard, approaching on soft slippers.

"Ah, Snaith," Verjouce sighed, even before the subrector appeared.

Snaith craned his crooked neck about the busy room, but

his eagerness to deliver his message was tempered by his surprise at finding the chamber thus occupied. He skittered over to his employer, and as he leaned in, the persistent wasps parted. Verjouce listened, his face expressionless, and when Snaith was done, the Director addressed the Taxus brothers.

"Taxus Estate, should you somehow produce the other paper you received from the calligrapher—an old and worthless scroll, I assure you, and of no use to you or your family— I might be more amenable to an exchange. I will give you some time to think about it. I am nothing if not generous. Snaith—perhaps the Estate would like a tour of the catacombs? I find it has a way of stimulating the memory."

Chapter Sixty-three

The Chapter Room

Don't feel so bad." Rowan smiled weakly. "I failed Irresistible Meals three times."

"I did not simmer the moonstone on the wrong heat!" Ivy protested.

No matter how she approached it, Ivy could not discuss the topic of scourge bracken, Snaith, or her experience at the final exam. She was seeing that the nature of this particular poison was one that was determined to be deeply private. Greasy-looking fireflies bobbed and reared around her field of vision, but oddly, with their arrival, she began to feel some strength return to her limbs—as if the insects fortified her.

Snaith and the other scarlet-clad Watchmen had deposited her and Rowan in the Chapter Room—she knew this because Rowan had told her so. He was clearly alarmed. The Chapter Room was in fact a large, carpeted chamber that featured an ancient-looking wooden table scattered with dripping, smoking candles. It served as the Guild's epicenter, hosting general meetings, demonstrations, and important visitors. It was a place for elders, and Rowan knew it as such, but most of all, Rowan knew it for all its horribleness. For it was also where punishment was meted out, with an audience.

There were decorative carvings in a banner that circled the entire room. The markings reminded Ivy of much of what she had seen at Dumbcane's shop. To the casual observer, they were mere woodcuts—stories of foragers and thick forests, patterned leaves, berries. Adorable stray children and wood-cutters' cottages. But the scourge bracken within Ivy called forth the worst of the shadows, and the shapes took on a nightmarish quality: huntsmen brandishing axes and caul-drons boiling unnamable things—tales of madness and dis-ease. Rowan was oblivious.

In a recess of the room, a lone Outrider stood guard, but as Ivy peeked at him, his cloak and mass of hair spewed a deep, swirling darkness that threatened to overtake the chamber's dim lights. Watching him, too, was Rowan, and the taster felt the hairs on the nape of his neck rise, but for a different rea-son. He realized he was seeing his future—captured, he now faced certain punishment. For his crimes he would lose his tongue and be forced to serve the Guild's most deadly desires.

"I wonder what will happen to Rue," he asked, changing the subject. "She disobeyed Snaith—that can't be good."

Ivy nodded miserably. The same thought had occurred to her.

"I suppose we can congratulate ourselves—in truth, I am

surprised we made it this far." Rowan's wretchedness was growing. "What hope did we really have of resisting the Guild's defenses?"

Ivy tried again to formulate words, but she knew she would simply recite cupboard inventories or obscure *Field Guide* footnotes every time she opened her mouth. She wanted so badly to comfort and be comforted. She moved closer to Rowan, resting her head on his shoulder, silently.

Her thoughts turned to Axle. A reunion with him seemed to be such an impossibility, and when she realized this, she sank even deeper into the shadows. Professor Breaux had said Dumbcane was sentenced to drink poison hemlock—what might Verjouce be saving for Axle?

It was almost a relief to be dragged before the Guild's Director.

"Three parts iodine, one part smoke bush, a soupçon of this-tle, and a thimble of distilled essence of wanderlust." Ivy was reciting a favorite potion of hers.

The only problem was, it was in answer to Vidal Verjouce's simple greeting:

Trespasser.

It wasn't spoken, this salutation. Instead, Ivy heard his awful voice in her inner ear. The Director sat amid ever more angry wasps and a few new, powerful hornets. The insects seemed energized and patrolled their territory not with their usual laziness but with a vengeance. Beside Verjouce stood the crooked figure of Snaith, triumph and pleasure oozing from his pudgy face. But she saw Axle above them—oddly, crammed into a gilt cage—and she allowed herself a moment of small joy.

Ivy had her own medley of insects with which to contend. The scourge bracken inside her was attracting not black, barbed things but flying creatures of the night. The fireflies hovered around her head still, and she felt deeply queasy as they bobbed about her field of vision, small stars extinguished and reborn.

"Nauseas. Three parts bicarbonate, one part nux vomica." Ivy's apotheopathic training was present, but she still was not in control of her mouth.

Now that Rowan's most dreaded moment was here—now that he faced the Director as a prisoner of the Tasters' Guild—he refused to allow his knees to buckle. He forced himself to look about the room. Verjouce was a sinister vision of black ink and insects, a shocking one, and his splotched face was turned toward Ivy. Axle caught Rowan's eye from his caged perch, and they exchanged furtive looks.

You, Ivy, have dared to taste the Kingmaker.

Ivy frowned momentarily. Kingmaker?

And, to my great disappointment, you are still alive.

Vidal Verjouce turned to the young taster.

"Rowan Truax," Verjouce said aloud. His name, spoken by

such a revolting voice, was like a rude push. Rowan staggered. The only other time the taster had heard his name uttered by the Director was when he had received his taster's robes, and that one time was more than enough. "You are quite a disappointment."

Rowan swallowed but said nothing.

"You were a mediocre student. A failure as a taster. You brought shame and dishonor to the Oath. But"—a sinister smile flickered across the Director's lips—"you have succeeded at one thing. You have delivered me the girl."

"Cattail thrushweed nevermore stew!" Ivy shouted pitifully.

But a shift occurred within the young taster—as if a light now shone on some nether region of his mind. Rowan felt a surge of anger course through him.

"Dishonor?" Rowan shouted. "You dare to speak of dishonor? Where is the honor in poison? Poison, by its very nature, is cowardly! It is the deceitful tool of the weakling, and you are its master!"

The wasps closed in tighter, forming an even more distinct crown, bulging and popping into spiky peaks.

"Hold your tongue—or I shall have the pleasure of holding it for you." Verjouce's face was contorted in anger, glowering at Rowan. From the shadows behind him, standing perfectly still, Ivy's eyes detected what others' could not—a pair of Outriders like statues on either side of the Director. They emerged now into the grim light—and Rowan went pale.

"Not afraid yet? You will be the first, then, to walk gallantly as you join their ranks."

"Shall I procure my sharpest blade?" Snaith asked evilly.

Ivy thought sickeningly of the revolting-looking crescent in Snaith's collection—its jagged edges and ripping teeth—and knew now why it had repelled her so.

But as Vidal Verjouce stood, detailing explicitly what pleasure he would take in working with Rowan in his new tongueless capacity, Ivy finally noticed Six. Rudely forced from the Director's lap, the cat had landed on the stone table, and his claws raked the surface with an awful noise.

"Six!" she called, the word wrenching from her mouth intact.

She stepped forward to the cat—he was preposterously dirty and covered with murky stains. The room swam about her eyes—the Outriders advanced further into the chamber's light, flanking their master, alert.

But the reunion was surprising. Six arched his back in some unknown fury—hissing crazily, fur flying from his large body in distressing clumps, spittle landing in a foamy spray. The fireflies spun dizzyingly about Ivy's head, and she stumbled back to Rowan's side.

"I am his master now," the Director mused. "Me—and scourge bracken." Verjouce's laugh was the sound of a saw being sharpened.

Ivy managed to quote randomly from the *Field Guide*'s

myriad uses for river mud and swat a few of the lazier insects at her brow. She looked woefully at Six.

"Cat's got her tongue," Verjouce purred to Six, his long fingers scratching the cat's chin.

He turned to his scarlet-clad Watchman.

"Call in the Estate," Verjouce told Snaith. "Perhaps they are ready to bargain."

Chapter Sixty-four

Breaux's Bouquet

A s Rowan braced to be turned over to the Estate of his former charge, he allowed himself a moment to think about what life might have been like for him had he been a better taster. Turner Taxus would be alive, for one. Taxus had been a reasonably nice employer, and Rowan's position in Templar was a pleasant posting. But he was forever tasting food that might be deadly. He was living a life designed by the Tasters' Guild and the Deadly Nightshades, a life of poison and intrigue. It was not a natural existence. Hadn't Axle told him on so many occasions that food was life—eating was joy, not sorrow?

But as the heavy door opened, it was not Snaith who returned with the Estate of Turner Taxus in tow; it was instead Rowan's favorite Professor, the one who on so many occasions had tried to lead him to the very conclusion he had just formed. And Professor Breaux was carrying over his shoulder a bundle of hay and sticks and leaves, a heavy burden— elaborate and intricate, with several species of flowers poking out at odd angles, many upside down. It was curiously out of place.

He paused to nod to the captives and, wiping his brow with a wink, emerged into the inhospitable room.

"Snaith?" Verjouce called.

"It is I, Director," Breaux responded. The Professor lifted his load from his bent back and deposited it on the floor before Ivy and Rowan. It was a rudimentary bouquet, tied with a thin rag. He kicked it further in the children's direction with the toe of his sandal.

"Delivery," he whispered at the pair.

"Professor Breaux?" Verjouce asked.

"Yes, Vidal."

"You have no business here," Verjouce determined.

"Ah. I believe I was summoned by your associate Snaith. I fear my granddaughter has gotten into a bit of mischief."

As if on cue, the lead Watchman returned, this time with the Taxus Estate.

The Estate, fully overwhelmed by their stay at the oppressive Tasters' Guild, were changed men. Gone were their swaggers. Gone, even, were the twinkles in their eyes. They followed Snaith blindly, wishing only to never again visit the city of Rocamadour or its catacombs below.

For Ivy the room was a dance hall of darkness, shadows popping and surging, her firefly halo disengaging and reassembling dizzyingly on some incomprehensible whim. She was descending into a further layer of shadow when her eyes alighted on Breaux's odd bouquet. It was a collection of his own particular favorites, and Ivy rejoiced at once in the flowers—they grew, were *alive,* and were not of the awful, harrowing world of scourge bracken. She peered closer at them, battling the shifting gloom.

Dog's mercury, calamint, frogbit.

Hawthorn, heartsease, mugwort.

Her dulled mind took in the collection of numerous plants, and then something clicked.

Flower Code!

Professor Breaux had laid at their feet an arrangement that detailed exactly where they could find the lost book of the Pimcaux Doorway.

o you have my property?" Verjouce asked the Estate.

Quarles's neck spasmed, and he grew still. The tour of the catacombs had been effective.

"Good. Then I propose a simple exchange," Verjouce continued. "Truax here"—Verjouce indicated Rowan, and it was now that the Estate finally noticed him—"for the paper. Are we agreed?"

The Taxuses were elated. They looked from Rowan to Verjouce and back again. Their brief stay at the Tasters' Guild had sapped their spirit so effectively that it was their only wish to return to the barbed roadway empty-handed—and to their local tavern—without a backward glance. With shaking hands, Quarles felt in his breast pocket and proceeded to reveal a tattered, ill-kept paper.

Snaith approached the Estate in his crablike way and extended his arm from a hunched back. The Watchman, having received the crumpled scroll, began to shuffle back to his master while the Taxuses marched over to Rowan and each roughly grabbed an arm. Yet a great curiosity welled up within the Watchman now as he handled the precious document. He paused, unfurling it. He saw the image of a door blazing with a circular knocker, made long ago from inks that infused the work with magic, or mischief.

The Estate was stalled in a moment of uncertainty. Were they done, free to leave? Caught between them, Rowan's eyes were drawn to the golden serpent on the page—glimmering, and nearly alive.

"Snaith?" Verjouce called to his servant. "Bring me the parchment."

But Snaith was captivated. There was great artistry before him, and it cannot be said that only the good of heart appreciate true beauty.

From his perch, Axle, too, had a bird's-eye view.

"Ivy!" he called down. "The ouroboros door! The missing page!"

Many things happened at once.

Ivy plucked up her remaining strength and flung herself at Snaith. Trails of the fireflies' deep purple light streaked through her vision and were met by infuriated black wasps. Suddenly the room was alive with the clashing of insects—so many insects—but the glint of the golden ouroboros on the scroll was as bright as the sun, a beacon.

Snaith's unfortunate posture and his ruined sense of

balance proved a poor combination. He fell, swatting both the mad girl and the stinging swarm, and something worse—much worse.

"Snaith—what is happening?" Verjouce called out, agonized at the sound of scuffling.

It was here that Six redeemed himself. Angered perhaps by the mad buzzing of the clashing insects, or urged on by some memory of chivalry, the enormous cat pounced upon Snaith, scratching wildly—a mass of stink and spittle. He raked his claws down upon Snaith's fat cheeks, threaded his teeth into an earlobe, and kicked at the Watchman as if he were a rag doll. And Snaith reacted as anyone might: he curled up in a ball, a hermit crab retreating into his shell. Still, the wasps stung at him—devouring his face, his crooked spine, his lumpy ankles.

Ivy stood, dizzy but free. In her hand was the image of a door—the way to Pimcaux.

Rowan tried to shake loose of the Taxuses' grip, and nearly did, but suddenly, horribly, the worst happened. Behind him rose the diamond-shaped window, and as he felt the Estate's hold finally release, he stumbled backward, one step, two steps—had there only been room for a third! Instead, he felt the window shatter about his body, a crackling like boiled sugar candy, and somehow—inexplicably—a beautiful chime-like sound accompanied the taster's exit as he left Verjouce's chambers, exchanging somber stone for thin air.

Chapter Sixty-six

Truax

Ivy fled down, down, down the spire's stairs, running, slipping, recovering, all the while with one foot in the shadowy world belonging to scourge bracken and another desperate to escape it. She gripped the stolen parchment in shaking hands while eager fireflies buffeted in her wake. But her mind was on one thing only. Rowan—the image of his fall, his arms spread wide as if to catch the sky.

Sobbing, she reached the dark stone streets. She raced, following the Flower Code directions Breaux had prepared, knowing the tide of Outriders was not far behind. Lavender and rosebud—taking a left, then right. Another lavender. All she had now, she found herself thinking, was movement— escape. Everything else was gone. If she kept moving, somehow she would get to Pimcaux. Somehow she would cure the King.

Suddenly fiery eyes blinked amid the shifting shadows, and she suppressed a startled scream. She had stumbled upon the vultures' fountain, now transformed by the scourge bracken within her into a crumbling, horrid thing. Black slime bubbled from the broken pipeworks, and tattered, dead vines encircled the statues. The great birds reared tall and awful, flapping their wings and letting loose flying embers that sizzled in the fountain's well. She pressed against the wall, shutting her eyes and forcing herself to breathe calmly, until with a start she realized the doorway she was crouched in looked familiar. An ox head. It led to Snaith's Irresistible Meals.

Appallingly, Ivy heard the sound of wings beating above her, and she cringed, covering her head. The bird was very, very close, and truly awful in its size. She felt the wind from its approach and ducked, waiting for the slash of its sharp talons.

Instead, a familiar hand.

A warm one, infused with life, not steeped in shadow. In the way that good friends are always the best medicine, the hand pulled her up from the scourge-bracken reverie and seemingly plucked her back into the world of the living. She looked from between her fingers and gasped.

Rowan!

But how was this possible?

Her friend smiled his particular welcoming smile and proceeded to fold his wings. Ivy realized Rowan had somehow managed to secrete away a pair of springform wings, made from familiar linen and tensed wire.

"What fun!" he confided, heart beating a rapid song in his

chest. "I'd been waiting to try these out since the forest!" He would, eventually, tell her how his flight against the thunderheads, soaring over the somber city of Rocamadour, had been the achievement of his dreams. But for now, he had seen from his bird's-eye vantage point a collection of scarlet Watchmen and Outriders disgorge itself from the Library, and he knew time was pressing.

Indeed, a sharp sound of approaching footsteps was heard, and turning, the pair ran on, Ivy never releasing her grasp on Dumbcane's stolen parchment. Finally, the two arrived in the low-slung Warming Room.

They skidded to a halt.

In preparation for Dumbcane's ink-making enterprise, the vast chamber was ablaze with an immense fire—the heat hit the children's faces like a scorching breath. Everywhere lay piles of litter and filth. The great firepit was smoking with thick brush, and an enormous bellows fanned the embers. Clinking, monstrous chains guided the assembly line. Outriders—more than Ivy thought was possible—patrolled the workshop, and Hemsen Dumbcane wandered about testing the contents of various cauldrons, readying coils of copper tubing and enormous sweaty beakers. Now and then the scribe would mutter and call for assistance, beckoning an Outrider to procure more water or produce more heat.

Ivy and Rowan watched the bony calligrapher as he peered into a small vial of gluey green syrup. Swirling it, he then sniffed at it tentatively and scowled. Cursing, Dumbcane threw the tube against a nearby wall, shattering it.

"What is he doing?" Rowan whispered.

Ivy shook her head. Axle would know, she thought. Axle—still a captive of the awful Director. Her heart sank.

Rowan beckoned her away from the light, and with their backs against the smooth wall, they inched around the horrible operation. Her ever-present fireflies, a halo atop her head, were mere sparks before the bonfire.

Along the sunken hall they crept, and ahead, their destination—the simple steps leading down into hallowed ground. Waiting to guide them belowground—just as Breaux had indicated in his bouquet—was Peps.

Chapter Sixty-seven

The Crypt

The ribbon of gloamwort was still there, tacked to the wall as Axle had left it. It was little trouble at all to follow it, even behind Peps's hesitant steps (because what trestleman in his right mind would return to the land of the dead?). For Ivy, the trip into the darkness was marked by the unnatural brightness of the gloamwort. The string bobbed and weaved, tensed and sagged—seemingly beckoning her along in a dancing line—sometimes taut, sometimes slack. Finally, the threesome arrived deep below the Tasters' Guild, at the oldest part of the maze beneath the city.

"I'm sure glad something good comes from passing this way," Peps murmured in the dark. "Breaux paid a visit to Malapert," he explained. "The Librarian told him he hid the few books he saved right here."

"Where?" Rowan asked.

"Breaux's . . . bouquet . . . had . . . *hedge mustard*," Ivy blurted. Her head was clearing slightly, but Ivy's words were still coming too slowly for her liking. Especially now, in their haste. "But . . . then it was . . . vague. Bryony. Buckbean." She took a deep breath, concentrating.

"Hidden, enclosed room?" Rowan quoted the definitions.

"Yes."

"Caulwort, de-thorned."

"What does it mean when it's de-thorned?" Rowan asked impatiently.

Ivy felt in her robes.

Axle's impressive *Field Guide* details some of the history of the catacombs beneath the Tasters' Guild, but there were no known maps of the twisting tunnels. They were in the oldest part of the maze, and there was simply nothing listed about their current location. Ivy knew this because she held in her hand her copy of the book. Yet it was still the best reference for deciphering the more obscure elements of Flower Code—and she bent over her *Guide*.

"De-thorned . . . caulwort," she muttered, paging through the long lists at her fingertips. "Um . . . here we . . . go. Oh." She paused, rereading the passage. "Oh, no—" Ivy straightened, looking about the underground chamber aghast.

"Ivy?" Rowan asked, worried.

"I think . . . Malapert hid the books . . . there," Ivy announced, pointing, seemingly, at Peps. It was a great relief to talk sensibly again.

Confused, the trestleman frowned, touching his chest.

"Surely you don't mean—" Peps began, but stopped himself just as quickly. He paused, turning slowly, and peered into the shadows. Stepping away, Ivy and Rowan were now treated to what lay behind him. A gaping hole in the masonry hidden in shadow and flanked on either side by two lumbering urns.

A tomb.

A giant keystone hung low in the ruined portal. No plaque to mark the dead within. Just a faint breeze, a slight sucking sound of the wind.

Peps cleared his throat. "Couldn't Malapert have just found a nice, snug cupboard to store them in?"

Rowan dislodged the ancient cobwebs and paused on the threshold.

"Wait!" Ivy called. She clutched the tattered ouroboros parchment in one hand, advancing unsteadily.

Rowan gripped the small torch Peps had provided, and, holding hands, he and Ivy walked up the three uneven steps to the opening. Together they entered the darkness of the hallowed ground.

Chapter Sixty-eight

Hallowed Ground

At first Ivy thought it was a trick of the poison within her—making the room lurch as if a dark field of grain were swaying in the wind. But Rowan noticed it, too, as soon as his eyes adjusted.

"What is this? What grows beneath the earth, without the sun?" he asked.

But just as quickly, he knew the answer. He had seen, at Malapert's, things grow in impossible conditions. But these plants were not cinquefoils and brought with them none of the uplifting joy that the golden flower possessed, the lightness of heart or being. Nor were there blossoms, or buds. Just velvety black spikes and oddly curling leaves that rustled in the ill wind. Their smell at once beckoned and repulsed.

"Oh, Rowan," Ivy whispered.

"Tell me it's not what I think it is."

"It's a tomb. It grows on hallowed ground. . . ."

"No!" he practically moaned.

"Just find the book—and quickly." Ivy looked about. "And then we need to replace the page that Dumbcane stole—the ouroboros page. But whatever you do, *don't touch* the weed!" Her head reeled—the awful growth was coaxing her, beckoning. It seemed to pulse, summoning her.

The books were there—stacked haphazardly in several dark recesses built to hold bones. There appeared to be a few dozen—Malapert had been overcome with regret and saved many more than they thought possible. Their enormous covers were singed, the pages darkened with smoke. Standing on tiptoe, Ivy could just reach them.

"Sweet pea and inverted heather," Ivy recited for Rowan, who hadn't gotten a proper look at Breaux's Flower Code.

"Sweet pea, that's easy. *Small*, right?"

Ivy agreed.

"Hmm. Inverted heather. Heather means *clarity*, but when it's upside down, it's—what *is* it?"

"Disguise."

"So," Rowan continued eagerly now, "small and disguise."

"I think Breaux wants us to look for the smallest book in the collection," Ivy guessed. "It might be disguised."

"They're all the same size!" Rowan moaned. "Look!"

Ivy inspected the Verdigris tomes. They were as she expected—enormous, leather-bound journals with stenciled titles upon their spines, each written in the old tongue. None could be remotely described as small.

Desperately, she looked around the crypt. The floor was a carpet of scourge bracken. Deep in the tomb's recesses, there was only shadow. Shadow, and more of the ossuaries within the walls.

"Stay here," Ivy ordered.

"What are you doing?" Rowan's voice nearly cracked.

Taking a deep breath, Ivy planted one foot in front of her, entering the dismal growth.

"Ivy?" Rowan called desperately—but she was determined. "You said not to touch it!"

"There is another book over there," Ivy replied. Although her voice was calm, she was anything but. Both legs were now entrenched in the dark plot of scourge bracken, and it rose sickeningly around her to mid-thigh. "Besides, I will be fine—I survived eating it in Irresistible Meals, didn't I? This could hardly be any worse."

It was a reunion of sorts. Although Dumbcane had extracted the worst elements of the weed and concentrated them in his inks a thousandfold, the scourge bracken beneath her feet made Ivy feel as if she had been thrown down a deep well—the world of shadows again reared up on her. Snaith's paunchy visage swam before her eyes. A look of triumph played across his face as he sharpened his awful knife.

The smell was stronger, of course, and as she made her way through, she wisely held her breath. It was the smell of decay, coming impossibly from something alive. And its touch was sticky, soft, and velvety. A deadly caress.

Her halo of fireflies was rejuvenated, dancing around the room—but this time they lit her way. Against the far wall, with the purple-tinged light from the insects, she saw it.

A lone book. But what book was this? It appeared to be an outdated instruction manual for barrel-making.

"Foxglove," Ivy gasped. It was the last element to the bouquet.

"Foxglove?" Rowan repeated. "Foxglove is . . . what *is* it?"

Ivy steadied herself. She needed to breathe and wondered if she dared.

"Foxglove: *false* and *insincere!*" Rowan cried out. "A small book . . ." He puzzled. "A small book, disguised under a false cover!"

Ivy grabbed the manual and sprinted back.

"It's about the right size," Rowan assessed as Ivy caught her breath.

Its binding was sagging, the gold-stamped letters of its title twinkling in the light of Peps's torch. Ivy reached for a better look. She blew away years of dust, revealing a plain, nondescript cover.

"Let's see," she said, unfurling the ouroboros parchment beside it to compare.

She opened the book tentatively, and as she did, a shower of golden petals rained down upon the tomb's entrance. They tinkled like crystal, tiny amber stained-glass windows as they touched the stone floor.

"Cinquefoils!" Ivy and Rowan said together.

The book was filled with the dried, pressed flower of the King.

Chapter Sixty-nine

The Pimcaux Doorway

hey emerged quickly with the book to the comparatively bright tunnel, where Peps nervously waited.

Although the cover promised to teach the many intricacies of cask construction, the inner pages told another story. It read:

BOOK OF THE OUROBOROS

Inside, the text was written in the tiniest of letters, and although the book itself was broad and wide, the script remained so small that there was little hope of deciphering it. Ivy examined the inner binding carefully and, looking up, nodded.

"I think this is where it goes," she said, finding the spot for the stolen page from Dumbcane's shop.

She took a deep breath and turned to the trestleman.

"Peps." Her voice wavered. "Are you coming?"

"To Pimcaux?" he asked, and indeed, it was as if the

thought had not presented itself to the trestleman until now. "No," he said, more gruffly than he meant.

Ivy nodded.

"I made a promise to myself—I will not leave this infernal city without my brother."

Both Ivy and Rowan knew there was no breaking a promise to a trestleman. Her eyes were filling with tears—darkly splashing on the parchment in her hand.

"But I would so appreciate it if, should you see my Wilhelmina"—he pointed at the charm that hung from Ivy's neck—"you tell her Peps is waiting for her."

"Of course!" Ivy managed a smile.

"Well, then." He waved his hand about in a show of impatience. "Off you go!"

Ivy looked at Rowan, who was a shade paler than usual. The two remembered the power of the magic in the Good King's books, having seen it for themselves in Axle's study. Rowan nodded. He was ready.

Ivy smoothed Dumbcane's pilfered paper, inspecting the gleaming ring of the serpent swallowing its own tail. She thought of its ancient meaning—not Taste, as the Guild proclaimed, but Renewal, Healing. The ouroboros, she realized, was now a symbol for her own journey. King Verdigris awaited her somewhere on the other side of this door. He awaited healing.

She held her breath. There was more to the page than she

had seen at the scribe's shop—a mere copy that Dumbcane had abandoned incomplete. The text was written in a golden ink that even in the dimness blazed like a liquid star. And among the ancient curlicues and flourishes of the Good King's hand were a roiling sea, ships lolling, a lighthouse's beacon.

"Cover your eyes," she warned her friends.

Ivy, with her shadowy, distorted scourge-bracken vision, placed the paper in its housing, reuniting the torn edges and charred corners in a seam of little sparks. The ragged fibers of the binding knitted themselves back together, a small, tidy zipper. The shining knocker grew remarkably lifelike and, as at Axle's, Ivy reached forward and lifted the thing, knocking.

And as the scorching light poured out of the ancient tome upon the young girl and her traveling companion, even the somber catacombs were illuminated by the glory of the golden sun.

Part III

Pimcaux

There are creatures who exist in the element of pure air—
birds, for one. Coasting, soaring, buoyant like light itself.
Then there are those of the waters—fish, frogs. Each are
separate kingdoms: air the kingdom of the Winds,
and water the Alewives.

—The History and Magic of Alewives
Axlerod D. Roux

(Quoted here from the lost manuscript.)

Chapter Seventy

Not Pimcaux

The golden atmosphere twinkled and faded away.

Great, drifting shadows lurked above Ivy, lashing about with an awful hissing—wretched scratchings of stone against stone. In the dimness, she felt at once restless and diminished.

This was not a world of light.

Slowly, the thick, plaguing fog cleared somewhat. In its absence there was a harrowing ruin, a once-great folly, and a royal-looking garden, only it appeared as if it had endured a flash fire. Yet she knew it, although it was greatly changed. Black, unharvested stalks stood about in odd clusters, blighted growths turning their silhouettes into unfriendly figures. A wrecked iron gate clanged dejectedly. This was the garden of Dumbcane's abecedarium, the garden she had seen when she cured Peps, the one where she had inexplicably found herself after eating scourge bracken.

Ivy looked around. It was now so much bigger, as if, in giving itself over to the land of shadow, it had spread out wildly. A hunched gardener was at work on a bald hedge, clipping the dead thing uselessly. As she watched his progress, an anxiety welled up inside her, and when the pale man turned, she was shocked to see the forger Dumbcane toiling in the charred remains.

You have come.

Ivy gasped upon hearing the voice—it was not that of the hopeless Dumbcane, who seemed completely unaware of her. It was a voice of inflection, rich with malevolence, and raspy with the effects of scourge bracken.

It was the voice of Vidal Verjouce.

She spun around the ruined garden, only to realize the voice had been directionless, in her head. The speaker was nowhere, and everywhere.

At her feet, she felt a familiar matted warmth and, looking down, saw Six, purring loudly and rubbing his chin against her shin. Her attire had changed, though. Gone were the robes of the Tasters' Guild she'd worn, and in their place an intricate lace dress, as black as night and possessing in its spidery pattern no distinct design—as if the despair of the growth around her had infiltrated the chaotic weave.

She shut her eyes and, steadied by Six's presence, asked a reasonable question.

Where am I?

You are a guest, Ivy, in my Mind Garden.

You call this a garden? Her eyes flew open.

Dumbcane was now busying himself nearby, and Six let loose an offending growl at the scribe.

Why have you brought me here? With a jolt, she thought of the catacombs, of the book that served as a Doorway to Pimcaux. Of Rowan.

From behind a charred trellis with crumbling vines, Ivy finally saw Verjouce emerge.

It was not I who brought you here. You are drawn to Kingmaker just as I am.

That is a lie!

With horror Ivy saw the man approach. Six had settled into an indifferent preen atop a pile of dead coals. As Verjouce closed in, his hood fell away. Here, in the retreat of his own devising, he was free to imagine himself at an earlier juncture. In his Mind Garden, the blind Director had orchestrated the return of his eyes. They were there, just as on the day he was born, no scars, no awful pits. He stared at her with them.

How nice to see you, Ivy.

Ivy felt a cold surge of fear at his transformation.

You possess an enviable gift. Dominion over nature. You infuse all plants with their former glory, their true selves. You make them infinitely more powerful. Just think of your effect on Kingmaker! With you by my side, I shall have more power than I ever thought possible!

Kingmaker does not grow. It is extinct. Ivy tried her best to be convincing.

We both know that is not so.

Ivy thought of the horrible infestation directly beneath the Tasters' Guild and swallowed hard, pushing the image aside.

Join me.

It was an order, not an invitation. He narrowed his eyes, and Ivy was acutely aware that she preferred him blind.

Never!

He snapped his fingers, and Dumbcane suddenly became alert, his beady eyes falling on Ivy, instantly in focus.

Thick, heavy ash began blowing by; a wind picked up.

The wrought-iron fence, a thing of beauty now crippled and twisted, caught her eye. Upon a finial, clasping an orb in its talons, was the figure of a black bird. A crow.

Just think of it, Ivy. Father and daughter together at last. Ruling all the land with the might and strength of a true King.

Ivy looked at him in horror.

You are not my father!

But she knew. Sorrel Flux had tried to tell her. Axle and Cecil had tried to protect her from it. Vidal Verjouce stepped close now, and lowered his loathsome head until she could see the madness in his face.

But something else was there, too. With a sick, sinking feeling, she knew it at once. A family resemblance. His eyes—he had plucked them from his own face, ridding himself of any trace. They were the same as hers—her worst fears confirmed. It was as if she were looking in a mirror. She watched his eyes as they mocked her look of horror.

No! It can't be true!

A wave of revulsion threatened to drop her to her knees.

Truth? The horrible man grinned. *You want truth?*

Suddenly, from the gate, a creaking like a rusted hinge, and the snapping of metal. The air whipped about. The iron crow had found its wings and tore itself free from the bars. It busied itself first by flapping and pecking the servant Dumbcane, and then it settled upon the young girl's shoulder.

Ivy was so surprised to see her lost Shoo, she was struck mute.

Listen to the crow. Those who seek, look to the crows, for crows never lie, she heard Vidal Verjouce say. It was familiar, this saying, and it tugged at her.

Tell the girl, he commanded the bird. *Tell her who I am.*

Shoo turned to her then and spoke. But his words were the noises of tarnish, a broken bell. What at first had seemed like her beloved Shoo was nothing more than an iron dressing upon a decorative fence—its eyes were blank and glazed, its weight suddenly unbearably heavy.

This was not her crow, she realized—her crow was in Caux, trapped forever in the tapestry. This was a bird from her father's evil mind; its vocabulary was mostly incomprehensible and sent a chill up her spine. It chattered away, her shoulder aching from its grip.

"Your father! Your father!" the creature rasped.

Repelled, she fell back, and the world began fading away.

Crows never lie. You see, I am your father.

Chapter Seventy-one

Wilhelmina

T here, there." Ivy opened her eyes to a sunlit room, a small patchwork quilt, and the tiniest woman she had ever seen. Quite a bit smaller than the tallest of trestlemen, her hostess had about her head a spray of silver curls like a heap of seafoam, and around her neck a choker of ample dark pearls. She wore, Ivy noticed, a smartly tailored black dress, one with sparkles in all the right places and a million small clasps up the back. The alewife—for, indeed, this is what the lady was—was tending to Ivy's forehead delicately with a damp sea sponge, and just as Ivy began to register that she was in a room of golden sunlight and not the despotic garden of Vidal Verjouce, her head exploded in sharp pain and her body was wracked with chills.

"Shh," the lady advised as Ivy groaned. She handed her a delicate teacup, a warm brew of what seemed to be pure gold.

"She's been like this all night," Rowan's voice said worriedly. He had not left his friend's side. "She keeps talking about crows. 'Crows never lie.'"

"Crows never lie?" the lady said thoughtfully. "Yes, well, I suppose that's true."

There was a knock on the door, and it soon opened. Another alewife, her hair high in a dollop upon her head, looked in. Her expression was stern to begin with, but a storm cloud passed over her face as she allowed herself a moment to take in Ivy and Rowan. She turned sharply to Ivy's nursemaid.

"Wilhelmina, come see me, please. Outside."

Wilhelmina rose, winking at Rowan, unperturbed at her summons.

"Drink up, my dear. It's cinquefoil tea!" Wilhelmina advised Ivy.

The stern alewife turned, her hair bobbling as if of gelatin, and after Wilhelmina passed beside her, she gave the children another reproachful look and shut the door.

"Wilhelmina?" Ivy looked to Rowan for confirmation.

"Yes! Peps's Wilhelmina." Rowan nodded, leaning in. "Ivy, I was so worried!"

Ivy smiled weakly. "So we're in Pimcaux?" she asked.

"Of course! Where else would we be?"

Ivy thought for a moment of the dismal Mind Garden, relieved that it was perhaps a dream.

"We came through the Doorway in the catacombs—don't you remember?" Rowan found himself happily babbling, so relieved was he that Ivy had emerged from her swoon. He rambled on about escaping Snaith, and talked even of his own experiences in Irresistible Meals, and then eagerly described his flight over all of Rocamadour in his springform wings.

"I still have them, of course; you can never be too sure when you might need to fly. Ivy, we're in Pimcaux—just think! But the oddest thing—you have on the most peculiar black dress!"

Ivy's stomach sank as she looked first at her arms, then the rest of her. She was indeed bound in the erratic black lace. Her feet were tucked into shiny black shoes, and there, in between them, lay the strangest thing of all: Six, curled upon the bed in a patch of sunlight. Her head pounded and she shut her eyes, breathing in the sea breeze.

"Alewives," Rowan explained, "rule over troubled waters. They are the ones to appeal to, should you ever find yourself ship-wrecked or drowning. I guess it's only natural they live in light-houses."

Ivy smiled weakly. "We are in a lighthouse?"

"Yes! Isn't that amazing? From what I can tell, it's quite a spectacular one. Ivy," Rowan began tentatively, "what does it mean—'Crows never lie'?"

With a sinking heart, she thought of Shoo.

"It was in Uncle Cecil's letter. It's an ancient writing of some sort. *Those who seek / Look to the crows / For crows never lie.*" She paused. "I miss Shoo," Ivy confessed. She did, terribly—even more so after her experience in the Mind Garden.

Rowan nodded numbly, thinking of the magical panels and

the crow's uncertain fate. He squeezed her hand. They continued chatting in hushed tones until the door was again thrust open—this time affording the children a bit more of a view—as the alewife returned to her bedside vigil.

"Well, imagine that! Who knew? You have the most refreshing smile!" Wilhelmina approved. "This is the first time I've laid eyes on it. I do see why those handsome D. Roux brothers were so taken with you."

Ivy brightened even further at the mention of Axle and Peps.

"And that charm—what memories! I am glad to see it again. How you convinced Peps to give it up, I'll never know." Ivy felt for the alewife charm Peps had given her what seemed like so long ago. The ribbon was warm and comforting around her neck.

"You had a close call," Wilhelmina confided. "Closer than you might imagine."

Ivy's smile was extinguished at the memory of her detour.

Wilhelmina leaned in further, after looking once at the door behind her.

"They are not happy that you've brought scourge bracken here," she confided. "Not happy at all."

Ivy's heart sank.

"Once you ingest it, its darkness grows inside you—takes up residence. It is now a part of you forever. Ivy, you will never feel right again in the shadows."

Ivy shivered—the thought of such darkness made her flesh crawl.

"But"—the alewife smiled brightly—"you're now a wounded healer! Isn't that just wonderful? And none of that will matter much to *them* when you've cured the King!"

To truly heal, one must know grave illness. That is what Rhustaphustian must have meant, Ivy realized. She sat up, ignoring a sharp pain in her ribs. The dress was maddeningly tight. She looked quickly at Rowan.

"The King! Where do we find him?" she asked Wilhelmina urgently.

The alewife looked pensive and then upset.

"Well, there is a small problem."

"Problem?" Rowan asked worriedly.

"Yes, problem. I'd consider Foxglove a problem indeed."

"Foxglove?"

"Mr. Foxglove," Wilhelmina sighed. "King Verdigris's new advisor."

"Advisor?"

"Advisor and biographer. He's writing a book—although, come to think of it, we've yet to see a single page."

"What sort of book?" Rowan asked.

"A kind of memoir, he says. Of the King. He's forever jotting down notes in his journals; he seems quite thorough."

"Why is this Mr. Foxglove a problem? Surely he would want

what's best for the King?" Ivy cried, knowing at once that, sadly, there were people who sometimes wished hurtful things upon those they pretended to serve.

"Best for the King?" Wilhelmina drooped. "Mr. Foxglove only wants what's best for Mr. Foxglove."

The alewife looked from one child to the other.

"But, here, let us not get ahead of ourselves. I'm sure your mother will be of great help, Ivy!"

Chapter Seventy-two

A Change of Attire

ilhelmina busily tidied the small chamber and would not talk further—Ivy needed to rest. At the mention of her mother, Clothilde, Ivy's stomach turned over and she sagged back into the soft cushions feeling utterly exhausted. She barely knew her mother, but what she did know she was not sure she liked. A reunion seemed unthinkable.

"Perhaps, Rowan, you would like to explore?" Wilhelmina asked the taster. "Pimcaux is really such a lovely place to visit—all sun and sea—and I'm sure you're eager to get started."

Rowan hesitated, looking at Ivy.

"She'll be fine," Wilhelmina assured him. "You've been a good friend to Ivy—that is plain to see—but now she needs to recover her strength."

Rowan reluctantly agreed and rose stiffly—he had been sitting in the small chair for entirely too long.

"But first"—Wilhelmina assessed his clothing—"you'll

need a change of attire. Your mourning wear—Ivy seems to have come prepared."

"My morning wear?" Rowan was confused. He thought briefly of his favorite combed cotton pajamas and matching robe, a gift from his mother—and a luxury of the past. He looked around helplessly.

"*Mourning* wear," Wilhelmina explained perkily. "We are all in mourning here, have been for some time. In sympathy. The King lost his daughter, you see."

"Oh!" Rowan understood. Come to think of it, the alewives were all wearing black. "I don't have anything," he pointed out. He now realized just how tattered and dirty his olive-drab apprentice robes were.

"Not a problem. Come with me." And she ushered the taster out the small, rounded door frame into the bright landing beyond. There was a spiral stair, and he followed her down it to a small room, cluttered with buttons, pincushions, and notions. It was a bright and happy workshop, with rolls of fabrics and tailors' torsos poked with pins. Heaps of quilts and embroideries cascaded from tables and baskets alike. The room had a pleasing smell of clean, bright oil and industry.

As she unrolled a silver tape and began to take the taster's measurements, Rowan could not help but notice the most captivating collection of rings upon her fingers. One looked as if it were a bubble of the purest water.

"Wilhelmina?" he asked.

"Yes, dear?" The alewife selected a lightweight linen the color of summer shade, and Rowan thought about the reason behind the dark suit.

"I read in Axle's book about Princess Violet. That she was poisoned."

"Indeed," she said through a mouthful of pins. "She ate from a roast that was cut with a poisoned knife."

"How is it no one else died?"

Wilhelmina rummaged through the cluttered basket, rejecting various spools of black thread, until she found one of which she approved. Then she looked the taster in the eye.

"Only one side of the knife was poisoned."

Rowan thought of Defensive Dining, a gruesome requirement at the Tasters' Guild. There are as many ways to be poisoned as there are poisoners to think of them.

"But her killer was never caught."

"King Verdigris doesn't know who murdered his only daughter?" Rowan asked quietly.

The alewife shook her spray of curls. "No. King Verdigris is in hiding. It's whispered that his grief at Princess Violet's death has overcome his senses—his magic is potent and unpredictable, out of control. If the cinquefoils and weather are any measure."

"The cinquefoils?"

"Yes. They grow everywhere. The King's flower has become, well, a bit of a nuisance."

Rowan found that hard to imagine but kept silent.

"They say he will not recover until the murderer is brought to light. So we wait for news, and for the time when we might be permitted to discard these dreary mourning clothes for something more lively. Instead"—Wilhelmina's voice grew sadder—"we got Mr. Foxglove."

Soon Rowan was outfitted in a tidy suit and vest with mother-of-pearl buttons and a wide-brimmed hat. Wilhelmina escorted him down a further stair to a small stone door. Opening it wide, the taster was introduced to the bright sea air.

"Just down the path, you'll find the village," she chimed. "Oh, and do take an umbrella. The weather is slightly . . . unreliable."

Rowan squinted. There wasn't a cloud in the achingly blue sky. The tall gray lighthouse—a stalk of stone—sat atop the seacliff. Overwhelmed, he stood, looking around. From behind he felt a gentle shove—Wilhelmina was ushering him across the threshold.

"Go on!" she urged. "While the sun's still in the heavens."

Apparently, if Rowan's eyes were not lying, the sun was not only in the heavens—it was everywhere. The landscape of Pimcaux was a stunning one, a collaboration of rock and water, sun and air. A shocking, vibrant golden light permeated the atmosphere. It was as if the sea, in its vastness, took up the sun's reflection and dashed it against the shore—and from it the cinquefoils grew, sprouting by the millions, yellow, golden, growing upon rock and field alike. They sprouted from the worn stone path, the rock face of the cliffside—even upon the tiny windowsill beside him. An abandoned gull's nest cradled the King's flower. The small, magical blooms defied all natural law, taking up residence where they chose, flourishing, seemingly, on thin air.

Rowan set off for town with their perfume as his companion.

Chapter Seventy-three

The Ribbon Tree

By the time he'd scrambled down the zig-zagging path—edging through dangerous jackknifes, past curious nesting birds—Rowan was quite hot. Which is why, when the rain came, he welcomed it, at first. But this was no normal rain—no Cauvian rain, at least.

It splashed him with enormous teardrops, and although impossible, it appeared to be seawater. He fumbled with the small black umbrella Wilhelmina had thrust upon him, and soon enough he had raised it, although its proportions were designed for tiny hands. He had walked a small path along the rocky shore, past clumps of windlestraw and grazing sheep in a salt marsh. Before long he had reached the town. The rain was gone, the sun was again shining—and over the broad frosted sea, a rainbow had settled.

Here before him, in this most beautiful of moments, was the entrance to the town, marked by two things.

First, an archway.

Second, a very odd tree indeed.

The tree was gnarled and ancient—of what sort Rowan could not tell, and he absently wondered if it grew only here, in Pimcaux. If it were an old lady lifting her skirts, the tree could easily hide a horse and carriage beneath her petticoats. And further, from every available branch hung an impossible number of silken ribbons, every color under the sun, streaming out in the sea breeze, putting the rainbow to shame.

Rowan looked around at this strange sight and entered the town.

He was grateful now for the shade of the small streets, and he advanced along the walkway that led through the village toward the gleaming sea, window-shopping happily. The town appeared to be a fishing village, the storefronts a weathered clapboard. His feet crunched on the small crushed shells that made up the path. He passed several quiet shops: a breadmaker, a broadcloth merchant—for sails, Rowan reasoned. A small store that sold notions—mostly pearl buttons and silver clasps in its display. A fishmonger.

A slight man gripped a homemade broom, whisking away the cinquefoil petals that littered the ground. Rowan nodded and kept on.

A few storefronts weren't immediately obvious. One shop in particular caught his eye. It was at the end of a small alley and partially boarded up. No one had been inside for years—

the drifts of sand and clumps of sea grass upon the steps were further proof. Old gilt lettering still graced the thick wooden door, proclaiming the establishment to be that of a family of weavers. The peeling paint read:

Four Sisters Tapestries of the Ancients and Royal Haberdashery

Through the window he could see dusty looms and tattered rolls of silks and ribbons—ribbons just like those from the tree Rowan had seen at the town's entrance. Empty spools and piles of bent or broken needles littered the floor, forming a dangerous carpet. Cruel-looking metal combs lay discarded upon the table—perhaps used at one time to tear and shred ribbons into thread, Rowan thought. A searose bush had somehow found its way between floorboards and had taken up position beside the cracked window—its wondrous scent reaching Rowan's nose.

Yet the place was forlorn. It seemed steeped in misery. It was at once intriguing and sad, and unless Rowan felt like breaking and entering, he would never know more.

Without further thought, he wrenched a weathered board from a rusted nail and opened the door.

Chapter Seventy-four

Four Sisters

The shop was enclosed in a velvety dust, and Rowan's feet were most certainly the first to disturb it. He stood, hesitating on the threshold and then, hearing nothing, went in.

A peculiar thought struck him: he was beginning to wonder if the tree grew the colorful ribbons lying everywhere (and, indeed, this would prove to be true), for they were most definitely the same sort. Vast sacks burst with inventory, and careful hands had sorted the ribbons into piles by color.

Beside the combing station, there was a small spinning wheel, a stool, and rolls and rolls of what appeared to be partially completed tapestries. A discarded harp was forsaken in the corner. Rowan walked by it and absently ran his hands along the silver strings—the notes were remarkably clear. On a table nearby, an abandoned tea set rested plaintively. Tea leaves dried and scattered, tarnish moving in.

There was a shelf of fat spools, silken thread, spun and finished. And what colors! They had been carefully arranged by shade, and Rowan was certain not a one was missing. He blew a layer of dust away from peeling labels beneath each and examined them.

The writing was clear enough, but the names themselves were mysterious. A particular purple-gray was called *Eveningsong*, while *Forgotten Wish* was a sad, pale blue. A strange wave of emotion overtook him as he read, and he stood for some time collecting himself.

And then, before him, upon the far wall of the shop, his attention was drawn to what at first he took to be a painting. But not of oil and canvas. This was painted in thread, a tapestry of such artistry and detail that it stole his heart away.

He ran his hands along the woven surface and thought again of Shoo in the panel in Templar. His fingers brushed the intricate weave of four figures—the four sisters—and four of the most beautiful women he had ever seen. Each was clad in a gown of colored ribbon—one, Rowan decided, golden as the sun, the next of starlight, followed by evening sky, and finally a stark-white windcloud. It was she, this cloud-clad woman, who made his heart stop. He stared at her.

He recognized her at once.

Axle had said she was the great mystery of the Verdigris tapestries.

Here again was the maiden upon whom Ivy's crow Shoo stood, back in the tapestries in Caux. Trapped within the magical tapestries of Verdigris, frozen in time, frozen in weave.

Chapter Seventy-five
Six

Rowan emerged from the shop and was so thoroughly absorbed in his shocking discovery that he barely noticed the driving rain and loss of daylight. How had he passed the entire day within the haberdashery? His umbrella was dry and safe, and completely of no use to him, as he had left it inside the Four Sisters' shop. Thinking only of telling Ivy his strange revelation, he ran past many storefronts that now, evening lights ablaze, seemed to belong to a completely different town.

He was approaching the archway at the town's entrance when he saw Six.

He skidded to a halt—the sea grit beneath his feet spraying forth, a tinkle of broken eggshells.

The cat appeared to be waiting for him beneath the ribbon tree.

"Six?" Rowan called hesitantly. For all of their travels together, he still did not trust him.

In response, Six merely gazed at him levelly, and blinked. His large eyes were pools of silver and held in them—or so Rowan perceived—the distinct expression of mockery.

"I . . . uh . . . I've got to find Ivy," Rowan told Six, regretting at once his need to explain himself to a cat.

The taster skirted the enormous tree—in the low light, the ribbons had given back most of their color and were fiercely flapping in the sea breeze. He found the path after the marshes and began his ascent. The dip in temperature made his climb tedious, while the sleet slashed at his upturned face. He had to fight the urge to look back to see if Six was stalking him. An inner dialogue raged within him—what sort of person was afraid of a cat? And just how—and why—had Six escaped the lighthouse? (And for that matter, tracked them through the catacombs?)

Yet Rowan would soon be very much thankful for the company of Six. As he arrived at the foot of the lighthouse, with the bright beacon's light spilling forth upon the roiling sea, he was greeted with the stern face of the elder alewife. She explained to him curtly that Ivy was no longer there.

Wilhelmina had taken her, under the cover of nightfall, to see Clothilde.

Chapter Seventy-six

Klair and Lofft

vy had napped fretfully until evening, which now found her shivering, wrapped in a borrowed wool coat, upon the uppermost platform of the lighthouse. The jacket was reasonably warm, with a pleasing amount of buttons. But it was too small in the arms, and she folded her hands around her chest to keep them warm.

The night made her uneasy. It was a darkness filled with movement—things seemed to dart about her, causing her to jump in fright. The sea in the distance was a mucky spume, and the few flickering lights of the town below looked weak and unfriendly. As Ivy waited impatiently for the return of the beacon of light—its slow rotation was maddening—she realized Wilhelmina was right. She would never again feel comfortable in the shadows.

The alewife had brought her up here and instructed her to use the gift from Peps that hung about her neck. She placed the birdcall in her hand, and Ivy noticed that there were both sharp and dull edges to the needle-like thing. Wilhelmina introduced Ivy to the blunt side, the side with the opening, and told her to blow. After several unsuccessful tries, Ivy found that what was required was more of a hum and trill—rather than a whistle—and with that, she mastered it.

The song was low and eerie—a ship creaking in a rough sea.

Finally, there it was again—the stark lamp of the old lighthouse, shining through Ivy's golden hair and out into the ocean. The world of shadow fell away, but Ivy had little time to settle down. For at first there was the emptiness that is light against nothing but night—the slight spray of the waves, the drift of the wind. And then—so unexpectedly— emerging into the illumination, bright and frightful, were two white birds of such magnitude that Ivy opened her mouth to scream, but the sound was lost to the wind. Stepping back on the slick stone face, she would have lost her footing had Wilhelmina not steadied her.

"Hush!" the alewife soothed. "It's merely Lofft and Klair."

Ivy nodded, recovering from her fright.

"They're husband and wife, you know," the alewife added confidentially.

The birds alighted easily upon the low-slung balustrade and, after a graceful flap of their vast wings, perched together, expectantly. Wilhelmina approached them and spoke quietly to each. The birds appeared to answer the alewife softly and turned their regal necks to examine Ivy.

"We are in luck!" Wilhelmina said. "They will take us!"

Ivy nodded and attempted a smile, but as Wilhelmina busied herself with a pair of silken harnesses, Ivy's stomach lurched. Wilhelmina had explained that it was best to travel by dark, but somehow Ivy had not understood that meant upon the backs of two giant seabirds.

"Albatrosses," Wilhelmina corrected, in response to Ivy's meek protests. "How else do you expect to get around?"

"There's nothing wrong with my feet," Ivy pointed out. "And *they* stay firmly on the ground."

"Walk?" The alewife snorted. "In these shoes?" And here she laughed the hearty laugh of a sailor. "It's really quite uplifting to travel by albatross. You'll see. Just hold on to this, while placing your chest like so. . . ." She showed Ivy the short reins made from luxurious ribbon. "And put your other arm here. Oh, and don't let go!"

And with very little else to do, Ivy soon found herself on the back of the larger of the two birds—and, at the urging of the alewife, she introduced herself to her ride.

"My name is Ivy Manx," she said, quite loudly, against the rain and wind. And to be polite, she asked, "I wonder, are you Klair or Lofft?"

To her great astonishment, the bird responded.

Chapter Seventy-seven

Thin Air

I know you, Ivy Manx," Lofft said, after introducing himself.

"You can speak?"

"Of course." He seemed offended at the question.

After a moment of reflection, Ivy asked, "Do all animals speak here?"

"I can only answer for birds. And, yes, all birds speak—although they don't always understand each other."

"Do crows speak?"

"Crows most of all! They are always talking. They hold caucuses and chat merrily for days and days. If you want something done, ask a crow."

"Oh—I so wish I spoke Crow!"

They flew on in silence as she contemplated her inaugural conversation with Shoo, but soon she grew weary of this. He was a prisoner of the tapestries, she remembered desperately. Who knew if she would see him again.

The night air was a mixture of many things—darkness,

salt, the crashing of waves below. Ivy began to turn her attention to the flight. Sitting upon Lofft's back was a bit like gliding on a wave. The albatross soared masterfully, barely even flapping his wings.

"How is it that you know of me?" she finally asked.

"We are very old, we two," he said, indicating his wife. This seemed to be his answer, as he said no more.

"Where are we going?"

"To the north a little ways. There is a compound."

"And that is where my mother is?"

"Yes."

"Do you know my mother?"

"I do."

Silence.

"But I knew your grandmother, Princess Violet, better."

"I don't know my mother very well."

"That may or may not be fortunate," he replied.

"And my father . . . Well . . ." She shivered.

"You cannot choose your parents any more than you can choose your feathers. They are there when you hatch."

Indeed, she thought. She certainly had hatched with quite a pair.

She saw the landscape now, beneath her. Pale rocky shores and the occasional cluster of homey lights. The clouds had moved off to sea, and what remained were insistent stars that painted the skies in unfamiliar constellations. Pimcaux smelled of salt and pine, and although she had never before visited, she felt achingly at home, wanting very much for this moment to last forever.

They were nearing the compound. Ahead there must have been a clearing, she guessed, atop a sheer cliff. And quite soon thereafter, they began descending in neat spirals. From her vantage point, she saw many smaller buildings and gardens within the walls of the main structure. The enormous birds finally alighted roughly on the lawn of a large, illuminated manor house. The walls before them gleamed, even in the low light. It was as if the sea and sand had forgotten their eternal quarrel and formed together a perfect polished stone.

"Thank you, Lofft," Ivy said shyly.

"No." The bird bowed his stark-white head. "It was my privilege, Noble One."

Wilhelmina was at the entry, a large iron portal with a great knocker. The knocker was unfortunately placed, and neither Ivy nor the alewife could reach it. As Ivy turned to watch the pair of albatrosses depart with rousing, shrill cries, Wilhelmina commenced rapping her knuckles against the door—and a surprising amount of noise ensued. She knocked and knocked until her knuckles were red and a fair few of her jewels looked the worse for wear.

Finally, distant footsteps approached.

"My dear, there's one last thing. . . ." The alewife paused.

Ivy waited as a frown flitted across Wilhelmina's face.

"Your mother— Your mother is . . . How shall I put this? . . . Not quite herself."

Ivy blinked. What did that mean?

But before she could ask, a rough-looking guard flung open the door, and Ivy jumped into the shadows. Peering out into the gloom and seeing no one, he moved to shut the door— when an afterthought occurred to him. Lowering his gaze, he was startled at the alewife standing before him. Wilhelmina cleared her throat.

"If you please, could you deliver this to your mistress?" She handed the guard a paper-thin starfish.

The man stared for a moment at the star in his hand, small and sea-green, upon which, in tiny dainty script, was Wilhelmina's name. He looked around again. Shrugging, he turned away on his errand.

Ivy relaxed into what she thought would be a long wait.

Instead, Wilhelmina grabbed her hand, and the twosome quietly followed behind him, breaching the thick walls of the manor. Approaching the vast marble stairs, Ivy thought she understood why Peps was so fond of this particular alewife.

Chapter Seventy-eight

Clothilde

From somewhere above came the tinkling of a piano.

It was not a particularly skillful tune; in fact, it struck Ivy as the product of a student who was not inclined to practice the lessons. Yet it was a melody, which was nice for two reasons. First, it distracted the girl from any escalating fear at seeing her mother and, in turn, the King. And, second, it served to cover their footfalls as they mounted the vast stone steps that were the centerpiece of the grand hall.

It was the only way up, Ivy had noticed, too, and this made her nervous that they might encounter the deceived guard on his way down. This, however, was not a possibility, as the guard had decided not to deliver the message to Clothilde, the King's granddaughter, but to Mr. Foxglove, who paid his salary. He was waiting politely while the man in question finished up a long trill upon a gilt piano.

Wilhelmina paused before a small stone basin. It was

shaped like a seashell, and although it contained a mechanism to propel water into the air in a graceful arc, it had been silenced at Mr. Foxglove's request. (Mr. Foxglove in general did not like the sound of running water.) There is nothing as sad to an alewife as a stilled fountain, as fountains are a place where the elements of air and water meet—a place of joy for those who inhabit watery arenas. As Wilhelmina ran her hand through the placid water, Ivy noticed that her touch left in its wake an incision—very much as if for the moment the water had ceased being liquid and was instead a clear jelly.

Ahead was a wide door, and peering in, it became clear to Ivy that this was where they were to find both the piano and its player. Something about this encounter made the hairs on the back of Ivy's neck stand up, and she felt an inexplicable flash of melancholia, which she put down to the improbable tune they were hearing. She thought it very unlikely she would be able to endure much more of this particular music without sobbing.

The alewife had stopped. Ivy marveled at the woman's pluck. Wilhelmina was quietly motioning to someone inside, waving and jumping about on her delicate black shoes. Then she stepped aside.

A great shadow filled the stone archway as someone advanced upon them quickly. The shadow grew and stretched, and soon fell upon Ivy. As the darkness enveloped the girl, a harrowing chill spread about Ivy's chest. The image of Vidal Verjouce and his awful Mind Garden lurched before her.

The shadow paused, waiting.

The curtain of darkness pulled away slightly, and her mother's white face materialized, enormous, like a moon. She wore a dress of such blackness that it sucked the very light out of the air. It was a thrilling thing—the deepest smudge of black velvet that wrapped itself around her white shoulders and encircled her waist before losing itself on the floor below. Her long hair, pulled back in a bun, was now as black as a raven.

She looked at them with an oddly blank expression.

"Yes?"

"Clothilde, I have brought you a visitor." Wilhelmina smiled. "Look who's here—it's Ivy!"

"Hello, Ivy." Clothilde smiled.

A moment passed, and Ivy frowned. Why was Wilhelmina talking to Clothilde as if she were a child?

"So nice to meet you," Clothilde added, an afterthought. She looked agreeably from the alewife to the girl.

This was bizarre behavior indeed. Her mother's character was one of such force and will that this polite and quizzical figure before Ivy seemed like a stranger.

"This is *Ivy*, Clothilde," Wilhelmina clarified. "Your *daughter*."

"Daughter?" she repeated. "Surely not. I would remember having a daughter!" Her laugh was that of a little girl.

"Ah, but you do remember!" Wilhelmina explained patiently.

"I do?"

Clothilde turned to inspect Ivy, running her pale hand through Ivy's gold-flecked hair, touching her cheek. A flash of emotion passed across Clothilde's face.

"A daughter," she whispered. Her eyes settled on Ivy's shoulders, and she recoiled as if stung. "Where did you get that dress?" she whispered hoarsely.

Ivy opened her mouth but then snapped it shut. Even if there had been enough time for her to explain, she felt the mysterious urge to quote a recipe for sarsaparilla soda.

"Never mind the dress for now, Clothilde—" Wilhelmina seemed about to deliver instructions when it suddenly became clear that the piano had stopped its playing. And the person who was no longer tickling the ivories had now made his way over to them.

"Ah," Mr. Foxglove said in a voice like an oozing fungus. "The entertainment has arrived."

It was a voice Ivy was incapable of forgetting.

A shrill, nasally one, belonging to her onetime taster and general miscreant, Mr. Sorrel Flux.

Chapter Seventy-nine

The Grange

Once, really not that long ago, Rowan Truax had commented that he doubted seriously a cat might do anything useful at all. He had remarked upon this— either to himself or to anyone who happened to be nearby— on at least three separate occasions recently: on the *Trindletrip*, in the sewers of Rocamadour, and in the chambers of Verjouce, where Six was happy to befriend his enemy. Cats, he was fond of saying, existed merely to please themselves and were given entirely too much credit otherwise.

But Rowan was about to do something he never thought possible: apologize to a cat.

Six was still waiting under the ribbon tree when Rowan stumbled back toward the town from the lighthouse. It became apparent to the taster that the cat was waiting for *him*. Once Rowan realized this, he was in a quandary. Should he trust a cat with suspect loyalties? (Didn't all cats have suspect loyalties?) Did he really have a choice?

"Have you been waiting for me, then?" Rowan asked.

Rowan was horrified as Six came up and rubbed his filthy coat upon his legs. Clumps of hair stuck fast to the black suit Wilhelmina had made for him, like burrs. With a mad purr in his throat, Six looked up at Rowan, and stepping away, he slowly blinked. Puzzled, Rowan took a step forward. The cat, too, took a step—toward the small village.

"After you." With a resolute sigh, followed by a sneeze, Rowan gave in. He followed the matted beast through the village. Although he had made his way along this very street twice earlier in the day, now, with the growing darkness, it was a passage transformed. Looking about as he kept behind Six, the shops and signs were glowing with an opalescent eeriness, and Rowan found to his great displeasure that the signs were no longer legible—the words were much longer and made up of an impossible number of odd letters and harsh consonants.

WHYLLSTIBLE FLNKENSTOLIE TA VWOT L'STRUUBE

read the sign at the end of the small alley that earlier held the Four Sisters' Haberdashery. Rowan saw nothing as he remembered it, and scowling into the dimness, he could see that there was, apparently, no shop at all but rather an old dilapidated shack, a few torn fishing nets strung up beside it. With growing confusion, he was tempted to explore the alley further, only Six was but a mere lurking shadow ahead and he dared not lose him. Rowan was vaguely aware of being watched, and although he saw no one, he could not shake the feeling that there were people—many people—gathered behind the dark windows that he passed by.

Cat and taster emerged finally upon a small path at the sandy beach in the twilight. Built of wood slats and lined with fragrant clumps of wild-growth yarrow, it meandered pleasantly along sea- and cliffside. Rowan followed Six for what seemed to be many, many miles, even after the path ended and became rocks, and led them beside a wondrous waterfall that dropped thrillingly from high above, ending in a deep pool nearby. Then, up—up, almost climbing. The cat seemed to wait as Rowan found his way, until they emerged at a beautiful mansion of polished stone.

Rowan knew at once that Ivy was here.

"Six," he said, ignoring the persistent tickle in the back of his throat, "thank you for being my guide. I owe you an apology. How can I ever repay you?"

To which the cat swished his tail and, of course, said nothing.

But Six was not finished with his tour. Great shadows stretched out from the lighted windows, sprawling themselves unfavorably upon the lawn. Six walked through these, beckoning in his way for Rowan to follow. Reluctantly, the taster did.

There was a series of outbuildings to the compound—a gatehouse that straddled the road, a caretaker's cottage with a small garden, and further away, upon a slight hill, a grange. As they neared the barn, a chill ran down Rowan's spine.

Although Six led him on, they never seemed to get any closer. The place was entirely uninviting—dark, broken-down. It smelled of pasture. But that was not the most repellent thing about the eerie barn. Rowan somehow knew it to be occupied. Had he not known Ivy Manx as he did—had he never met her at the Hollow Bettle, had he remained a servant of the Tasters' Guild for all his days—he could not have understood what it was he was sensing.

He realized the grange was deeply enchanted.

Chapter Eighty

Mr. Foxglove

ell, well, well." Mr. Foxglove—or Flux, as the case may be—gestured with a manicured hand as the guard led Ivy and Wilhelmina into the large parlor with the aid of a long, barbed spear. "I've been expecting you. Although, I'll admit, I can't imagine what took you so long."

Ivy stared at her former taster.

Sorrel Flux, she noticed, had undergone a transformation of sorts. His appearance, once quite an afterthought, seemed to be of some new import to the scrawny man, and he now donned a showy boutonniere in the buttonhole of a slick black suit. Upon his head there was no longer a tatty Guild hood but a small beret at a canted angle. A stain populated his thin upper lip—either an odd patch of hair or some forgotten snuff.

"You're Foxglove?" she asked, incredulous.

"*Mr.* Foxglove, to you." Flux sneered. "I'd offer you something—a bite perhaps—but I'm still recovering from our little stay together."

"I should have finished you off when I had the chance." Ivy glared. Her fingers twitched and ached for her poison kit, sitting useless back in Rocamadour.

"Manners, manners. Is that any way to talk to your host?"

She looked at Clothilde, standing beside him, her face unreadable.

"I see you have met my muse," Flux purred.

"Muse?" With a jolt, she realized he meant her mother.

"Every writer has a muse!" Flux condescended. "Someone to inspire them, guide them—fetch them tea."

"Mother." Ivy cringed to hear her voice crack. "Where is the King?"

But Clothilde had not heard her.

"She can't tell you," Flux announced gleefully. "My darling"—he now spoke to Clothilde—"isn't it time for your . . . *medicine?*"

He snapped his fingers, and the guard cautiously approached. He proceeded to skillfully dispense a thimbleful of a sickly yellowish syrup into a small glass of water, holding it out to Ivy's mother at arm's length. Clothilde grasped the tumbler, and for a moment it appeared as if she might drop it.

"The poor dear—she was suffering so when she left Caux," Flux reminded Ivy. "But my many years at the Tasters' Guild endowed me with a vast repertoire of—shall we say—*medicines* with which to treat her. How lucky that I came upon her—just in time."

336

It was true, the last time Ivy had seen her, Clothilde had looked unwell, desperate and stricken as she called out to Ivy from the door to Pimcaux.

"What are you making her drink?" Ivy demanded. Her former taster had a fondness for potions—he had poisoned the visiting sentries at her uncle's tavern when she and Rowan were fleeing it, as well as countless others in Templar.

"Your concern for your mother is touching. Misplaced but touching. This is the very woman who tried to drown you in the waters of the Marcel! You were a mere baby—but no doubt just as much trouble. Ah—if only she had succeeded, this tedious conversation could have been avoided."

Turning to Clothilde, he coaxed, "Now, now. Be a good girl or I shall lose my temper and require that dreadful child of yours to drink some, too."

The fog that clouded Clothilde's eyes seemed to clear somewhat as her gaze settled on Ivy. But in the next instant, she smiled sadly and swallowed the draft. Her expression again became oddly waxen, retreating to a vacant place.

Appalled, Ivy narrowed her eyes at Flux.

"You'll never get away with this! You seem to have everyone here fooled, but I'll tell them just who you are—"

"Then, Ivy, you shall never see another birthday." He pinched some life back into the crease of his pants leg and yawned.

Ivy looked at her former taster crossly. Talking was

getting her nowhere. She took a deep breath. Ivy had an idea. It was a terrible idea, one that she knew would greatly upset her dear friends in Caux (and one that was surely breaking a promise to a trestleman), but the Prophecy was at stake. She needed to distract Sorrel Flux, and she would do it with ink.

Ivy summoned a smile to her bright face. "You are a writer, you say? I did not know you were a wordsmith," she said sweetly.

"I am." Flux nodded defensively. "See?" He pointed to what was impossible to ignore—the vast room was filled with the detritus of a scholarly profession: everywhere were papers (mostly doodles, it seemed to Ivy), pens and ink bottles, broken quills, all in great disorder. Tacked to the walls were incomprehensible scrawls and half thoughts. Leatherbound journals were stacked haphazardly to the ceiling. In a corner, crumpled balls of parchment formed a small mountain. It was evident that Flux considered his surroundings as proof enough of his profession, for he wore upon his yellowed face a look of complete satisfaction.

"How wonderful!" Ivy enthused. "Writers command such great respect."

"Indeed."

"What do you write?" Ivy asked shyly. "The biography of the King?"

Flux eyed the girl evilly but could not resist answering. "Something like that."

338

"Of course, it is such a lonesome profession, one filled with self-doubt and anxiety. So very difficult."

Flux hesitated.

"What would you say if I told you I knew of something that would make it infinitely easier?"

Flux polished his nails upon his shiny vest. This child was so immensely tedious, he thought. How he had endured her company for an entire year, he had no idea. She was persistent, and pesky, and needed to be punished.

"Vidal Verjouce has this special *ink*—"

Flux's pasty mouth snapped shut at the mention of his former master; his eyes grew wide and calculating.

Ivy paused modestly.

"Yes?" He leaned forward.

"Well, whoever uses it finds himself capable of great genius—and amasses incomparable fortunes. No more toiling over the empty page—the ink will instead do all the work for you, while you collect the glory."

Ivy watched as Flux digested this information.

"What is it made from, this ink?" he asked, skeptical.

"Oh, it's the simplest thing. Scourge bracken!" She smiled agreeably.

"Scourge brack—" Flux coughed the words. "But that's impossible! It is long extinct." His pasty face had settled into a look of suspicion.

"Apparently not! And your former master has great vats of

it," she continued, warming up to her deception. "I've seen them myself, in Rocamadour. In fact, he's making more as we speak. He's amassed an army of Outriders to assist him. I, for one, don't see why he should have it all for himself."

"Rocamadour. You don't say. . . ."

"But first," Ivy continued piously, "about King Verdigris . . . ?"

Flux drummed his fingers for a short second. If what this awful child said was true, his former master had been successful in uncovering the most potent weed ever known. Vanishing were his scholarly ambitions, replaced by ones of tyranny and power—kingly dreams.

Ivy held her breath. She had come to her own conclusion about her former taster. Were he to get his hands on the deadly weed, he would be no match for it. And, certainly, nothing would be worse than it was currently—with Vidal Verjouce already in possession of its powerful forces.

"That is easy," Flux sniffed dismissively. "Try the grange. Something moved in there a while ago and is scaring the animals. I thought it was a specter."

Chapter Eighty-one

The Masquerade

lthough Mr. Foxglove was masquerading as a writer—in particular, the King's biographer—he had never interviewed the royal ruler. In fact, he had never actually *seen* the King directly. Mr. Foxglove assumed, rightly, that the King was dangerous and unpredictable before his illness, but now the old man's great magic was undeniably deranged.

He was also, quite to Flux's liking, missing.

Arriving on the sandy shores and golden pastures of Pimcaux from the bleakness of the Templar palace was like discovering a new color, or taste—or both. The thrill lasted approximately as long as it took Flux to shed his tattered robes and steal something slightly more suitable from a schoolboy. (He also pilfered the poor boy's sack, in which he found the genesis of his new identity—a small notebook.)

He set out to do what he did best: to find the most powerful person he could and insinuate himself into his lavish life. He was most certainly up for the challenge. And challenges there were, for the King's magic was fearsome, and he had in place some difficult obstacles.

There were three tests.

Upon his arrival at the King's retreat, Flux drew closer to the stone compound only to find great, gnashing trees that knit their ancient branches—in a symphony of cracking and straining—before him and threatened to carve deep gashes in his yellow hide. But his figure was slight, and he had little problem passing.

Next he came to a pool of incredible tranquility, and as he gazed upon himself within it (remarking on several occasions at his own good fortune for being so easy to admire), creeping, viny tentacles from the picturesque water lilies slithered up and around him, and he was nearly drowned.

Finally—and here he noticed he was no further along in his journey; if anything, he seemed only to be getting further away from the manor—an orchard sprouted before him. A patchwork of dappled moss led through it.

He sighed.

Golden light peeked from behind a thundercloud, bathing all before him in temptation. There were many trees, profuse with fruit. But Flux was not hungry (he was never hungry) and had spent long years of his life at the Tasters' Guild, where his appreciation for untested fruits had been extinguished.

(Had the King only constructed an enchanted beer garden, it would have most certainly successfully ensnared him.)

Instead, he took a small, overgrown footpath into which he had seen a weasel dart, and it passed through a crumbling stone wall and brought him out upon the sea. A fortress of polished stone rose from a cliff, and Flux slid into residence quite easily, posting some papers he called his writing credentials, and brandishing a quill he had found at the bottom of the schoolboy's sack.

"I will begin today on the King's biography," he announced to the pale and sickly Clothilde. "And should I uncover the identity of the person responsible for Princess Violet's poisoning"—the taster paused dramatically—"then it will be my humble pleasure to mend the King's broken heart."

Writing this part of the King's biography would be easy. Flux smiled, for he knew quite well who the killer was.

Yes, life was to be a whole lot easier here in Pimcaux for the turncoat Flux—or Foxglove, as he soon made himself known.

Chapter Eighty-two
Reunion

aving told Flux everything she knew about Verjouce's ink (and much more that she didn't), Ivy was outside with Clothilde in a matter of moments.

"Leave the midget here, as insurance." Flux had pointed at Wilhelmina.

The alewife winked at Ivy and nodded encouragingly, so, taking her mother's hand, Ivy led her down the marble steps and out into the moonlight.

Flux had sent along the guard, a man named Moue, who lagged behind with tentative footsteps. Moue was decidedly unenthusiastic about his new assignment—the kitchen servants had said the barn was full of bad spirits, and he was in some doubt as to whether a visit there was part of his job description. (If there were such a thing as a clock that told the time remaining in one's life, Moue's would be winding down quite quickly.)

Inwardly, he decided to follow the two just until the barn

doors and go no further, and this was made easier by the fact that the visitors were already ahead on the short path that led up the hill.

Moue had fallen behind, and from this point of disadvantage, he heard a shout. Hurrying (why was he hurrying? he wondered), he soon suffered a shock too strong for his poor system. Rearing above him at the hilltop was the most awful of specters. Moue knew from his childhood that a spirit might take any form it so desires. Giant lizards, half men, sea serpents. The one before him now was a wild-eyed and great-toothed tiger, with slashing talons and awful, festering black sores upon his skin.

Moue expired upon the spot, leaving Six to sniff him uninterestedly. Behind the large cat, Rowan had emerged from the shadows and, after a happy reunion with Ivy and a moment of explanation, joined her and the docile Clothilde at the barn doors. They pondered what to do next.

"I think I should go in alone," Ivy finally said. The barn looked quite old, even in the darkness, and she realized she had always had a fondness for barns. Honeysuckle grew weed-like at the entrance. The night wind was picking up and blowing through the gaps in the wooden siding.

"No," Rowan said firmly. "I've come this far by your side— and I made a promise to Axle never to leave."

Ivy looked to her mother, who was standing back. A dazed frown creased her forehead; her now-black hair had come loose from its neat bun and was blowing wildly.

"Someone needs to watch her," Ivy pointed out.

"She'll be fine," Rowan responded curtly.

"Mother?" Ivy called, but the word sounded false on her lips. Ivy turned to Rowan and, reaching for his hand, pushed open the sagging door.

Together, they entered the domain of the King.

Chapter Eighty-three

The King

"Hello?" she called, for nothing else came to mind. "Great-grandfather?"

Rowan and Ivy gripped each other as a slight dizziness struck them both. They felt as if they had passed through an invisible mist of sorts, which tingled as it clung to their skin. Blinking, they saw it was an unlikely twilight. Before them was not the interior of a barn at all but a vast forest of ancient oak.

Rowan peered behind them. The door was gone—Clothilde, too—and the forest stretched out in all directions, endless.

Ivy bent down and picked something up.

"An acorn!" She cupped it. It was surprisingly heavy.

"It's solid silver!" Rowan gasped.

Looking around, closer now, they saw that the oak leaves appeared to be made of silver as well; they tinkled pleasantly in a slight breeze.

"Acorn," Ivy whispered. "Means *eternal life*, right? Do you think it's Flower Code?" Ivy was beginning to see a larger connection between herself and the world all around her, but before she could say so, Rowan spoke.

"Or *imminent death*," Rowan whimpered, remembering. "It depends on how it is presented."

Ivy was silent.

"Axle says that nature has retreated and does not want to be interpreted. Right now, I hope he's right," Rowan added.

The pair stood before a path. It was a meandering one, and as they stepped forward, the great oaks accompanied them along their way, bowing low in welcome and knitting a basket above Ivy's and Rowan's heads from smaller branches. A jackdaw twittered a complicated song.

They walked for some time, lulled by the wood. Astonished, the friends watched as the acorns and oak leaves turned from silver to gold, and then back to silver.

"Haven't we already been this way?" Rowan demanded. "The leaves are silver again, and I could swear we passed that low branch there earlier."

Ivy stopped and looked around.

"I don't know."

A wind had picked up, and the metallic sound from the trees was a fury of chimes. A few acorns fell roughly to the ground beside them.

"I think you're right—we've been walking in circles," she decided. Suddenly the forest seemed more like a maze.

"I think we're lost," Rowan said hopelessly.

"Nonsense." Ivy crossed her arms. They were so close to the King—she could feel it!

The light was dimmer now, and a storm was picking up. Above, the great trees bent and swayed, and soon a hailstorm of silver acorns began pelting down upon them.

"Oww!" Rowan, who had been attempting to collect the acorns, gave up and ran for cover.

Whosoever speaks to the trees speaks to the King, Ivy thought.

"I am Ivy Manx!" she shouted. She raised high the acorn that she still clutched. For her efforts, she received a nasty strike to the cheek—a welt rose up, and indeed, a bruise would appear and last for weeks.

"Ivy!" Rowan called, desperate. "They're coming down everywhere!"

There was no safe haven from the streaking acorns, and Rowan cowered beneath his arms. Whereas one silver acorn was a novelty to the former taster, hundreds falling from the sky were suddenly an abomination—and, clearly, quite dangerous. Rowan shut his eyes.

"I am Ivy Manx—and you will let me pass!" he heard his friend say.

Something happened then.

With a loud crack, followed by a reverberating rattle, the world shifted.

Ivy was suddenly back in the barn, and she was alone. Flecks of dust caught shards of moonlight from above, filling the air with glittering constellations. Pinholes in the roof threw down spears of silver, and Ivy saw that above the grange's first story rose another, blanketed in dust and pigeons' roosts. Severe windows pierced the walls in several places along the way and provided Ivy with enough light to wonder at the dim vision that now rose before her.

A set of pillars, unlikely in a barn, of the densest marble and highest polish stretched the height of the room, and they were crowded with ivy and creepers—heavy and old. Ivy's eyes were drawn to the recess between the pillars, but something was there that stirred great fear within her. Gathering her courage, she looked, and saw an unforgettable throne of such majesty she inexplicably started crying.

A figure was seated on the throne.

The man before her was grave and dispassionate, and very old. It appeared to be raining on him—a gentle, persistent rain, and one that the King showed no proclivity to address. His blue eyes were clouded over, but he sat tall and defiant. His hair grew long, a cloud of spun wool that cascaded to his shoulders and draped to the floor—where it intertwined with his similarly long beard. Each was covered in silk ribbons, everywhere, tied at chaotic intervals. His robes were of an unnameable green—the color of spring, perhaps, or summer, or the underside of a rock. They were plush with embroideries, woven strands of gold and rich colors that moved about seemingly on their own. The garments fell heavily to his knees. His hand rested on his lap, in which he clutched a book, bound with chains and sealed with an ancient lock.

"Ivy," came a voice, a voice of the wind, of the wood. "Your name means *friendship*."

Ivy was silent.

"Let me gaze upon you. You remind me of someone whom I loved greatly."

Ivy took a tentative step forward, and as she did, she noticed the King shrink—as if struck. She stopped.

"You have her face. Violet—my daughter's."

Ivy examined the King's dull eyes—they were the saddest she had ever seen.

"King Verdigris," she began, "the Prophecy . . ."

King Verdigris's grip tightened upon the locked book in his lap, and she stepped forward again. Once more the King cringed.

Ivy looked closer at the throne upon which the ancient King rested. This was not easy, as there was an embroidered tapestry draped across the King's knees. The tapestry itself wanted to be admired—it was of the same quality as the very ones in Templar, and seemed lively and pulsating. But it was the throne now that Ivy wished to see, and it appeared to be of the densest wood, with a dark stain. Upon further examination, Ivy saw that it was not solid but rather a mass of trained branches impossibly growing in concert in the shape of a cathedra, or royal seat. The rain poured down upon it, soaking and strengthening it.

With a sick feeling, she realized the throne was fashioned of hawthorn. *Hawthorn binds people and imprisons souls,* she remembered Axle saying. There was no place where one might say the King began and the throne ended. And still the rain fed the awful scene. The ornate chair was a part of him, growing into and from him, and with each of Ivy's steps, the barbs stabbed further into the great King's flesh. King Verdigris's old skin was thin and transparent, and beneath it a thicket of veins could be seen—a dark, brown, woody color.

If grief and sadness had physical form, it would look very much like this throne, Ivy thought. How had the King allowed this to happen? She began weeping.

"How am I to help you?" she sobbed. Her tears landed with loud authority upon the sawdust floor, and small pools sprang up, reflecting the moonlight at her feet.

"There is something I need you to do," the King said.

She noticed a box before her. She leaned down to examine it—after assuring herself that this action would cause the King no further pain. It was tied with a ribbon.

"What is this?" she asked.

The King lifted a thin finger, and the box sprang open. Inside, Ivy saw a peculiar pair of matching stones. They were beset with deep, patterned grooves and were a pale gray, tinged with pink.

"Plant these," the King directed.

"What are they?"

"They are an old King's burden."

"A burden?" Ivy looked again in the box, frowning. They were not rocks at all but the pits from a summer fruit—a plum, perhaps, or a peach, but different, too. New and foreign. They smelled strange.

"Where shall I plant them?" She felt the pits. They were a bit too heavy for their size, and something about their touch was repellent. She returned them to their box quickly, closing the lid.

"In Caux. Where they belong."

Ivy nodded.

"How will I know where to plant them?"

"You will see when it is time. But do it quickly—before they become your burden, too. Although I fear they already are."

Just how a matching set of plum stones could be so much trouble Ivy now wondered.

"Find me here when you are done. I will be ready for you."

Caux! Ivy stood, frozen, an awful feeling welling up inside her. *Breaux's warning!* She had forgotten to take with her something that grows from the earth of Caux! How was she to ever get home?

She wheeled about, looking for Rowan, but the barn door was nowhere to be found. She was back among the silver and gold of the great oaks.

Chapter Eighty-four

The Thorn

Ivy reeled, turning back to the King.

"Please—I need to speak with my friend!"

But the King and his awful throne were gone, and what remained was a small patch of damp earth, as if it had just rained. A barn owl was perched upon the nearest tree branch, and, seeing Ivy, he opened his mouth to cry but changed his mind, snapping it shut. The bird was simply enormous, snowy white, flecked with gray.

She fought to stay calm, but this was a preposterous exercise. On silent wings, the owl now flew a small ways off—settling again on a low branch, bobbing his neck and staring calmly at her with his round eyes. Grasping the box with the plum stones inside, she turned and set off after him.

It was not long before Ivy saw something through the trees. Rowan stood before the barn entrance against Pimcaux's night sky—he was but a speck in the distance. He was still so far away, and Ivy had the impression he was calling to her—both his hands were cupped beside his mouth, and he strained forward. Evidently her mother had overcome her apprehension, for she was by his side, pulling his arm. Ivy watched as Rowan tried to shake her off, but Clothilde's grip was too strong.

Ivy ran, turning once to look for the owl, who was, quite strangely, flapping silently by her side. The golds and silvers of the leaves streaked like comets behind the bird as he kept pace with her. More tingling—as if she ran through a curtain of cobwebs—and she was there. She nearly stumbled into Rowan.

"Ivy! I thought you were lost! Where did you go?" He shook free of Clothilde's grasp and, casting her a rebellious look, straightened his suit. "She wanted to leave without you—"

"Mr. Foxglove is coming!" Clothilde announced urgently. "He must not find us!"

Ivy barely listened. She pulled at the taster's coat, untidying it again, and for her efforts received a scowl.

"Rowan! We forgot to bring something that grows from the earth—the earth of Caux! Professor Breaux's warning!" she cried, searching first Rowan's exasperated face, which became immediately pale and downcast at the thought of his future in this new land.

"Think!" Rowan was panicked. "You must have something!"

Ivy shook her head. "My poison kit is in Rocamadour! There is nothing. Oh, Rowan! What are we going to do? We need to go back! King Verdigris told me to plant these in Caux." She brandished the small box. The stones clinked inside. "It's *urgent.*"

"Hurry!" Clothilde wrung her hands, peering behind her desperately. "He's nearly here!"

Ivy looked at her mother crossly and thought about the disturbing figure of the King upon his hopeless hawthorn throne.

Hawthorn! she thought.

"Rowan," Ivy cried, remembering. "Your thorn!"

Ivy pushed Rowan's jacket and shirt aside and inspected the dark barb that was all that remained from the hawthorn forest, just below the skin. She pinched at it, but Rowan's skin had healed over. She needed something sharp.

"Mother—come here."

To her surprise, Clothilde dutifully obeyed.

"I need one of your hairpins—quickly."

Her mother felt her hair, now unusually wild, and, sure enough, produced a silver hairpin—one that had pricked Ivy's little finger atop the Craggy Burls what seemed like so long ago. Taking it, Ivy touched the glinting shaft to Rowan's ribs. An eerie, cold numbness spread across his chest. As Ivy plucked at the thorn, Rowan felt nothing. But he contemplated an unusual thought: the remnants of the ancient tree that imprisons souls, the hawthorn of Caux, seemed to be of some use after all. If Ivy was right, it would be bringing them home.

At last, Ivy had the thorn. The wound was clean and already beginning to close. The barb wasn't much to look at—small, brown, a splinter of dead wood. Sharp. But when Ivy held it up, it began to grow. First, it sprouted to life with merely a small tendril, unfurling cautiously, but soon it was growing small leaves, and not long after that it abandoned all tentativeness and expanded with growing strength and thickness. Ivy placed it on the earthen landing beside the grange and stepped back. It had fashioned itself into a twisting arbor.

An archway of bramble.

Looking through, Ivy could not see much within the doorway—a small, friendly-looking splash of greenery, as if very far away, through thick mists and swirling cloud, there might be a sort of garden. The archway formed a shady hall, a long and winding path. She was aware of a scented air calling to her with all the verdure of Caux.

From behind them came the sound of coughing, sputtering, and a litany of curses. Flux was nearing.

Ivy looked about the King's domain, the dark hill and the field below—stretching to the night sea. The strange stars were out, shining upon the velvet ocean. Above her somewhere were Klair and Lofft, and she thought a quick goodbye. Ivy clasped Rowan's hand in hers. Holding the box from the King tight against her chest, together they stepped through the garden archway.

Chapter Eighty-five

The Ring

Sorrel Flux had reconsidered his decision to let the Manx girl attend to her loony great-grandfather. His interest was piqued by the mention of this ink of which she had spoken, and he debated the ink's various merits to himself for several minutes until its importance had grown to great proportions. His mind kept returning to the simple fact that if his former master, Vidal Verjouce, was devoting himself to its manufacture, then there must be some gloriously horrible—and momentous—reason. Like a moth, a small and unlovely moth, it was Flux's character to be attracted to a flame.

And this ink flickered like fire.

So Sorrel Flux wrapped his cape around himself tightly and, with eager footsteps, flitted by the perky alewife in his parlor. Crossing the field to the old grange, and stepping over the prone body of his guard with little emotion, he determined to finally put an end to that awful Manx child once and for all. She was of no further use, and since there was very little that

Flux liked about children in general, he would take great pleasure in plying her with something deadly—returning the favor for the year he had suffered in her dreary tavern. Only the most awful of poisons, the most painful of poisons, would do. He drew himself up.

Incredibly, before him stood the tiny alewife. How had the midget gotten past him?

He blinked.

"Step aside," he intoned. If necessary, he could easily jump upon her.

Wilhelmina skipped forward.

"I don't think so," she quipped in her eternally optimistic fashion.

"No?" Flux laughed, a slight snort, and then a hiccup, finishing it off.

"No."

And with that, she drew from her small, dainty hand one of her wondrous rings, a jewel as delicate as a soap bubble. She raised her hand and threw the thing, and it landed at Flux's feet. As it hit the ground, it bounced once, and Flux looked down at it nervously. Still, there it sat. A full moment passed, and Flux looked at Wilhelmina wickedly.

With a grim smile, he leaned down to grab it—it was, after all, sparkly and reflected him nicely—and it was then that Wilhelmina's ring made a remarkable transformation. No longer a ring at all, it was now, amazingly, a vast lake that separated her from Flux, a lake with thick drifts of sea fog upon it. And the shock of the appearance of such a deep pool before him caused the already off-balance Flux to topple in.

He was, at best, a poor swimmer, having had little to do with water as a child. And since he had swallowed a great deal of it in his surprise, and since his heart was heavy with malice, he was finding it quite hard to stay afloat.

Sorrel Flux gasped and choked—and began to sink.

Chapter Eighty-six
Caucus

Stepping through the thorn door, Ivy and Rowan did not return to the Tasters' Guild—quite thankfully for both of them. Nor did they arrive at Templar, which had grown lonely and dispirited in their absence as the people of Caux restlessly awaited the fulfillment of the Prophecy. They did not find themselves at Axle's trestle, amid his many stacks of enchanted Verdigris books, the quiet river flowing beneath it.

Instead, they stood before the seven majestic tapestries, returned to their home deep beneath the forest floor in Underwood, the garden archway growing from the living roots of the regal retreat's wall. It took Rowan a moment to realize that they had arrived before the final panel, the one that held Ivy's crow captive. The garden scene rippled, and here and there little bluebells popped into bloom. But one important thing was missing from the tapestry—or, rather, two. The mysterious lady in white—and Ivy's crow, Shoo.

Rowan turned to Ivy, but she shouted first.

"Underwood is alive! Isn't it wonderful?"

Rowan nodded. Indeed, the brown and dying roots from Southern Wood above were growing once more, infused with life. Upon the walls, the tapestries before them rippled as if made from wind—lines stretched and puckered, and in a dizzying display the borders of the panels became indistinct.

All except one.

The nighttime panel was silent, eerily so. It was quite lifeless. As the children inspected it, Rowan was again reminded of the sensation of being pulled in.

"I know this place," Ivy whispered. The rough wool obliterated the light within, and the once-tidy garden of Verjouce's imagination was overrun with spiky weeds. Seeing it again filled her with dread. "It's my father's Mind Garden."

From behind them came a voice, and both Ivy and Rowan jumped. They had not arrived alone.

"It took Cecil long enough to return the tapestries to their rightful place," Clothilde sniffed, brushing an inchworm from her arm. She turned next to the task of smoothing her black hair into a neat bun, returning the hairpin to its proper place. Standing quite straight, Clothilde was suddenly the picture of her old self. She looked about Underwood as if she owned it.

Stepping far away from the shadows of the menacing Mind Garden panel, Ivy examined the grand hall. Something marvelous was happening. The tapestries were emerging again—just as they had in the queen's dining room in Templar—their vivid images spilling forth from the weave into reality. A carpet of green grass nudged its way beneath her feet. Wildflowers tickled her ankles. The tapestries were infusing life back into the dying roots that made up the magical underground castle, saving Underwood from its parched and failing existence. Ivy and Rowan could hardly recognize it.

"Ivy—" Rowan wanted to tell her about the Four Sisters' Haberdashery, and the mysterious tapestry inside, but the three were distracted by a pair of darting blackbirds flitting between them. The birds alighted upon a branch heavy with ripe pears that sprang from one of the panels. Several grackles now joined the songbirds, chattering. In fact, as they watched, the branch was burdened with dark birds of all sizes: gray jays; ravens; rooks; nuthatches; and small, darting hummingbirds. They overwhelmed the tree, speaking in shrill chirps and all at once. They were utterly agitated and sang of urgent things. Ripe fruit thudded to the ground.

And then, all at once, the birds grew silent.

After a time, the sound of wingbeats filled the air—at first from some distance, and then in a full roar. A wind blew Ivy's golden hair. Atop the highest branch a final bird alighted—black as coal. He settled in, crowning the tree with his outstretched wings, a few stray woolen strings dangling from his tail. The old crow let forth a caw. It was hoarse and dry, but utterly familiar.

The tree erupted in welcome—drowning out Ivy's cry.

"Shoo!"

In the din, Rowan looked around. If Shoo was here—where was the beautiful woman in white the crow had perched upon? Shouldn't she have been released from her woolen prison, too? Yet there was no sign of the sister from the tapestry shop. Just Ivy and Clothilde.

He looked again, carefully. Wait—there was something.

A pool of dark water congealed by the archway—he had somehow overlooked it. Soggy, wet footprints led away, into the thicket of Underwood.

Sorrel Flux eyed the airless underground cavern with disdain as he emerged from the thorn door. He was drenched and dripping, water sloshing from his silk stockings and fine boots. He cared not in the least. This was no place for him—all this noise and birdsong. No, he had an errand of utmost importance.

Flux slipped away behind a cloud of jasmine. He had ink to find.

APPENDIX

(Excerpted from *The Field Guide to the Poisons of Caux*,

by Axlerod D. Roux—chapter 62, page 746—

"The Secret Language of Flowers.")

acorn ⤳ eternal life; inverted: imminent death

arrowroot ⤳ Beware of danger.

barberry ⤳ sourness of temper

bryony ⤳ enclosed

buckbean ⤳ chamber, room—usually for sleeping

calamint ⤳ success

caulwort ⤳ birth, new life; de-thorned: tomb

crimped gill ⤳ tiredness, fatigue

dog's mercury ⤳ deceit

elderberry ⤳ journey forth

elm ⤳ dignity

fern ⤳ sincerity

forkedtongue ⤳ to decipher

foxglove ⤳ honesty; inverted: false, insincere

frogbit ⤳ rivalry

garden marigold ⤳ May I be of some assistance?

hawthorn ⤳ hopeless

heartsease ⤳ restoration

heather ⤳ clarity; inverted: disguise

hedge mustard ⤳ hidden

ivy ⤳ friendship

jasmine ⤳ wealth at any cost

lady's slipper ⤳ resting comfortably; inverted:
                    endangered